THE PIT GIRL'S SCANDAL

DAISY CARTER

CHAPTER 1

South Wales - 1838

"Be sure your sins will find you out..." Reverend Bowen let his dire warning hang in the air as he leaned over the pulpit. His gaze raked across the heads of his congregation, and he felt a gratifying sense of satisfaction at the way so many of the eyes looking up at him blinked guiltily. "The Lord sees and hears everything," he boomed, determined to keep his flock on the straight and narrow. He smacked his fist on the lectern to give added weight to his words, noting who seemed to be most uncomfortable so he could be sure to visit them during the coming week to dispense more moral guidance.

Ten-year-old Betty Jones tried not to fidget as

his dark eyes paused and looked directly at her. The sermon had lasted almost an hour, but her mind had been drifting for at least half the time as she enjoyed the way the sunlight shining through the stained glass window cast a rainbow on the flagstone floor between the pews. *Did the Reverend hear me singing on my way to work?* Betty's mouth went dry at the terrible thought, and she felt the heat flood her cheeks as he looked at her even harder. It was as if he could see right into her innermost thoughts and secrets. *I promise I'll only sing hymns next time...nothing too jolly.* Her silent prayer seemed to do the trick, and Reverend Jones suddenly snapped his bible shut with a loud thud, making some of the folks at the back of the church who had been dozing off wake up with a start.

"Miss Mostyn will have the collecting plate at the back of the church, so please give generously on your way out. The only parish notice this week is that Mr Crundell has asked me to remind you that the Inspector of Mines is still due to visit, so you must be sure to obey the rules at all times. We don't want word getting back that Nantglas Colliery is anything but the best, especially since the viability of some coal mines has been brought to the attention of Her Majesty."

After a ripple of worried mutters, the congregation of All Saints Church, Pencastle surreptitiously stretched their cramped limbs and stood up, their duty done for another week. They dropped the meagre few coins they could spare onto the collecting plate towards the fund for the new church roof and hurried out of the cool, dark church into the welcome sunshine of the early spring day.

Drifts of yellow daffodils nodding in the breeze made Betty smile, and she slipped her hand into her father's, skipping along next to him.

"Do I have to stop singing, Pa?" she whispered, tugging on his hand to get his attention. "I don't mean to sing out loud, but sometimes I just forget myself. Is it bad of me?"

Emrys looked down at his daughter, reminded once again how much she looked like her mother, Fay. They both shared the same warm hazel eyes and glossy brown curls that framed a heart-shaped face. He chuckled and shook his head. "You sing like a nightingale, our Betty. Never let anyone take that away from you. Although perhaps it would be better to make sure you keep it a bit quieter at the pit, eh?"

"Are we having mutton stew for dinner, Ma?

I'm starving." Jack Jones, Betty's younger brother, was untroubled by whether he had broken any rules, more worried about the rumble of hunger in his stomach.

"All you ever think about is your belly, Jack. Morning, noon and night, you're thinking about food." Minnie and Jack hurried along after Betty, squabbling noisily, while Fay Jones paused at the lychgate of the church to chat to one of the villagers. They were a handsome family, in spite of being just as hard up as the rest of the villagers. Emrys had broad shoulders and the gnarly calloused hands of a miner, but there was also a gentleness to him. He paused to pick a primrose, tucking it into Fay's shawl once she'd caught up with them. They had been married eleven years, and he still couldn't believe his good fortune that she had agreed to be his wife.

"Yes, it's mutton stew, and I've baked fresh bread to go with it." Fay ruffled Jack's blonde hair fondly and felt her heart lift with happiness. She took a deep breath, enjoying the fresh air as they strolled along the rutted track towards the row of cottages at the edge of the village where their home was. It was a far cry from the elegant Georgian house she had grown up in as the only daughter of a wealthy corn merchant. Her widowed father had been horrified when she'd announced she was courting Emrys, telling her that she would live to regret marrying so far beneath her. When she'd gone ahead with the wedding, he had cut her out of his will and his life without a moment's hesitation. It had been a source of quiet grief to her until they had had a loving reunion days before he'd died. But Fay couldn't help where her heart had led her. She had loved Emrys since the very first day she had laid eyes on him at the village fête when she had dropped her handkerchief, and he had returned it to her. Their wedding had been a quiet affair, and they had welcomed Betty into the world ten months later, followed by Jack and then Minnie several years apart afterwards.

"We're lucky your ma is such a good cook," Emrys said over Jack's head, giving his wife a gentle smile that still caused her heart to skip a beat, eleven years and three children later.

The sound of footsteps behind them made Betty turn around. "Coming to the pub, Emrys?" Wynn Parry's question had a challenging undertone as he swaggered after them. He had a swarthy complexion and had been good-looking once upon a time, but the years of too much time spent in The Red Dragon pub had taken their toll. Now his features looked coarse, and he had the air of a man who knew his best days were behind him.

Betty could feel the twitch of tension in her father's hand around her own.

"Not this time, Wynn, thanks all the same." Emrys's pace quickened slightly, but Wynn kept up.

"Going home for a nice family meal are you?" Wynn continued as though he wanted to goad a reply. He gave his wife Catherine a sour look. She was scurrying along several paces behind him and she lowered her eyes, knowing what was coming next. "I expect your Fay could teach Catherine a thing or two about keeping a man happy. I can't remember the last time I had a dinner that wasn't burnt or ruined." He guffawed loudly as though he'd said something funny. Catherine forced a chuckle, trying to make light of it, but nobody else laughed.

"Well I like Ma's cooking," Dylan Parry piped up. At eleven years old, he was only a head shorter than his father and he stuck his chin out defiantly. "It fills our bellies and the Reverend said we should be grateful for small mercies, Pa."

"Dylan's right," Betty chimed in, always quick to agree with her best friend. "His mam's fruit cake is just as nice as ours, Mr Parry."

Wynn scowled slightly at the way Dylan had outmanoeuvred him. The boy always defended Catherine, but he would get his own back later, in the privacy of their own home. Nobody challenged Wynn Parry's authority and got away with making him look like a fool, he reminded himself.

"You go and relax, dear. You've worked hard this week." Catherine tightened her shawl around her thin shoulders, hoping that Wynn might overlook Dylan's reply. "And you're quite right, perhaps Fay could teach me some new recipes."

Wynn shrugged nonchalantly, thrusting his hands in his pockets and jingling the coins in there. "S'pose I'd better spend my bonus by myself then, Emrys. You could have earned as much as me if you were a bit smarter down the pit. The trouble is, you're too busy helping the youngsters settle in. It's every man for himself down there. That's why I always get the weekly bonus...it's the mark of a real man." He puffed his chest out, full of his own importance. "You'd better run along home then, like an obedient little husband." His parting words were laced with sarcasm and he chuckled as he turned the corner to head to the pub.

"You shouldn't let him talk down to you like that, Catherine," Fay said as they watched him swagger away. "You're a good cook, I'm sure." She patted her friend reassuringly, noticing the yellow stain of an old bruise on her arm, which Catherine hastily tried to cover by pulling her sleeve down.

"He doesn't mean anything by it," Catherine said with a nervous smile. "Come along Dylan. We'd better get home. You know your pa won't want dinner to be late."

Dylan nodded, tucking his mother's hand into the crook of his elbow gallantly, as he'd seen Emrys do with Fay. "I'll help you peel the potatoes, Ma. You can put your feet up for half an hour."

Betty waved goodbye and the two families parted company. The Parry's lived on Finch Lane at the bottom of the hill and her family was halfway up, in Limetree Lane.

"Why does Mr Parry speak to you like that, Pa? He always sounds mean and I don't like it." Minnie pulled a face as she kicked a pebble along the dusty track.

"Ancient history, Minnie."

"What do you mean? Mrs Parry is always kind,

and Dylan is Betty's best friend. Mr Parry should be nice too."

Emrys tucked his arm around Fay's waist and pulled her close, smacking a kiss on her cheek. "When I met your ma at the village fête, Wynn fancied himself in with a chance of courting her as well. He challenged me to a go on the coconut shy and said that if he beat me, he would start walking out with your ma. He was so sure he was going to win, I can remember it like yesterday."

Minnie's eyes widened with surprise. "So what happened? Did he win?"

"No, I knocked a coconut off quicker than he did. And then, quite by chance, I caught your ma's eye when she dropped her handkerchief, and I picked it up for her. We were married within a year." He shook his head with a rueful smile. "I don't think Wynn has ever forgiven me, and poor Catherine bears the brunt of his temper."

"Not that I would have even given a man like Wynn Parry a second glance," Fay added with a grimace. She smiled fondly at Emrys and her children. "Your pa stole my heart and that's all there is to it."

"I'm glad about that," Minnie said. She opened the wooden gate that led to their small front garden, already looking forward to a precious hour in the afternoon where she would be allowed to do as she pleased.

As Betty followed her family up the short path to their cottage, she was surprised to see Dylan appear at the end of the lane hurrying towards them with a grin on his face. "Ma said I can go out for half an hour before we start on dinner. Do you want to come with me?" He waved the fishing rod in his hand. "Is that alright, Mrs Jones? Might catch a couple of trout if we're quick. I saw some in the pool last night."

Fay nodded and hastily handed Betty her old apron in exchange for the starched white one she wore for Sunday best. "Don't be late back," she called. Dylan had already grabbed Betty's hand as they ran down the lane and their shouts of laughter drifted back to her making her smile. She was fond of Dylan and secretly hoped he might end up courting Betty when the time was right as long as Wynn didn't find some way of ruining things out of spite.

BETTY CLUTCHED her side as they got to the bend in the river. "Stop...I've got a stitch." She bent over to catch her breath as Dylan kicked off his hobnailed boots and attached a wriggling worm to the hook on his fishing rod.

"Get your toes in the river. That'll soon wake you up after that boring sermon."

Needing no second asking, Betty kicked off her boots, slipped her long woollen socks off and hitched up her skirts to dangle her feet in the tumbling water. The cold made her gasp and she smiled at the way their feet looked almost like marble as they sat in companionable silence so as not to disturb the fish. There had been heavy rain the previous week and the river was higher than usual, eddying in a deep pool in the curve in the riverbank opposite them. It was Dylan's favourite fishing spot, and they came to sit there most weeks. The first acid green leaves of the silver birch trees were just beginning to unfurl, and the hedgerows were dusted white with sprays of blackthorn flowers.

"I don't reckon they're biting today," Dylan said quietly. He jerked the rod slightly to make the bait more enticing, watching the surface of the water with narrowed eyes. There was a sudden splash further upriver as a fat trout leapt into the air to catch a fly as if to taunt them.

"Never mind, it's just nice to be out here away from the noise and dirt of the pit." Betty leaned back on her elbows with a happy sigh and looked up at the white clouds that were drifting overhead. The Aberglas river rose in the nearby mountains, tumbling through upland moors and the thick woodlands higher up the valley, before winding sinuously through the village on its way towards the coast many miles away. During the long, hot days of summer, the village children swam in the still pools under trailing willow fronds and it provided a welcome haven of peace and quiet in the mining community.

"I'm sorry about what Pa's like. He'll be drunk by the time he gets home…again."

Betty's heart went out to her friend. She knew that Wynn was quick to use his fists when he'd been drinking and she wished there was some-thing she could do to help Dylan. "Maybe he'll be better this week after what the reverend said?"

"I doubt it," Dylan replied gloomily. "It's not me I worry about, it's Ma. She thinks I don't hear them arguing or notice the bruises…I hate him, Betty. I really do." He yanked the rod out of the water and his bad mood was dispelled as a silvery fish flopped on the grass next to them, caught on his hook.

"We got one. Well done." Betty jumped up and knocked the fish on the head quickly while Dylan put fresh bait on his line and cast it out again. "Your ma will be happy to have that for supper. Maybe that will keep your pa happy too."

"Things will be different one day, Betty. You'll see. We'll be together with our own little cottage and Ma can live with us, safe away from Pa. He can drink himself to death for all I care…as long as we have each other I'll be happy." Dylan's dark eyes sparkled with amusement as he saw Betty's surprised expression. "Who else would we marry but each other?" he added with a chuckle.

"I…I suppose so. We've known each other forever and you are my best friend." Betty felt a warm glow in her chest as she considered Dylan's words.

"And you're mine too," Dylan said emphatically. He leaned over and gave her a peck on the cheek, before busying himself with his fishing rod again. His tanned face had flushed red and he looked bashful. "There. We've had a kiss so we'll always be together, won't we?"

"I reckon so, just don't tell my pa what you did," Betty said with a wry smile. "I'm already in enough trouble with Reverend Bowen for singing too loud." She stood up and shook out her skirts. Even though the kiss had been innocent, the thought of her and Dylan making a life together sometime in the future felt like being wrapped up in her favourite patchwork quilt on a stormy night, cosy and safe.

"I don't think we'll get more than one fish today, not now he's arrived." Dylan pointed towards a large heron that flapped lazily along the opposite riverbank before settling in an oak tree. The canny bird watched them with beady eyes, and Dylan pulled the rod out of the water knowing that the fish would be long gone. They both pulled their socks back on and laced up their boots.

"Where do you think we'll live then?" Betty wanted to know more about how Dylan imagined their future and she shot him a curious glance as they strolled back up the track towards the village.

"I'll be earning a bonus every week down the pit by then and we'll rent one of the cottages at the top of the hill." Everyone in Pencastle knew those were the best houses in the village because they bordered the fields. The air was cleaner up there, away from the endless coal dust that infiltrated the lower houses on a windy day, coating everything in a grimy black film. "We'll have two girls and two boys, and I might even be pit manager one day."

Betty grinned at him, happy to play along. "We'll have a vegetable garden and a few chickens under the apple tree. And Ma and Pa will sit outside in the sun with your ma. Maybe Minnie and Jack will both be married too by then and live on the same lane as us with their families."

"I like the sound of that." Dylan stopped and turned to face Betty, his face suddenly serious. "I'm not joking, Betty. I want to give my ma a nice life as soon as I'm able to and for you and me to be together. It will be a happy marriage, though. I don't want you thinking I'm anything like Pa," he added firmly.

"I know, Dylan. That's what I want too." Betty stood on her tiptoes and returned the childlike kiss on his warm cheek before running up the lane to her home. As they parted company, the hard-edged silhouette of the Nantglas Colliery stretched up into the sky beyond them. It would shape their lives, just like it did for all the villagers, demanding their blood and sweat to keep the black coal coming from the bowels of the earth. But on that spring day, with the first daffodils nodding in the breeze and the starlings chattering overhead, Betty had no worries to darken her thoughts. She hummed loudly, singing her favourite tune, buoyed up by the first blossoming of innocent love she carried deep in her heart.

CHAPTER 2

South Wales - 1846

"What are you doing down here?" Wynn Parry's gruff question sent a shiver of dislike down Betty's spine. The weak light from his Davy lamp was barely enough to pierce the wall of darkness that pressed in on them from every angle and he held it higher, looming over her.

"Betty Jones...I thought it was you." His face in the shadowy light looked like a grotesque gargoyle making her stumble backwards.

"It's none of your business what I'm doing," Betty retorted, tilting her chin defiantly. "I'm eighteen now, not some little child you need to check up on."

"You know women aren't allowed below

ground. You'll be getting us all into trouble if you aren't careful. This is no place for a weakling like you, you're as feeble as your father anyway." He reached up to knock the cap off her head and his lip curled with disdain as Betty's curls tumbled around her face.

"Leave us alone, Mr Parry. We'll get on with our business and you get on with yours." Betty quickly coiled her hair and jammed the cap back on.

"You want to watch out, girl. I could make your life very difficult if I wanted to." Wynn's comment dissolved into a humourless chuckle and he pushed past her, leaving her alone in the pitch-black darkness of the Blaeny shaft again.

Betty breathed in and out to steady her nerves, praying that Wynn's words were just empty threats. She squatted down and her eyes gradually adjusted enough to tell where the rough-hewn wood of the wall met the stony floor beneath her feet. Wynn was quite right. Since the Mines and Collieries Act had been passed four years earlier, women were prohibited from working underground in the coal mines.

But how else will we earn enough to pay the rent and feed ourselves? The question which had haunted

Betty's every waking moment for the last six months slid into her mind yet again. She blinked back the tears which pricked the back of her eyes. There was no time to cry, not when the coal needed shifting.

At first, the change in the law had come as a relief. Before that, she had worked deep underground with her pa and Jack and Minnie. Emrys had strained every sinew at the coalface for years, hacking the coal from the clutches of the rocks with fierce determination to provide for his family. The three children had shovelled it into the wooden tubs which they would harness to themselves and drag upwards through the narrow tunnels, often on their hands and knees like beasts of burden. This was their life, for twelve hours a day, five and a half days a week, stopping only to eat a slab of bread and dripping and wash it down with cold, sweet tea by the guttering light of a tallow candle. Emrys had always insisted that Fay would not work underground with him, knowing that a woman of her genteel upbringing would barely survive such hardships. But Betty, Jack, and Minnie could not be spared. In spite of their tender ages, Emrys relied on them to bring up enough coal to keep a roof over their heads and put food on the table.

Once the Act had been passed, only Jack and Emrys had been allowed to work down the shafts and at the coalface. Betty and Minnie had joined Fay at the surface as tip girls, much to the annoyance of the older men who regarded the surface as their domain. It was a less grueling place to work out their days until they became too sick or old to continue.

"T'aint right, the women taking our rightful work out from under our noses," the cantankerous Dai Llewelyn had grumbled on their first day above ground, pulling his collar up against the persistent drizzle. "I've a good mind to tell Lord Griffiths what I think about these new rules next time he rides through the village," he had added, even though everyone knew the owner of the mine and much of the land around it, as well as most of the cottages in the village would be unlikely to listen to such concerns.

"My hands are tied. It's the law and I don't like it any more than you do," Ezra Crundell had replied. He had shot Betty a dark look, leaving her in no doubt that she would have to prove her worth or risk being underpaid. The men already earned double what the women did, as it was, even though they did the same work.

They soon got into a new rhythm, but Betty quickly realised it was still backbreaking work. Now her days consisted of dragging tubs of coal to their cart, emptying it onto the screening tables, and sorting the coal from stones with the other women until their muscles burned with tiredness.

Each family was paid by the weight of the coal they could bring up, and it seemed as though, no matter how hard they worked, it was never quite enough to make ends meet. Emrys prided himself on taking time to help those weaker and slower than himself, much to Wynn's amusement, which meant he never earned as much as he could have done. And Wynn never missed an opportunity to make a snide comment about his old rival to whoever would listen.

Betty shifted again in the dark tunnel, rubbing her legs to stop them from cramping up as she waited for Jack. *At least Pa was an honourable man,* Betty told herself as she picked up the faint sounds of a tub being dragged towards her. *Was.* Would she ever get used to her dear pa not being with them anymore?

At the end of last winter, on a day when their

breath had curled around their heads, and the mist hung in the valley bottom like a grey wraith, seeping through their clothes and leaving everything permanently damp, Emrys had coughed up blood as they had been trudging home.

"It's nothing. Just a bit of dust tickling my throat." Even though he didn't make a fuss, Fay had blanched at the sight of the scarlet stain on his handkerchief and the way his words sounded wheezy, like an old pair of bellows.

"Chicken broth, that's what will cure it." Fay had sent Betty back out into the night to go to the butcher's to buy chicken bones and a carrot and onion with the last of their money. Then as word got around, Catherine had crept to their door once Wynn had gone to the pub to give them a posy of dried herbs to hang by his bed.

All week long, their cottage had been filled with the agonising sounds of Emrys desperately trying to drag air into his lungs, each breath a bit more laboured than the last. Betty had squeezed her eyes tightly shut, praying that the Lord might spare him, unable to imagine life without her darling pa. And Minnie had reverted to her childhood trait of sucking her thumb for comfort when Betty pulled the patchwork quilt up to their chins.

They tried to snatch a few hours' sleep before daybreak because the work down the pit never stopped, even for a family sickness. Then eight days after Emrys had coughed up blood, the cottage had fallen silent. Emrys had taken his final breath at the age of just thirty-nine years old and life changed irrevocably for the Jones family.

The sound of dragging and scraping snapped Betty back to the present and she pushed the upsetting memories of their pa's death away, preferring to think of the gentle bear of a man he had been instead. "Jack? Is that you?" She kept her voice quiet and lowered the tone of it, not wanting to attract attention from the other miners. Even though she knew Mr Crundell was not too particular about staying within the law, it kept life simpler if she looked and sounded like a boy at a glance by those who didn't know her.

"Almost with you," Jack grunted.

Betty could see her brother's hunched back as he dragged the tub of coal closer. Although she was already breaking the law by going underground in the pit to meet him, they didn't dare risk having her working at the coalface with Jack. They compromised by having Jack be the one to dig out the coal and load the tubs, bringing them to Betty who would then make the final part of the journey to take the coal to the surface. It was slower than how they had used to work, and she felt the usual prickle of anxiety that they should try and work faster. "Quick, hand it over and get back down there." She felt for the rough straps of the harness and hitched them over her shoulders, wincing as they dug into her tender flesh. Even though she tried to pad the straps with rags, she invariably had bruises and scrapes all over her. She had been doing the job for so long that the pain was a constant companion she had grown accustomed to.

"See you for the next one in half an hour," Jack muttered. He was already hurrying away with the empty tub Betty had returned for him. In the darkness, he sounded more like Emrys each day and she had a sudden vision of them doing this for the next five, ten, twenty years or more, eking out a living as best they could.

What else would we do? This is all we know. Betty's favourite daydream she escaped into as she heaved the coal along the tunnels towards her cart was to imagine a different life. *I'd be a famous singer on the stage. Minnie would be my dressing room assistant, and Jack could be my manager.* She smiled to herself, ignoring the stab of pain in her shoulder muscles, picturing herself in a velvet gown looking out at a sea of rapturous faces as she sang. *But that would mean leaving Dylan behind.* Betty paused to catch her breath as she reached the wooden cart and a vision of his kind face slid into her mind, making her heart beat a little faster. Even though they weren't yet formally courting, she was confident that it wouldn't be too long until Dylan made his feelings for her more publicly known. As he had told her all those years ago by the river, it was silly to think they might end up with anyone else.

Thinking of Dylan gave Betty a fresh burst of energy and she heaved the tub onto the edge of the wooden cart, balancing it carefully so she could tip the precious contents out. Every piece counted and she coughed as a cloud of coal dust flew up into her face as the coal rumbled on top of what she's already put there. Stashing her tub in an alcove for safekeeping, she wiped a cloth across her eyes and leaned against the back of the cart to start moving it. Just when it felt as though she might burst a blood vessel, the wheels creaked forwards on the track and she felt the momentum start to pick up.

"Keep on going, our Betty. You can do it. Nearly there." She muttered the words to herself like a mantra, over and over again. It was what Emrys had used to say to encourage her, and by the time the cart's wheels were rolling along nicely, she even managed a brief smile as she remembered the way he'd always told them they were capable of more than they realised.

After what felt like an age, Betty finally saw a pinprick of light ahead. It was the entrance to the Blaeny shaft and the sight of it after the choking darkness never failed to lift her spirits, no matter what the weather was like. Beads of sweat ran down her forehead, making her eyes sting, but then she felt the first caress of the fresh air that always blew in from the entrance and picked up her pace even more. "I'll show you who's feeble, Wynn Parry," she growled, walking so fast that she was almost breaking into a run as the cart trundled along in front of her.

"Whoah there! Look out, you fool." Dai Llewe-lyn's shout echoed around the pit as Betty burst into the daylight with her cart, blinking from the exertion. He stomped away, muttering about how there was no respect for the elders of the mine anymore and Betty pulled her cap lower over her eyes. The last thing she wanted was to get him riled up even more than he usually was and attract unwanted attention.

"Taking your time today, I see." Ezra Crundell gave Betty a thin smile as he waddled over to her, snapping his pocket watch closed. His grubby waistcoat strained over his belly and he wiped some crumbs from his beard. Unlike the men who grafted in the mine, who were usually wiry and muscular from their labours, Crundell's position as the manager gave him ample time to eat. His rotund figure and the way his small eyes looked like two currants sunk in soft dough was deceptive. People who didn't know him might be lulled into thinking his generous proportions indicated a jolly, kindhearted fellow, but Betty knew nothing could be further from the truth. Crundell was a mean and miserly man, through and through.

"Sorry Mr Crundell, we're going as fast as we can," Betty said hastily. Even though each family was paid by the amount of coal they brought up, the mine owners also expected the manager to maximise production, and Mr Crundell never let them forget it.

Ignoring her apology he leaned over the edge of the cart and peered at the contents. "It's not the best coal…too much slack in there for my liking." He plucked out some of the smaller pieces and prodded his pudgy fingers in the fine dust with a frown.

"It's because Mr Parry hogs the best part of the coalface," Betty stated, matter-of-factly. "Jack has just as much right to work the good part but since Pa died, Mr Parry has forced Jack to work his leftovers, after he's taken all the best coal out for himself. It's not fair, Mr Crundell, and you know it."

Crundell scowled at her. "Are you accusing me of favouritism, *Miss* Jones? When you shouldn't even be down below ground and I very generously turn a blind eye."

Betty gulped and lowered her eyes. If he stopped her from going down to help Jack, their income would fall dramatically but she hated the way Mr Crundell and his cronies held all the cards. She had long suspected that Wynn had some sort of hold over Mr Crundell, but what it was, she didn't know. The upshot of it was that Wynn Parry always had the best position at the coalface, where he could fill his tubs with the lucrative larger chunks of coal at double the speed of most men. Meanwhile, Jack had to make do with the leftovers, hacking out what smaller pieces were left and scrabbling on the ground to scoop up the coal dust as well, simply to earn a few extra shillings each month.

"No Sir," Betty muttered. "I appreciate you letting me help Jack since we lost Pa...I...I don't know how we'd manage otherwise."

Her apology seemed to appease him and he puffed his chest out. "Folks say I'm a fair man, Miss Jones and I'm sure you would agree." After Betty had nodded obligingly he strolled away. "Jenkins will tally up what this is worth and I suggest you keep your head down for the next few weeks. That nosy parker Mr Morgan could call in at any time, it's been a while since we had an inspection, and I don't want him getting wind of anything untoward happening that might affect my bonus."

"Did I hear my name?" A scrawny man sidled up to Betty and she suppressed an inward sigh. Fred Jenkins was the foreman and Mr Crundell's right-hand man when it came to ensuring the pit workers didn't get a penny more than they were owed...or better still less if he thought he could get away with it. He sniffed loudly, looking at her load of coal with a gloomy expression. "Oh deary, deary me, the quality of this ain't very good, is it Miss Jones. It's even worse than what Emrys used to call a good day's work and that ain't saying very much." He grinned at her, revealing a mouthful of dirty, broken teeth. "Never mind, eh? There's plenty of folks who would like to live in your cottage if you can't pay the rent no more. I wouldn't even mind it meself, being as it's up the hill and out of the horrible smog that lingers below. 'T'was only the fact that your ma helped Emrys with some money that you got such a nice home," he added with a tinge of resentment.

"That won't be necessary, Mr Jenkins," Betty said, summoning a meek smile. "We're making enough to cover the rent and feed ourselves, even if some of the other men are determined to make life difficult for us. If you could tally the coal and write it in your book, Ma and Minnie are waiting at the tables to riddle and sort it."

"All in good time, all in good time." Fred strolled around the cart, knowing full well that every passing minute would be eating into how much the Jones family could earn. "Seems like a lot of slack and rubbish, but I reckon it's a decent weight." He licked the stub of his pencil and jotted a figure down in his ledger, angling it away from Betty so she couldn't read it over his shoulder.

"All done, Miss Jones. Better get on your way."

"Thank you, Mr Jenkins." Betty pushed the cart to the table where her ma and Minnie were waiting.

"You took your time," Minnie grumbled. "I overheard old Mr Crundell saying our coal is practically worthless." She rubbed her bloodshot eyes and yawned. "I'm so tired I could practically fall asleep standing up."

"I'm sure our coal isn't as terrible as they want us to believe." Betty waited for one of the men to offload her cart, enjoying the breeze on her face for one pleasurable moment. "I don't understand why they all seem to dislike us so much." As if to underline her point, she caught sight of Mr Crundell, Wynn Parry, and Fred Jenkins standing in a huddle on the far side of the yard, deep in conversation. Every few seconds they glanced in her direction and she felt a shiver of foreboding when Wynn threw back his head with a bark of laughter, before slapping Jenkins on his back in a jovial manner.

"They're in cahoots about something, that's for sure," Fay said thoughtfully. She sighed as she wielded her rake over the coals on the riddle, pausing to remove a stone. Even though Betty, Jack, and Minnie were doing their best to work hard, she missed the protection being married had afforded her. Without Emrys, she felt vulnerable. It wouldn't take much for them to lose their home, and she had seen the way some of the men eyed her up, like a hawk looking at its prey. She could never imagine marrying another man, but she knew there were plenty of rogues who would happily take what they wanted from her regardless. Wynn had taken to loitering nearby whenever he had a chance and she knew he was not the sort of person who would give up easily once he'd set his mind on something.

An hour later, the sun was starting to sink over the hills. It had been an early spring that year, but there was a nip in the air once the sun had gone down. "I'm going on home, Minnie. I can light the fire and start making dinner." Fay tightened her shawl and gave her daughter a weary smile. "You'll be alright to walk home with Jack and Betty, won't you?"

Minnie nodded cheerfully. "I don't mind at all, Ma, if it means dinner will be ready. My stomach's rumbling so loudly I'm surprised they can't hear it over the clatter of the machines."

Fay took her rake to the storage shed and put it in its usual spot, ready for the following morning.

If Mr Crundell knew they had hit their daily targets, he allowed one woman from each household to leave a little earlier so they could get home and start on all the other chores. He had given her a curt nod a few minutes ago to indicate she could leave if she wished.

Walking down the track to the village, Fay was lost in her thoughts. She had taken this route so many times she could have done it with her eyes closed, just like all the people who worked at the pit. Just as she reached the edge of the village, she spotted a flash of yellow in the grass. It was a primrose and she picked one flower, holding it to her nose to enjoy the light scent of it before tucking it into her shawl. "I miss you so much, Emrys," she murmured. Primroses had been his favourite because he said they heralded sunny days ahead and he had always picked one for her if he saw one. The sudden sound of footsteps following her made Fay turn around and her heart sank when she saw who it was.

"Maybe it's time to think about the future instead of the past." Wynn swaggered towards her and raised his eyebrows suggestively. "There's no point pining after him, Fay. He's gone and you need someone to take care of you."

"I have Betty, Jack and Minnie," she said hastily, stepping backwards. "Jack's the man of the house now and we're getting by alright."

Wynn's gaze locked on her and he stepped closer again. "That's as maybe, but who keeps you warm at night, Fay? I know you would have married me if it hadn't been for that stupid man running the coconut shy. I should have won, not Emrys, and you know it."

Fay sighed. "That's all water under the bridge now, Wynn. Catherine is your wife, and Dylan's a good lad...you have a lovely family if you could but see it."

"Lovely?" Wynn's mouth twisted with distaste. "Catherine could never match up to you, and Dylan's always taken her side...he's nothing but a snivelling pup tied to her apron strings." Suddenly he grabbed Fay's arm and pulled her against his chest, locking her in an embrace that she couldn't wriggle free from.

"Stop it, Wynn. You're hurting me." Fay tried to pull away but he tightened his grip.

"There's nobody to stop us being together anymore. Why do you insist on spurning me, Fay?"

"Because I love Emrys and always will," Fay cried, wrenching herself free. "And I will never do what I think you're suggesting. It wouldn't be right…Catherine is a good woman…just leave me alone. You should be ashamed of yourself." She turned and stumbled away, blinking back the tears that pooled in her eyes.

"You owe me…you'll regret turning me down, Fay…just you wait and see…" Wynn's parting words rang out in the cold evening air and he turned on his heel to stride to the pub. Holding Fay in his arms and then seeing the look of disgust in her eyes had reawakened all the animosity he had felt towards Emrys Jones over the years. Wynn knew with certainty that one day he would get his own back if it was the last thing he did. He just needed to bide his time and wait for the right opportunity.

CHAPTER 3

*B*etty hummed as she pegged the washing out on the line in their small garden that backed onto a dirt track with an identical row of cottages behind it. Although it was only a modest space, it had been Emrys's pride and joy and in the little spare time away from the pit they were allowed, he had carefully planted seeds and nurtured them until they grew into plants, so roses and hollyhocks jostled with whatever vegetables would grow in the rich soil. Now that it was May, a haze of blue forget-me-nots brushed against Betty's skirt and she bent down to admire the tiny blue flowers. She was not as green-fingered as her pa had been, but she hoped she would be able to keep the garden tidy and productive in his memory. The wind was blowing from the west which meant she could hang the washing out without the risk of it being covered in black dust from the pit, which was another reason to be cheerful.

"Ma's been down in the dumps for weeks," Minnie commented with a worried frown. She draped the last of the wet bedsheets on the line and attached two wooden pegs to hold it in place as the breeze filled it like a sail.

"I know." Betty's good mood evaporated, and the gnawing anxiety that was never far away returned, giving her a hollow sensation in her stomach. "Something's bothering her, but she won't tell me what it is."

"More than whether we'll cover the rent, you mean?" Jack had strolled out to join them. "Wynn Parry has been crowing even more than usual about his latest bonus. I wish I didn't have to work right next to him at the coalface. He knocked my tub over yesterday, and I had to refill it again which left us short. He reckoned it was an accident, but I'm not so sure. He seems to delight in my misfortune."

"Nothing that horrible man does is ever an

accident," Minnie scoffed. "I really don't know how Dylan is so lovely with a man like him for a father."

At the mention of Dylan's name, a rosy flush coloured Betty's cheeks. He had walked her home several times last week and although they had just chatted about village news, she could sense that her feelings for him were changing. She still saw him as a friend, but now when he smiled at her, it made her feel slightly breathless as though her heart had skipped a beat. She wondered if this was what love felt like.

Like Minnie, she found it hard to believe Wynn and Dylan could be father and son. They were different in practically every way. Thinking about Wynn reminded her of something. "I noticed that Wynn has been stopping to watch Ma's work at the riddling tables more than usual too," she said. "Does he say anything to her, Minnie?"

"He doesn't need to," Minnie sighed. "Every time we look up, either Mr Crundell, Fred Jenkins or Wynn seem to be hovering nearby. It's as if they've got something against our family and they're trying to find fault. It's making Ma quite jumpy…me too if I'm honest."

"We'll just have to keep our heads down and

make sure we don't do anything to annoy them," Betty said firmly. She knew that their pa would have wanted her to be the sensible one, as the eldest of the three of them, so she needed to nip these concerns in the bud before they took hold. "We'll do our best, make sure Fred Jenkins records our loads fairly, and ignore any comments that they make to try and provoke us. We have just as much right as any other family to make an honest living at the pit. Pa worked hard and we shall too." Even though her words were emphatic, Betty couldn't help but feel worried privately. Their mother had been quieter than usual over the last few weeks and she noticed that she had been eating less.

"Morning all." Dylan's cheerful greeting over the back fence made Betty smile. "I caught a few trout this morning. Would you like a couple? I've already given Ma two for us and Pa's still out cold from being drunk last night, so he needn't know."

"Yes please," Minnie cried before Betty had a chance to reply. "We've had mutton stew six nights in a row. I'm desperate for something different."

"Count yourself lucky you can still afford a hot meal every evening, young lady." Dylan gave Minnie a brotherly nudge with his elbow as he handed over the two fish which were skewered on a stick, already gutted and ready for the frying pan. "I heard some of the mines are thinking about cutting wages. Let's hope Mr Crundell doesn't think it's a good idea too. I wouldn't put it past him."

"Will you come in for a cup of tea and a slice of bread and jam, Dylan?" Fay peered out of the back door, hearing the commotion and her face brightened when she saw Dylan glance at Betty before nodding.

"If it's not too much trouble, Mrs Jones. I'd like that very much."

A few minutes later the kettle was whistling merrily on the range and Betty added a pinch of tea leaves to the pot. They still had a few jars of strawberry jam left from last summer's pickings and she opened a new one, along with a pat of golden butter to go with the slices of bread Fay had already cut.

"Won't you sing for us, Betty?" Fay asked after they had devoured all the food. She had taken the smallest slice and only eaten half of it, claiming she had lost her appetite. Jack had swooped in and finished what was left, but it gave Betty cause for alarm. Her mother seemed to be wasting away under her grey dress.

"Yes go on, we could do with cheering up. Sing us something from the travelling show that came to Pencastle last summer." Jack drained the last of his tea and sat back in his chair.

"How about The Maid of Milton Marsh? I liked that song." Minnie's eyes sparkled with anticipation as Betty stood next to the hearth and smoothed her dress down.

"Alright, as long as you don't think anyone will overhear and report back to Reverend Bowen. You know he only likes us to sing hymns."

Dylan jumped up to shut the window, then settled back in his chair again. Watching Betty sing always tugged on his heartstrings and made him feel something that he couldn't quite put a name to. Was it love or a deep yearning to protect her? He wasn't sure, but one thing he did know was that he couldn't imagine not having Betty as his friend.

Betty took a deep breath and sang the haunting love song, starting quietly but then allowing her voice to soar like a lark high in the sky as the melody took her down memory lane, reminding her of the golden evening they had sat in the meadow watching the travelling performers.

"That was so beautiful," Minnie whispered as the last note died away. She dabbed her hanky at the tears which had pooled in her eyes. "It's not fair that you got all the talent. Betty only has to hear a song once, and she can sing it perfectly, you know," she explained to Dylan. "I mean, where does her musical ear even come from?"

"Aye, it's a mystery when the rest of us sound about as musical as a donkey with indigestion," Jack said with a snort of laughter. "Especially Minnie," he added, ducking as his sister whacked him with the tea cosy.

"It's from my side of the family," Fay said, making Betty turn to look at her with surprise. "Not me of course," she explained. "I can hold a tune, but nothing like you dear. It was someone else…" Her words trailed off and her face fell for a moment, making her look sad.

"You never told us that before. Who is it—"

"Never mind that, Minnie," Betty said hastily, cutting her question off. "We don't need to harp on about my singing. It's just a pleasant diversion anyway, nothing more and nothing less." Betty hurried over to the table and clattered the plates as she cleared away, sending Minnie a warning look. They knew that most people in the village considered Fay to be higher up the social classes than them and that her own father had cut her off when she had married their pa. But Fay never talked about her family and they had never been encouraged to either. Emrys had told them once it was too painful for her and Betty wanted to respect that, even though she was curious to know more.

"Can Betty be spared to walk to the river with me, Mrs Jones? It's a lovely day and we can pick some sorrel for your stew."

"Of course, Dylan. Make the most of having a day off, we'll all be back at work again, soon enough." Fay picked up the sampler she was working on and threaded her needle while Minnie buried her nose in the well-thumbed version of The Old Curiosity Shop that the church ladies had let her borrow.

"I'M WORRIED ABOUT MA," Betty confided as she and Dylan strolled along the riverbank and came to the edge of the woods. She stooped to pick some wild garlic leaves and the air filled with their pungent scent. "She doesn't seem to be eating as much as she used to and I know she's fretting about us not earning enough money." She stopped short of saying anything about Wynn's behaviour at the mine. Dylan had been working down a different shaft for the last few months and probably had no idea about the way his father took the best coal for himself, not caring if others had to go without.

"I noticed that she seemed quieter than usual just now. But remember she lost the love of her life when your pa died; it's only natural she might grieve for a long time."

Dylan bent down and picked a violet, handing it to Betty with a shy smile. "I always used to wish my pa would be more thoughtful and pick a flower for Ma now and again, the way Emrys used to for Fay...no chance of that, though. He doesn't have a kind and caring bone in his body." He chewed his lip, looking downhearted. "Just because Pa is a drunk and a bully doesn't mean I have to turn out like him, does it?"

Betty threaded the flower into her shawl as she shook her head vehemently. "Never, Dylan. You're not like your father at all so don't ever think you might end up like him. You're thoughtful and put others first, for starters."

"Steady on," Dylan chuckled. "You'll be making me blush at this rate." His expression grew more serious and he sighed. "Pa's drinking more than ever and I think he's been having a dalliance with a woman from down the valley. When I challenged him about it, he denied it, but I don't believe a word he says anymore. He doesn't care one jot about me and Ma."

"I'm sorry, Dylan. It must be hard to see him treat your ma badly." Betty decided there was no point pretending Wynn was nice. They both knew his true colours, and she owed it to Dylan to be a good friend and support him however she could. "Let's just enjoy our walk for now," she added. She slipped her hand through the crook of his arm and gasped as he winced. "What is it? Have you hurt yourself?"

Dylan gave her a rueful smile. "Not exactly. Pa did more than deny the rumours of his affair." He rolled up his sleeve to reveal an angry red welt on his arm that was already turning into the deep purple of a painful bruise where Wynn had grabbed him with all the force of his brawny muscles and boiling anger.

"He hit you? Oh, Dylan, the man's a brute." Betty's cheeks were red with indignation at what

Wynn had done to her dearest friend. "Is there any way you and your ma can get away from him?"

"I wish there was." Dylan shrugged and held back a bramble that was blocking their path. "If he carries on drinking the way he is, maybe he won't be around much longer. I know it's bad of me to say it, Betty, but I wouldn't miss him if he was gone. I feel so helpless about the way he treats Ma."

"You mustn't blame yourself. He's a grown man who should know better."

"It would have been better if God had taken him instead of your father," Dylan said matter-of-factly.

They strolled on in silence for a few minutes, each lost in their own thoughts. "You have a real talent with your voice, you know," Dylan said after a while. "It's a shame there isn't a way you could earn a living that way instead of being down the pit."

As Betty knelt on the mossy woodland bank to pick sorrel, Dylan gave her a sidelong glance. Every part of him wanted to ask if they could start courting, but something held him back. He had heard the gossips in the village, ruminating about how Fay wasn't really one of them, because she came from a well-to-do family. And Wynn had always been particularly scathing in his condemnation of the Jones's marriage. Behind closed doors, he had said on many occasions how nothing good ever came from marrying out of your own class, and at some level, the message had become absorbed into Dylan's beliefs as well.

"I wish I knew more about Ma's family," Betty said, perching on a fallen log to enjoy the sun on her face for a moment. "Grandfather Hughes is a mystery to me and Pa always told us never to talk about it."

"Even if you don't know anything about them, at least your ma has raised you to be educated," Dylan replied. It was common knowledge that Fay had wanted her children to be well-read and the children of the village had teased Betty when they were younger, calling her a bookworm with ideas above her station, just because the Jones family were different.

"Not that it's done much good," Betty replied with a shrug. "We're destined to work at Nantglas Colliery just like all the villagers, and we'll never do anything else. Any hopes that Ma might have had about us doing something else ended when Pa died." She shrugged as though it was of no concern. "I don't mind. As long as I can do what I need to keep our home, I'll be happy."

Betty sounded accepting of her situation, but the words made Dylan's heart sink. "You're not like us, Betty," he said, taking her hand in his own. "You have a lively mind, and you're beautiful. Who knows what you could achieve if you looked beyond Pencastle and the colliery."

He realised with sudden certainty that even though he loved Betty more than he could say, if he asked for her hand in marriage, she might end up doomed to be an impoverished miner's wife all her life. He thought about how workworn his ma was, and how the harsh conditions at the mine were taking their toll on Fay as well. He wanted something better for Betty but didn't know how he could be the person to provide it. He was barely managing to stop Wynn from beating his ma black and blue most weekends. Worse still, when Wynn was drunk lately, he had taken to mumbling about how he wanted to get revenge on Fay and everything she stood for.

"We'll have a nice life, Dylan. I've got the people I love most around me, and we'll have our own family too one day like you said all those years ago…do you remember?" Betty gave him a coy look and picked her basket up. She hoped Dylan might take her cue and speak about getting married too, but he seemed distracted so she pushed the idea aside and they headed back up the track. "I enjoyed this, maybe we could do it again but we'd better get back before your pa comes looking for you."

"There's something I want to say…" Dylan blurted out as the first cottages came into view. He decided to put his concerns aside and declare how much he loved her. Betty seemed happy to stay in the village and work at the colliery, and he realised that if they were married, at least he could do his best to love and cherish her the way she deserved.

"What is it?" Betty felt breathless as she saw Dylan's flustered expression, and her pulse quickened.

Dylan stepped closer and took hold of Betty's hands, and she looked up into hiswarm brown eyes. "Betty…will you…would you consider…"

"What are you doing with that hussy?" The harsh words rang out, echoing off the cottages on either side of the lane. Wynn was striding towards them, his chin jutting forward like an angry bulldog.

Dylan and Betty sprang apart and turned to

look at him warily. "We just went to the woods for a walk and to pick some sorrel, that's all Pa. Mrs Jones said it was alright."

"I thought I told you not to mix with them Jones's?" Wynn spat. He stepped closer, and a fug of beer fumes wafted over them as his lips twisted with contempt. "She's not good enough for you, Dylan if you're thinking of bedding her. Her ma thinks she's better than us ordinary folk, and this little madam does too, I don't doubt."

"How dare you speak about my family like that," Betty shot back. She put her hands on her hips, determined not to be cowed by him. "Don't think we haven't noticed you trying to get Ma and Minnie into trouble at the pit. My Pa always said you were a wrong 'un, and the way you treat your own wife and Dylan is despicable."

Wynn's face darkened with anger and he jabbed his finger in the centre of Dylan's chest, making him stagger backwards. "Have you been sharing our business all about the village, you blabber-mouth? A little bruise on your arm and you're squealing like a piglet to anyone who'll listen. Wait 'til I get home from the pub tonight, and then I'll give you something to help you keep your mouth shut."

"Everyone knows what you're like, Mr Parry, so you've no need to take it out on Dylan. Maybe I should mention something to the constable? See how you like that." Betty saw Dylan's face go pale at her words, but it was as if she couldn't stop. "My Pa was twice the man you'll ever be, and Dylan is too," she snapped.

"Why...you...you...I won't let you get away with speaking to me like this, Betty Jones." Wynn's words came out as a snarl and he bunched his hands into fists, before turning on his heel and marching away, muttering angrily to himself until he disappeared around the corner.

"I'm sorry, Dylan, but I can't stand by and say nothing when he's so horrible." Betty gave him an apologetic look. "It's all bluff and bluster, isn't it? I expect he'll have forgotten about it by the time he sobers up again tomorrow."

Dylan nodded, but a sense of foreboding gripped him like an icy hand around his heart. As they parted company and he watched Betty walk the last few yards towards her cottage he had a terrible feeling that Wynn would never forgive Betty's harsh assessment of his character. His father was the sort of man who would bear a grudge for years, letting it fester and grow like a disease and he prayed that this time it might be different. *I love Betty, but if I defend her and cross Pa, he'll take it out on Ma.* The thought that swirled in Dylan's mind left him almost dizzy with worry. Whichever way he acted, he would be potentially endangering the two women he cared about more than anything.

CHAPTER 4

"*I*'m really not hungry, Betty dear. Just let me rest for today and I'll be back on my feet in no time." Fay waved the spoon of porridge away and gave her daughter a vague smile before her head fell back on her pillow again. "Just today…I promise I'll try and be back on the riddling tables again tomorrow…" Her last words came out as barely a whisper, but Betty could tell how troubled her ma was that she was missing work for a second day running.

"Don't think about work, Ma. Just have a good sleep. I'm going to ask the butcher for his best bones and make a tasty beef broth for you later on." Betty plumped the pillows beneath her mother's head and gently brushed her hair back from her forehead, which glistened with a sheen of perspiration.

"Is Ma going to be alright?" Minnie's face was etched with worry as she poured them all a cup of tea in the kitchen. The sun had barely risen and she glanced at the clock on the mantelshelf. They had to be at the pit by six o'clock in the morning in the summer months but it was hard to leave their mother alone all day when she seemed so frail.

"Maybe you should stay with her today, Betty? Minnie and I can get by," Jack said tentatively. His suggestion lacked conviction though. They all knew every penny counted and they couldn't afford for one of them to be off work as well as Fay.

"I think it's just exhaustion." Betty tried to sound hopeful but worry gnawed at her guts. When their pa had got ill he had mentioned several times that he felt weary before he'd started coughing up blood but like most of the miners, tiredness and aching muscles were just accepted as part of working life. They grafted, and too many workers died young; that was just the way it was. "The three of us will work as normal, maybe even a bit faster if that's possible."

Minnie yawned loudly and spooned porridge

into her mouth as fast as she could. "At least we've got a bit more food in our bellies today." She divided Fay's portion between their three bowls and ate hers with relish.

"And you say I'm always talking about food," Jack chuckled. "We'll do our best, and Ma will get better," he said firmly. "If I could work longer hours, maybe I could have some of the better coal that Wynn has overlooked." His face took on a thoughtful expression.

"That's not such a bad idea, Jack." Betty cleared away the plates and scraped beef dripping onto three thick slices of bread, adding a couple of hard-boiled eggs and one bruised apple they could share to the tin they took their lunch in. It wasn't much to last them all day, but it was all she could afford at the moment. On a whim, she added a teaspoon of sugar to the cold tea in each of their Dudley tins, hoping it would give them all a bit more energy for the long day ahead and make up for the meagre food rations.

"Imagine if we had enough money for a slap-up dinner tonight," Minnie said dreamily as she watched. "I'd have hot ham and parsley sauce, with potatoes…"

"And fresh bread to mop up every last drop,

followed by plum pudding and custard," Jack continued. He clutched his stomach with a grin as though he was full to bursting. "In fact, I'd have two puddings…apple crumble…and then a mug of hot chocolate to wash it all down."

A wave of guilt engulfed Betty. As the eldest, it was her responsibility to keep the family together, but she felt as though she was failing when every day was such a struggle. It was hard enough to put enough food on the table to make sure they could do the gruelling work at the mine, let alone afford the occasional small treat to keep their spirits up.

A sudden hammering at the door made them jump. "Who would be calling at this time of day?" Minnie grumbled. She started dragging a brush through her hair so she could plait it.

"I'll answer it. You'd better carry on getting ready for work." Betty dried her hands on her apron and hurried to the door, hoping it might be Dylan with a rabbit from his snares that they could make a stew from. She smoothed her hair and was already smiling as she opened the door, but the smile vanished as soon as she saw who it was.

"Good morning, Miss Jones. I thought I'd come early to be sure to catch you at home." Elis Jenkins lounged nonchalantly against the door frame, his bulk almost filling the space. He gave her a sly smile as his gaze lingered on her womanly curves. "It's been a while since I've seen you. Usually, I deal with yer ma, but I can see the passing of time has treated you well now that you're all grown up."

Betty crossed her arms across her chest and looked him in the eye. "Make it quick, please, Mr Jenins. We have to get to work, as I'm sure you know." Elis was Fred Jenkins' brother, and she disliked them both as much as each other.

"It doesn't do to be rude to the person in charge of your future, Miss Jones." Elis stood up straighter, suddenly more businesslike.

"In charge of our future? I'm not sure I understand. You're just a land-worker for Lord Griffiths, even though you like to behave as though you're more important," Betty shot back defiantly.

"Well, that's where you're mistaken. I ain't just maintaining walls and gateways no more, Miss Jones." Elis towered over her in a deliberately intimidating fashion. "I've been promoted to collecting the rent for Lord Griffiths since old Grundy got too feeble to carry on. And a nice little job it is too. It suits me down to the ground."

Betty stepped back a little, coughing to cover her surprise. Mr Grundy had been their rent collector for as long as she could remember, and he had always been willing to let the rent run overdue by a few days or more, as long as he knew it would be settled eventually. He had come from humble beginnings and knew what it was like to go hungry. But Elis Jenkins was a different kettle of fish altogether. He had travelled the country as a prize-fighter for several years, and his flattened nose and scar-pocked face bore testament to the beatings he had willingly taken part in. But an injury several years ago had meant he'd had to stop, so he had returned to the valley to work for Lord Griffiths. Elis delighted in throwing his weight around. He was known for getting embroiled in fights in the bar of The Red Dragon every weekend at the slightest provocation. But worse than that, rumour had it that he was spiteful too. For Lord Griffiths, Elis was the perfect combination of character traits and sheer brutish strength to get his rent collected on time after he had grown tired of Mr Grundy's lenient ways.

"Hah, you didn't expect that, did yer?" he said with a triumphant smile. "Yer Ma was always quick to look down her nose at me. She still thought she was Lady La-De-Dah, I reckon, even though Emrys was as common as muck."

"I don't know what you mean, Mr Jenkins. But we really must leave for the pit now, so if there's nothing more…" Betty started to close the door, but Elis jammed his large booted foot in the gap, making the door judder in its frame.

"Not so fast, Betty. Your rent is due, and I want to make sure you'll have every penny of it ready for me before nightfall tomorrow. Also, Lord Griffiths asked me to inform you that it's going up by two shillings a week, starting from the next time I collect the rent."

"Two shillings a week?" Betty gasped. She felt the blood drain from her face. "Ma isn't well at the moment, Mr Jenkins. Please can you be lenient and give us a bit more notice…I'm sure things will improve soon. She just needs a few days to rest."

"Ain't my problem, is it?" Elis shrugged and turned to leave. "That's the trouble with you Jones's," he sneered. "Everyone knows you fancy yourselves a cut above the rest of us with yer fancy book-learning and Emrys mollycoddling Fay all these years, just because she was born with a silver spoon in 'er mouth." He gave a humourless chuckle and strolled down the path. "It's time you learnt you're no better than the rest of us. Of course, my brother Fred quite likes the look of this cottage…

maybe you could live in one of the rooms down Mousely Lane instead...I hear they're nice and cosy." With that, he lifted his hand and gave her a jaunty wave before strolling away, whistling under his breath.

"Did you hear that?" Betty was trembling with anger and distress as she slammed the door closed and saw Minnie and Jack standing behind her. "He wants two shillings a week more for our rent from next week...I scarcely have enough put by to pay for this week's as it is. I wish Mr Grundy was still in charge instead of that bully."

"I can't believe he said we should move to Mousely Lane," Jack cried. "Everyone knows those old buildings are only one step up from the work-house, full of drunks and ne'er-do-wells."

Glancing at the clock, Betty realised they had to leave immediately or risk their wages being docked if they were late to work. "Hurry up. We can talk about it on the way up the hill, but we have to go now." She jammed her old straw bonnet on her head and hastily hung her apron up, grabbing their lunch. "Elis Jenkins might think he can frighten us into moving so his brother can steal our home, but I'm not having it. I'll think of some-thing. We have to keep Ma at home here. Moving her to a damp room down the valley would be the worst thing for her health, and Pa worked all his life for us to live in our little cottage. We can't let it all be for nothing."

Jack and Minnie nodded in agreement as they hurried down the garden path. "Whatever you suggest, Betty. We'll stick together and make it work. We won't let him get the better of us," Jack said firmly.

BETTY STRAINED against the leather straps of her tub as she saw the glimmer of light at the end of the shaft. With every step she took, her mind swirled with one question. *How can we earn enough to pay the new amount of rent and stay in our home?* She scarcely noticed the dull ache of pain in her shoulders or the cramping of her muscles. If anything, it provided a welcome distraction from her churning thoughts.

"Maybe we could team up with another family?" Jack had given her a fresh suggestion every time she met him in the dark tunnel to exchange his full tub with her empty one.

She had considered it for a moment, then

shook her head. "Everyone is already working within their families. You know folks don't like to partner with others. We need a solution that's just for us, Jack. It's only until Ma gets better."

Jack had nodded, even though she couldn't see it in the pitch black. Betty was right. The mining families guarded their own spots at the coalface as possessively as a terrier with a bone, and although his spot wasn't as good as Wynn Parry's, Jack knew that he could end up in a part of the mine that was even less productive. He had only been allowed to stay where he was because of the many years of hard graft their pa had put in before them, and the last thing he wanted was to change and end up with it being a backward step.

"Two more shillings a week. It's daylight robbery," Betty muttered to herself as she tipped the coal from her tub into her cart and started to push it along the track for the final part of her ascent out of the tunnel.

"What are you wittering on about, girl?" Dai Llewelyn gave her a curious look as she emerged into the daylight. He had warmed to her recently, affording her a grudging respect as he saw how hard she worked.

Betty sighed. "It's Elis Jenkins, Dai. He's putting

our rent up just when we can least afford it. Ma's not very well at the moment, but he paid no heed to that."

Dai pushed his battered cap to the back of his head and spat on the ground between them in an expression of annoyance. "Aye, the landlords and their thuggish rent collectors always want more. I reckon they'd work us into the ground if they thought they could get away with it." He lowered his voice and glanced over his shoulder. "I heard Mr Crundell and Fred Jenkins racked up some debts at the card tables recently. You keep your wits about you, girl. Don't let 'em see you wrong. Yer ma might be a bit posh, but she was always kind to me, even when I could have been a bit friendlier to her." He gave Betty an apologetic wink. "I know folks say I'm a curmudgeonly old fellow, but I know a kind heart when I see one." With that, he gave her an encouraging nod and pushed his cart towards the riddling tables.

"YOU SEEM to have time on your hands Miss Jones, enjoying the sunshine and chatting to Dai." Ezra Crundell's comment from behind her made Betty jump. For a large man, he had a habit of creeping up silently, which was rather discon-certing.

"I'm just going to empty my cart now," Betty said hastily. She started to steer it away from him, but he waddled around in front of her, blocking her path.

"What did Dai want with you?" he asked with a suspicious frown. "I think his mind is getting addled, so don't pay any attention to his gossip."

"He was just passing the time of day, sir." Betty wasn't going to let on what Dai had warned her about. She needed every nugget of information she could get because she would never know when it might come in useful.

Seeing as Mr Crundell had taken her to one side, Betty decided it was time to be brave. An image of her ma's pale face gave her the courage she needed, and she blurted out the question that had been taking shape in the back of her mind during the last few journeys to the surface with her cart. "May I have a quick word with you, please, Mr Crundell," she said, giving him what she hoped was a winning smile.

"As long as it's quick," he said distractedly. "Stop your squabbling will you, Esme and Lorna," he bellowed, scowling at two of the young girls on the line.

"The thing is...Ma's not very well, as you know..."

"Indeed. It's very inconvenient." Crundell turned back to face her. "I'll have to look for someone to replace her if she doesn't hurry up and stop this wretched malingering you workers seem so prone to."

Betty bit back the retort that was on the tip of her tongue and took a deep breath. She couldn't afford to let his petty needling get to her now. "I know you like our colliery to do well, compared to the other ones nearby, Mr Crundell. And that's a reflection of your good character." She smiled inwardly as Crundell nodded pompously, falling for her flattery.

"It's why I'm regarded as the best pit manager in the district, Miss Jones. I'm glad you've finally recognised that fact."

"Well, Jack and I wondered if you might allow us to work longer hours, Mr Crundell? We need the extra money now that Pa's no longer alive...and it might help you out as well, of course. If we could do a couple more hours after the official closing time...

just enough to fill one cart perhaps…it would boost your figures and help us get Ma better again in no time." Betty watched the emotions chasing across his pudgy features as he considered her request. First suspicion, then curiosity, and finally the one she had been hoping to see; a gleam of greed in his small eyes.

"Well…." Mr Crundell sucked his cheeks in and rocked forwards on his toes, like the seasoned negotiator he was. "I wouldn't normally allow such a breach of the rules, Miss Jones."

"I understand that," Betty said quickly. "And I would make sure that nobody but Jack and I knew about it. You have my word."

"I might need to think about it. Lord Griffiths, the colliery owner is already delighted with my performance, you see. There's no real need for me to better it." He stuck his thumbs in his waistcoat and shook his head before looking back at her as if a thought had suddenly occurred to him. "I do like to support several charitable bodies because I'm a very generous person, Miss Jones. Perhaps I could consider your request if you were to give me… shall we say…half of the additional money you would earn from doing the extra work." With a thin smile, he let his words hang in the air between them.

"Half of everything?" Betty tried to stay calm. She had expected him to want some sort of one-off bribe, but this was more than she had anticipated.

"Yes, half of the additional money. I think that's a very generous agreement, don't you? After all, you're asking me to break the law, Miss Jones. If anybody found out, I could lose my job."

Betty did a hasty calculation in her head and realised she had no choice. "Thank you, Mr Crundell. We'll start tomorrow night, once I've had a chance to make arrangements for Minnie to look after Ma and cover all my chores at home."

"Very good. And remember, this stays between us, Miss Jones, otherwise things could get very nasty for you and your family." Mr Crundell patted her on her arm and Betty tried not to recoil and show her distaste for him. "I think you and I could get along very well with this little arrangement, Betty. Who knows…maybe I could favour you in other ways as well…let's see how we go, shall we?"

"Yes…Jack and I are very grateful for your agreement, Mr Crundell." She forced herself to smile and turned towards her cart, feeling the weight of his gaze on her back. She glanced skywards, sending up a hasty prayer. *Please forgive me for bending the rules. It was the only thing I could think of to help Ma and get some more money in.* Betty felt a strange combination of relief and anxiety. She was glad their immediate money worries had now been dealt with, but she hoped she wouldn't come to regret giving Mr Crundell something he could hold over her. She had never knowingly broken the law in her life, and if anyone found out, she could lose everything.

CHAPTER 5

"*H*as everyone gone yet?" Jack's voice was quiet as he chewed the last mouthful of his apple. He was sitting with his back to the brick wall enjoying the evening sun on his face.

"Yes, I just saw the last of them heading down the lane." Betty stood up from behind the wall in the corner of the yard and lifted her arms above her head to stretch her shoulders which ached after twelve hours of labouring already. Since Mr Crundell had agreed to her request, she and Jack came up to the surface of the mine with everyone else at the end of the shift but had managed to evade suspicion by loitering at the back. The rest of the workers were intent on getting home as fast as possible, so nobody gave them a second look when they slipped away to hide. Instead, the villagers trudged down the hill, chattering like a flock of garrulous seagulls while Betty and Jack waited for the yard to empty.

"Come on then, Betty. Three more tubs of coal to fill your cart, and that'll be a few more coins for the rent." Jack yawned loudly and jumped up. The sooner they got back down the pit, the sooner they could get home.

Betty tried not to let her thoughts turn to the future over the next hour and a half as she dragged the tubs along the stony floor after Jack filled them. *Just think about today...and maybe tomorrow.* She gritted her teeth as she covered the last few yards with the third tub, leaning into the rough harness. Two weeks had already passed since Elis Jenkins had announced the unexpected increase in their rent. Betty had scrimped and saved every penny she could, telling Minnie that they needed to stretch every meal further by replacing meat with bread and potatoes, and by some miracle, she had managed to pay the new amount.

She grinned in the darkness as she thought back to Elis's visit last night. He had hammered on the door, reeking of brandy and thrusting his hand out for the money as soon as Betty swung the door open. "I reckon it was a fluke that you managed to pay last week," he had grumbled, swaying slightly in the light that fell on him from the kitchen lamp. "Let's see if you can keep it up, though? I'll take my dues in full, right away, ta very much."

Betty had dropped the coins into his palm and bobbed her head politely. "There you are, Mr Jenkins. Goodnight." His eyes had bulged with disbelief making him look comical as he hastily counted the money out from one of his gnarly hands into the other. It had almost made the back-breaking work worthwhile to see his expression, but Betty stifled her laughter, knowing it might trigger one of the bad tempers Elis was so renowned for, especially when he'd been drinking.

"It's all there...this time," he had harrumphed, sounding disappointed. "I'll be on my way then." He had lurched off down the path, muttering to himself under his breath about how his brother wouldn't be best pleased, and Betty had felt a wave of relief that she had got him off her back for one more week at least.

"I've filled the last tub for tonight." Jack's muffled voice behind Betty startled her.

"That was quick. If you tip it into the cart, we

can call it a night and get home. I'm ravenous. I hope Minnie has made us a nice dinner."

A few minutes later, they emerged from the shaft, pausing to check that there was nobody around before wheeling it to the hiding place Mr Crundell had agreed they could use, behind an old shed that was rarely used. Mr Crundell made sure that he tallied her first load the following morning himself so as not to arouse suspicions with Fred Jenkins, and so far, the plan seemed to be working.

As they hurried down the hill, the sun was sinking low in the sky, painting vivid streaks of pink and orange on the bracken-covered hillsides of the mountains. A pair of buzzards wheeled overhead, with their plaintive cry that always sounded rather sad to Betty, and she sighed. Working late like this was not so bad in the height of summer when they could still snatch a couple of hours of daylight before bedtime. But in the middle of winter, she knew it would be far more challenging.

A sudden rustle behind them made Betty and Jack spin around, and she smiled when she saw Dylan striding towards them.

"What are you two doing up here so late?" he

asked curiously. He had a bulging hessian sack over his shoulder and blood on his hands from where he had already gutted the rabbits he had snared. "One for the pot?" he added with a grin. "I got three tonight, so I can spare one."

"I'll see you back at the cottage," Jack said, accepting the rabbit Dylan had offered them. He gave Betty a warning glance, but she nodded, and he trotted off.

"Can I trust you to keep a secret, Dylan?" Betty fell into step next to him.

"Of course. You shouldn't even need to ask."

"Jack and I are working extra time down the pit at the end of the shift."

Dylan stared at her, looking shocked. "After hours, you mean? But what if Crundell finds out… he'll sack you on the spot. You know it's not allowed. You're not the sort of person to break rules, Betty; you never have been."

Betty shot him a rueful smile. "My back's against the wall, Dylan. Ma's not getting any better, and Elis Jenkins has put our rent up. What else could I do? You don't need to worry about Mr Crundell; he's making a tidy profit from our extra work. He's as crooked as they come when it suits him."

Dylan looked at Betty with admiration. "You never fail to surprise me. But one thing I don't understand…why has Elis put your rent up? Usually, it's only done in the New Year."

"Because he's the sort of man who does what he chooses," Betty replied with a hollow laugh. "I suspect he's trying to get us evicted so his brother, Fred, can have our house. But it's not as if I can march up to Lord Griffiths and ask him if Elis is singling us out, is it?"

"I'll try and help out however I can, Betty. But I daren't break the rules myself as Ma relies on me bringing in a wage, especially as it seems like Pa spends it practically faster than I can earn it, down at The Red Dragon."

"You're a kind and loyal friend," Betty said, shaking her head. "I wouldn't want you to put yourself at risk of getting into trouble. Just the occasional rabbit or fish for our dinner is more than enough."

"You'll get through this," Dylan said, desperate to reassure her. He hated seeing Betty so worried, but she was right, there was nothing she could do about Elis's rent demands, and they just had to hope Fay would get well enough to get back to work soon. It was a constant worry for him as well that the gruelling work would affect his ma's health the way it did for so many of the villagers.

"One more thing, Dylan. Please can we keep this between ourselves? The fewer people who know what we're doing, the better, and you know that gossip can spread like wildfire around here."

Dylan squeezed her hand, giving her a long look. "You have my word. And I promise I'll make sure Pa never finds out either. He seems to have it in for you and your family for some reason, and it's the least I can do for you, Betty."

THE FOLLOWING MORNING, the sun beat down on Betty and her family as they toiled up the hill. There hadn't been a drop of rain for almost a month, and the dust coated their boots. It would have been a perfect day to go for a swim in the river, but there was no time to spare for such leisurely activities anymore, not with Fay still languishing in bed, still too weak to work.

"I heard some of the colliery owners send their workers to the seaside for a day trip," Minnie said longingly. She lifted her hair from the back of her neck in an attempt to cool down, but the air was completely still, with no hint of a breeze.

"No chance of that with Lord Griffiths," Jack muttered. He kicked a stone disconsolately as they arrived at the yard. The longer work days were taking their toll even though they had only been doing it for a few weeks. "He should be called Lord Skinflint instead." He winced as pain suddenly shot through his ear.

"Show some manners, young man, or I'll clip you around the lughole again. It's Lord Griffiths, and you'd better behave respectfully, especially after this morning's announcement." Ezra Crundell gave Jack another prod in the arm with his pudgy finger before continuing to the front of the yard and hauling himself up the steps onto the wooden platform he used to speak to the workers.

"Quiet everybody, Mr Crundell wants you to listen good and proper to what he's got to say," Fred Jenkins bellowed, glaring at two children who were squabbling over a few pieces of coal. "Come over here so you can hear properly." He herded everyone up in front of the platform, and everyone fell silent, hoping it wasn't going to be bad news.

"As you know, Lord Griffiths is an extremely benevolent employer," Mr Crundell began, strutting back and forth as he warmed to his subject.

"About as benevolent as a miser lookin' at his last shilling," the woman next to Betty whispered loudly, making some of the workers in the crowd snigger. Fred Jenkins fixed the woman with a fierce stare, and she ducked her head.

"He has asked me to share some urgent news," Crundell continued. "He will be bringing a very important gentleman, Lord Leyfield, to visit Nant-glas Colliery in the coming days. Lord Leyfield has recently returned from abroad and wants to invest in the coal mine."

A ripple of excited whispers ran through the workers, and Betty felt her spirits lift. Perhaps they would finally get the pay rise which had been promised for the last two years but which had so far failed to materialise.

"Not before time," Jack muttered. "Some of the pit props are in a dreadful state down the shafts; it's a wonder we haven't had an accident. And it's high time we got paid more as well."

Betty nudged him to be quiet as Mr Crundell looked at them. "There is one small problem, though." Mr Crundell paused to make sure that he had everyone's full attention. "Apparently, Lord Leyfield is in two minds about which colliery to invest in. It could either be ours...or it could be

The Ferncoed Colliery." His face pinched into a sour expression at the mention of their arch-rivals, a much larger coal mine a few miles away in Pentood Valley. Mr Crundell had long hoped to become manager there, but Lord Griffiths had chosen someone younger, which still rankled.

"You can leave it to us to impress the toffs, Mr Crundell", Dai Llewelyn shouted. "We'll doff our caps and tell them we're a safe bet. I've worked here for over forty years, man and boy, and we deserve it more than those upstarts at Ferncoed."

"I think we'll need more than the words of a doddery old fool like you," Wynn shot back, rolling his eyes. "Why don't I show him one of my carts of coal, Mr Crundell. Lord Whatshisname will see how good the quality is, and that should be good enough to secure the investment."

"Aye, because you don't leave any of the good coal for anyone else," Jack couldn't help but reply, even though Betty sent him a warning look.

"Pushing yourself forward, just like usual, Parry," another wiry man commented with a bark of laughter.

"That's quite enough," Mr Crundell shouted as arguments threatened to break out between all the rival families who worked there. "I'm the manager, and I shall be showing our visitor around. All I need from you lot is to do as you're told, keep quiet, and work hard. Is that clear?"

Everyone nodded and shuffled off to their various positions. It had been a nice distraction to listen to Mr Crundell's news, but the minutes were ticking by and they couldn't afford to stand around idly chatting.

Wynn made a beeline for Betty and Jack, blocking their way as they headed towards the shed where their full cart of coal was hidden. "What are you doing over in this part of the yard?" he demanded.

"Just some chores for Mr Crundell," Betty said hastily.

Wynn gave her a hard stare, clearly not convinced. "You'd better not mess this visit up for us," he said eventually. "Just because your ma used to be a toff doesn't mean you are. If anyone's going to impress Lord Griffiths and his pal, it's me." With that, he swaggered off, leaving a cloud of stale alcohol fumes and the pungent scent of the strong tobacco that he favoured in his wake.

The day passed faster than usual because the whole mine was abuzz with anticipation about the forthcoming visit. Every time Betty came to the surface with her cart, she could hear snatches of gossip from the women on the riddling tables, each time more fanciful than the last.

"...I 'eard they might sink a whole new shaft which means we'll never need to worry about bein' out of work..."

"...five shillings a week payrise...that's what my Bobby reckons we're owed..."

"...they say he's as handsome as a prince and looking for a new wife since his own passed away...what do you think of my chances, ladies?"

Betty grinned at the last one. It was Minnie, of course, and she had a dreamy expression on her face as the women on either side of her cackled with raucous laughter that made the men frown. "I think you've more chance of kissing a frog than marrying a Lord," Betty called. "Now crack on with your work, otherwise it'll be bread and dripping for tea again."

Minnie pouted and tossed her head. "You've lost all your sense of fun since Ma got ill, Betty. Can't I even have a joke without you fretting about money?" She relented when she saw Betty's shrug of apology. "I know you're looking out for us, but I was only daydreaming...at least that doesn't cost anything, does it."

"Keep your chin up, Minnie," said Dawn, who stood next to her. "Fay's made of stronger stuff than you think. Lots of folks said her marriage to your pa wouldn't last five minutes once she'd realised how hard it was being poor. But all credit to her, she stuck it out, and they stayed in love. 'T'was like a fairytale romance, which is more than I ever had with my old misery guts of a husband."

After what felt like no time, the yard had cleared again, and Betty and Jack descended back down the shaft by the weak light of their tallow candle. As Betty waited for Jack, she thought about what Dawn had said to Minnie earlier that day. It was true; her parents had enjoyed a very happy marriage, even though money had often been short. Now that she was older, she could appreciate how much they must have loved each other for her Ma to turn her back on a comfortable upbringing where she would never have had to want for anything. The thought of it tugged at her heartstrings. That was the sort of marriage she hoped to have with Dylan, but the way Wynn was watching them like a hawk, the thought of them courting and then having a little cottage together with a family of their own seemed further away than ever.

Why is Wynn so bitter? Can't he just let go of the past and accept that Ma and Pa were made for each other? The questions flitted through her mind making her sigh again. Suddenly a small sound snagged her attention and brought her back to the present. It was like the sound of stealthy footsteps on the loose shale of the floor, and she strained her ears to see if it would happen again.

"Who's there? Is that you, Jack?" Betty's voice sounded faint in the thick darkness, and the hairs on the back of her neck stood up. "Is there someone there?" she demanded, a little bit louder. She wished she still had her candle, but Jack had taken it so they could save burning two of them until it was absolutely necessary. A sudden whisper of air rushed past Betty, bringing the scent of tobacco with it, and she froze. It smelt like the same one that Wynn Parry smoked, but there was no reason why he would be down the mine at this time of night.

"Did you call me?" Jack's cheerful shout drifted towards Betty, and she sighed with relief as she made out the pinprick of light from his candle getting closer.

"No…it's fine. I was just asking how much longer you were going to be."

Jack huffed and strained as he pulled the full tub up to her. His eyes glinted with intrigue, and he nodded towards the coal. "Take a look at this… Wynn left some of the good stuff lying on the floor today, so I've taken it. I reckon he's getting a bit slapdash, what with being hungover most days." He held up a couple of large lumps of coal with a chuckle. "His loss is our gain, Betty. What he doesn't know won't harm him. We might even make an extra shilling more than usual this week if Crundell is straight with his tallies."

Betty peered into the tub with a worried frown, glancing over her shoulder again. "Won't Wynn know you've taken it though, Jack? We can't risk him finding out about what we're doing."

"You worry too much," Jack replied happily. "He'll be busy drinking his wages away in The Red Dragon right about now, just like every night. It's about time we had a bit of luck, isn't it? I didn't take too much, and he's not going to miss a few good bits if I cover it with the dust and smaller pieces we usually bring up."

Betty nodded reluctantly. The thought of a few extra coins to make a nice stew for them all was tempting, so she decided that it wouldn't harm as long as they didn't do it every time. Glancing around one last time, she pushed away the notion that she felt as though someone was watching them in the darkness. *I'm just tired and worried about Ma, that's all. My imagination is running away with me, thinking I can smell Wynn's tobacco. He'll be down at the pub, just like Dylan always tells me he is.*

CHAPTER 6

*B*etty's high spirits were soon dashed when she saw Minnie running up the lane towards them after they had left the mine for the night. "Come quickly," she shouted. "Ma's not talking any sense, and I'm worried about her." Her long blonde hair flew out behind her, and her hands were still covered in flour from where she had been baking.

"I thought her breathing sounded bad this morning," Betty said, hurrying into the cottage. She threw off her bonnet and dumped her basket on the table.

"Ma...Ma, how are you feeling?" Betty perched on the edge of Fay's bed and rested her hand on her mother's forehead. Where it had been damp with a sheen of sweat the day before, now it felt hot and dry under her fingers.

"I...I'll be fine, dear. It's nothing." Fay gave them all a weak smile, but then a sudden coughing fit seized her, shaking her narrow shoulders. "Just a bit of sleep...that's all I need."

"She's been unwell for too long now. She should be getting better," Jack said with a worried frown.

Betty came to a decision. "I'm going to see if Doctor Cooper will come and have a look at her. I'll tell him we've tried all the usual things, but she's worsening."

"Can we afford to call the doctor out?" Minnie wrung her hands in her lap. "I tried my best, Betty, I promise. I made some broth, but she refused to eat. She told me we needed the food more than her." Tears pooled in her eyes as she looked at Fay's wan face on the pillow. Her cheeks looked gaunt, and she had dark circles under her eyes.

"I put a bit of money by, just in case. Hopefully, Doctor Cooper won't charge us too much. He was kind enough to let us pay less when Pa was ill, so we must pray that he'll do the same again." Betty didn't tell Minnie that the money she had in mind was for the rent. She would just have to deal with

Elis Jenkins when he came, whatever the consequences. Their ma's life was too important, and she couldn't bear the thought of losing her the same way they had lost their pa. "Just do your best to keep her awake until I get back," Betty instructed as she darted from the room.

Betty ran through the village as fast as her feet would carry her, calling to everyone she passed to see if they knew where Doctor Cooper's whereabouts was after she realised that he wasn't at home.

"I ain't seen him since this morning, maid, sorry." The landlord of The Red Dragon shook his head as he rolled a new barrel of beer off the dray cart.

"Try old Mary Lloyd's place," one of the women beating her rugs outside the front of her house said. "I heard she'd burnt her hand earlier today, and I saw the Doctor heading in that direction on his horse not thirty minutes ago."

Betty waved to her in thanks and picked up her skirts so she could run faster. Mary was Dai Llewelyn's sister who lived alone since she'd been widowed many years ago. When she was younger, some of the children of the village had spread rumours that she was soft in the head, and they would creep up to peer into her garden and steal apples from her tree for a dare. But Fay had always told Betty not to judge without knowing, and Emrys had forbidden them from taking part in the childish pranks. Eventually, Betty learned that Mary's desire to live a quiet life in her cottage on the outskirts of the village was because of grief from losing her husband and young child when their cart had overturned. Determined not to cast the poor woman out of village life, Fay had often taken her small gifts, leaving them on her doorstep and hoping that the old woman would take some comfort from knowing someone was looking out for her.

As Betty rounded the corner of the dusty track, she was relieved to see Doctor Cooper's grey mare quietly grazing on the verge outside the wrought iron front gate. She patted the horse's neck and paused for a moment to catch her breath before tiptoeing up the path to the wooden door. The whitewashed cottage was bigger than she remembered when she had come with her ma several times as a child. It nestled under a thatched roof, and there were tidy rows of vegetables growing in a kitchen garden to the side, flanked by flower beds full of hollyhocks and roses. She raised her hand to knock on the door but before she could, it creaked open to reveal a wizened old woman who looked up at her with a bright smile.

"Are you Fay Jones's girl?" Mary Lloyd peered past Betty as if worried that there might be more people with her. "You're the spitting image of her, so I'm sure you must be. Come in." She stood back to allow Betty inside and gestured to a chair at the scrubbed kitchen table where Doctor Cooper was sipping a cup of tea.

"I'm sorry to disturb you, Mrs Lloyd. I'm looking for the doctor, and someone said you'd burnt your hand, and he was here to see you." Betty knew she was gabbling nervously but Mary merely patted her on her arm.

"Not much gets past folk in Pencastle, that's for sure," she said with an amused chuckle. She held her hand up to show Betty the bandage. "I told Dai not to make a fuss, but he insisted the Doctor should check up on me. I splashed some boiling water on it, that's all. My eyesight isn't as good as it used to be. Would you like a cup of tea now that you're here? I don't get many visitors," she added, wiping a cup on her apron. "How's that lovely ma of yours?"

"That's why I'm here." Betty felt bad for all the

times she had wondered whether Mary Lloyd was as strange as the villagers had told her she was. The only thing she seemed guilty of was liking her own company. Her cottage was spotlessly clean and an elderly terrier snored by the hearth. "Ma's been in bed for days and I kept hoping she would get better with a bit of rest…but she's not looking too good today, Doctor Cooper. I wondered if you could come and see how she's doing?"

Doctor Cooper gave her a kindly look from under his bushy eyebrows, hastily gulping down the last of his tea. "Of course, my dear. I could tell when I came to treat Emrys that your mother was of a delicate disposition and I'm sure the work at the pit takes its toll."

"Doesn't is just," Mary said emphatically. "Them owners line their pockets, never mind how bad the workers are struggling to make ends meet. My brother, Dai will probably breathe his last standing on that cursed riddling line as he can't afford to stop work."

"We've tried broth, and Ma's had plenty of sleep…I'm just worried she might end up going the same way as Pa." Betty shuffled from one foot to the other, keen to get back home again.

"Give her a spoonful of this every day, Betty."

Mary pressed a jar of honey into Betty's hands. "Your ma always took the time to show a bit of kindness after I lost…after I lost my loved ones. Not like some of the villagers." Mary's eyes misted over, and she blinked rapidly.

"I have a couple more things to do here, and then I'll come immediately," Doctor Cooper said, standing up. "You run along back to her bedside and I'll see you shortly."

"Thank you, Doctor." Betty hesitated. "Will it cost much? It's just that we don't—"

"I know…don't worry. We'll sort something out." The doctor waved her concerns away, and Betty heaved a sigh of relief as Mary showed her out again.

"Look after your family, dear. They're all that matter when all's said and done." Mary watched Betty hurry away with a troubled expression, reminded again of the grief of losing her own husband and daughter. Life was tough at the pit, and not many families escaped without experiencing illness from the gruelling work.

"I'M SORRY MRS JONES, but your condition is worse than I first thought, I'm afraid." Doctor Cooper's face was grave as he stood up from where he had been listing to Fay's breathing. The wheezing in her lungs was clear to hear and he shook his head slightly.

"Surely there's something we can do, Doctor?" Minnie's tone was abrupt but Betty knew it was because she was worried.

Doctor Cooper snapped his leather bag closed and beckoned them away from the bedside. Fay had already drifted back to sleep again, but he didn't want her to overhear their conversation. "Fortunately you called me out just in the nick of time. Most of the villagers leave it too long and then there's nothing I can do or say, but it's good that you came to fetch me today, Betty."

"She'll be alright won't she?" Jack said hastily. "We've already lost our Pa…"

Doctor Cooper put a reassuring hand on his shoulder. "I know you won't want to hear this, but I strongly recommend that your mother doesn't work at the pit anymore. If she survives this illness, her lungs will always be weaker than they were. The dust up there, combined with working outside in all weathers would be the end of her if she doesn't stop now."

"So you think she will survive?" Betty whispered, feeling her spirits lift slightly. She had assumed the worst, but now there was a sliver of hope to cling onto amongst his words and that was what she would choose to focus on.

"I never like to speak in absolutes Betty, as I'm sure you can understand. But if she retires from working on the riddling tables, eats wholesome food, and avoids over-exerting herself, I do believe your mother will live to see a few more years at least. That's the best I can say."

"That's good enough for us, Doc," Minnie said, throwing her arms around him. "We were terrified she wouldn't even make it to the end of the week."

"Thank you…you have no idea how happy we are to hear this," Betty said with a smile as the Doctor's cheeks flushed pink, flustered by Minnie's hug. "I know it will be hard managing without her money coming in, but we'll find a way to make ends meet. Ma's wellbeing is all that matters, just like Mary said." She handed Doctor Cooper a couple of coins from the tin on the mantelshelf. She knew it was less than his usual fee, but he harrumphed and shook his head when she offered more.

"You'll need every penny you can get for food and rent, I expect," he said gruffly. "At least up the hill here this cottage is spared the worst of the smog and coal dust from the mine. Do what you can to ensure she stays here, Betty. She wouldn't last long in one of those damp buildings down the valley, of that I'm certain."

THE REST of the week passed in a blur as Betty and Jack pushed themselves beyond what they thought possible. Instead of stopping to eat, they wolfed down their food as they worked, to the point that Betty wondered how long they could sustain it. When Friday evening came around, Mr Crundell dropped their wages into Betty's hand, and she riffled through the coins, checking it was the correct amount.

"That looks a bit light," Jack muttered, leaning over her shoulder.

"You're right. Mr Crundell...can I have a quick word, please?" Betty ran after his portly figure, and he rolled his eyes as he turned around.

"What is it, Miss Jones. Mrs Crundell is expecting me home. I don't have time for any nonsense tonight."

Betty thrust her hand out, palm upwards. "You've short-changed us, Sir." Glancing over her shoulder, she lowered her voice. "We agreed you would pay us an extra two shillings a week for all the extra coal we've brought up. This is one shilling short. I'm sure it was just a mistake," she added, trying not to sound accusatory.

"Dear, dear...such a fuss over one paltry shilling." Mr Crundell smoothed his moustache and shrugged. "I have to make sure the books balance, what with Lord Leyfield's visit coming up any day. I'll make it up to you next week."

"But we need it this week, so I can pay the rent," Betty pleaded. "I had to get the doctor out for ma... please Mr Crundell...we're desperate. The Doctor said our mother has to stay in our house for the sake of her health...her life depends on it. She might die if we're evicted."

"Your mother's health is not really any concern of mine, Miss Jones. Apart from how inconvenient it is to be short-handed right when we need everyone pulling their weight. I was very generous in agreeing you could work extra hours, and I refuse to be hounded over one shilling. You'll have to wait until next week...or perhaps you'd rather end our little arrangement?"

Betty's heart sank. Mr Crundell held all the cards and there was nothing she could do about it.

"Very well, Sir. I'll just have to hope that Elis Jenkins shows some leniency."

Crundell had already strolled away, and Betty's words fell on deaf ears. Once the yard had cleared, Betty and Jack went below ground again and she used her annoyance at how unjust their situation was to fuel her anger. They filled the cart faster than ever, and this time, Betty had no qualms about Jack taking some of the better coal from Wynn's station at the coalface. They needed every advantage they could get, and she was determined not to be beaten.

"Do you think the weather will break soon?" Jack wiped his sleeve across his forehead as they walked home at the end of the evening. "I know I'll be complaining once it's the middle of winter again, but this heat is exhausting."

Betty looked westwards, where tall clouds were starting to build in the indigo sky. The air was curiously still as though the land was holding its breath, and the grass on the verges had already gone to seed, the green lushness of a couple of months ago a distant memory. "I hope so, Jack. The farmers won't be happy with the weather this year. It's been so dry, and Dylan said he's never seen the river so low."

"We'd better hope we don't have a storm," Jack grumbled. "Remember when Pa told us about the great storm of eighteen thirty when the Blaeny shaft flooded and eight men lost their lives."

Betty shivered at the recollection. Emrys had always drummed it into them that they should double-check the shutter doors were firmly closed behind them as they made their way through each section of the shaft. "They could save your life one day," he had said firmly. "Don't leave it to chance. Whether it's an explosion, fire, or even a flood, those doors are what keep you safe." Since his firm warning, it had become second nature for Betty to always check and check again they were closed, even when it was someone else's responsibility.

"I noticed that Wynn has been a bit careless with the doors recently," Jack said. "I meant to tell you, but it slipped my mind, what with worrying about Ma. I'm sure he's been drunk on the job a few times. Do you think I should tell Mr Crundell?"

Before Betty could reply, a figure stepped out of the darkness. It was Elis Jenkins. Betty tried to push past him to get to their garden gate, but his arm shot out and blocked her way.

"Friday night again already, Betty. It soon comes around, doesn't it." He grinned, and Betty could smell the beer on his breath. Clearly, he had already been to the pub. "You know what that means, don't you?" He rubbed his hands together gleefully.

"Jack, can you go in and check on Ma, please." Betty wanted to deal with Elis alone, and she waited until Jack had gone inside.

"I hear you've had Doctor Cooper out visiting," Elis remarked, smirking when he saw Betty's look of surprise. "I make it my business to know what's going on with my tenants. It's an expensive time for you then...what with your ma being ill." His comment sounded almost concerned and thoughtful, and Betty wondered whether she had misjudged him.

"Yes, it is," she replied. "But Ma's health comes before everything. I'm sure you would feel the same way about your mother too, Mr Jenkins."

Elis snorted with displeasure. "My ma was nothing but an embarrassment, drunk on gin most nights and bedding any man who would give her a few pennies for the pleasure. If you're trying to soft soap me, Betty, it won't work."

"I can't quite pay you all the rent tonight," Betty stated matter-of-factly. "But I promise I'll have it next week."

"Next week? No, no, that's not how this works, Betty. You pay what you owe when I come to collect it…or risk being evicted…" He crossed his arms, his mouth twisted into a sneer. "Old Mr Grundy was far too lenient, and Lord Griffiths wants things done differently. You have until Sunday evening otherwise the bailiffs will be here on Monday and we'll take all your furniture. Then if you're late again, you and your family will be out on your ear."

"Is your heart made of stone?" Betty cried. "Ma is at death's door, and you're quibbling over a shilling. Shame on you, Elis Jenkins. You're a stain on this community of hard-working folk."

Elis merely chuckled and reached out to squeeze her arm, making her wince. "You can say what you like, but I ain't falling for any sob stories about your ma being ill. What of it? If she dies, it's one less mouth to feed, Betty. Look at it that way."

"You…you're an odious man. I'll get that money for you, and then you can leave us alone." Betty pushed him away, her heart pounding with anger. "If your brother thinks he's having this cottage, he's sorely mistaken. I'll do whatever it takes because, unlike you, we love our Ma."

"I'll see you on Sunday evening then," Elis replied, unperturbed by her barbed words. "And now I'm going to get back to my game of cards. Good day to you, Miss Jones. Enjoy your last few nights in your cottage." He doffed his hat and sauntered away, whistling under his breath as though he didn't have a care in the world.

CHAPTER 7

"Betty, is it alright to come in?" Dylan's cheery voice put a smile on Betty's face as she ladled out the porridge early the following morning. He peeked around the door and held up half a loaf of bread. "Ma told me to bring this up for you. It's a little bit stale, but she said if you soak it in milk and add some nutmeg, it will help your ma get better."

"Are you sure that's the only reason you called in?" Minnie asked with a mischievous smile that made Betty blush. "Two little birds a-tweeting on the tree, saying I love you...do you love me?" she warbled as she poured out the tea.

Betty burst out laughing. "Mind you don't shatter the glasses with that singing, Minnie. It's not the most tuneful rendition of that fine music hall song."

"Here you are, Dylan. You may as well eat with us, and then we can walk up to the pit together." Minnie jabbed her sister with her elbow and passed Dylan a small bowl of porridge as he took off his coat and hung it on the hook behind the door. His brown hair was sopping wet, and the smell of damp wool came off his trousers.

"Looks like the fine spell is over. I can't say I'm sorry." Jack shovelled porridge into his mouth, speaking around it. "It's been hotter than I've ever known it, these last few weeks, even down the shaft.

"It will be good for the water levels in the river, this rain," Dylan agreed. "I might go fishing tomorrow after church. As long as the water isn't too churned up, there should be plenty of trout for the taking."

"Elis Jenkins is threatening us with the bailiffs again." Betty sighed as she sipped her tea. Thinking about their situation had made her lose her appetite. "We're working harder than ever, but we can never get ahead. I wish Pa was still here. He would know what to do."

Dylan covered Betty's hand with his own and

squeezed it reassuringly. His brown eyes were filled with concern, making her heart skip a beat as he gave her a crooked smile. "Remember you can always ask for my help, Betty. I know it's not the same, but I don't want you to struggle alone with your worries."

She nodded, feeling tears pricking the back of her eyes. "That means a lot," she murmured. "Thank you."

"Come along, you two lovebirds...we don't have time for chatting. I expect the yard will already be ankle deep in mud, and Mr Crundell will be in an even worse mood than usual." Jack stood in the doorway, peering outside. The rain was coming down in stair rods, hissing as it hit the parched ground, and the sky looked leaden and heavy with roiling clouds that were as dark as a bruised plum. "I wouldn't be surprised if we get thunder and lightning," he added as a breeze started to pick up.

As they trudged up the hill a few minutes later, Betty's thoughts felt almost as tumultuous as the weather. Even if they worked harder, there was always the risk that Ezra Crundell might go back on his promise or underpay them like he already had. The rain trickled down the back of her neck, and they slithered on the ground which had quickly become churned up by everyone's boots.

"You ain't going to make us work in this, are you Mr Crundell?" Dawn Watson pulled her shawl over her head and scowled as she raked the coals in front of her, snatching at any stones which caught her eye. "I thought you were going to build a nice shelter for us lot outside. You promised it last year, and we still have to work in the blazing sun and pouring rain."

"Yeah…how can you expect us to work our best when we're soaked to the skin?" A buxom woman standing next to Minnie hitched her sodden dress up and did a jig in the puddles under their feet. "We ain't ducks Mr Crundell…it might be alright for them, but not your best women on the sorting tables."

Several of the women made quacking noises, and before long they were all roaring with laughter.

"That's quite enough of this," Fred Jenkins bellowed, striding over to glare at them. "We've got the inspector due any day, and you think it's alright to lark around like fools? If you behave better, we might get the money, and then you'll get yer bloomin' shelter, won't you. Saints preserve us…I swear women should stay at 'home where they belong."

"Ah, stop yer fussing, Fred." Dawn gave him a saucy wink. "You can warm me up at the end of the shift…at least I've got some flesh on my bones, not like that scrawny wife of yours."

Fred stomped off, muttering under his breath. The yard was thick with mud streaked black from the coal dust that quickly caked everyone's boots, making every step laborious.

"It's like the storm of eighteen thirty all over again," Dai said with a pinched expression as Betty and Jack passed him. He shook his head gloomily. "I don't like the look of this, not one bit."

"Surely a bit of bad weather doesn't need to be a cause for alarm, Dai?" Jack picked up his tub and jumped as the first ominous rumble of thunder echoed across the valley, quickly followed by a bright, white jagged streak of lightning in the sky.

"It ain't the fact that it's a storm, lad. It's to do with how dry it's been these last few weeks. You never know where the water's going to flow, not when it's coming down like that over there, see?" He pointed a gnarled finger towards the rivulets of water that were starting to flow down the hillside whichever way you looked. It was as if all the springs which had been bone dry for months had suddenly come to life again and the air filled with the sound of gurgling water.

"Tell me you're not wittering on about the great storm again, Dai?" Wynn shot them a sour look as he hurried past. His eyes were bleary and blood-shot, and there was thick stubble on his chin as though he hadn't slept for days. "Is it any wonder we never get any investment here when you old timers are always harking on about the past? We should be looking to the future. It's folk like me they need to make this place a success, not feeble old men and women with airs and graces," he added, giving Betty a venomous look.

"It's time you lot were working," Ezra Crundell said forcefully as he waddled over towards them. He grabbed at the line of carts to stop himself from falling over in the mud. "We're not stopping just for a drop of rain. Get down the shaft and look lively. You Two could learn a thing or two from Wynn," he added, jabbing a finger at Betty and Jack. "He gets on with the job and doesn't stand around complaining."

"That's rich," Jack muttered as they entered the shaft. "Wynn looks like he's been sleeping in a barrel of beer. Did you smell the drink on him,

Betty? He's nothing but a drunken bully. I've got a good mind to ask Mr Crundell if I can go and work in the shaft where Dylan is instead. At least I won't have to listen to Wynn going on about how he's the best miner they've ever had."

"Let's just get through today, Jack," Betty said hastily. She knew her brother could be hot-headed when he got an idea into his mind, but the last thing they needed was to cause trouble with Wynn. It wouldn't take much for him to start a fight with Jack, and they were no match, even if he was the worse for drink.

"My feet are going to be sopping wet after today," Jack grumbled again. The rainwater was already trickling along the floor, and all they could hear was the sound of dripping around them.

"The storm will probably have blown itself out by the time we've filled the cart and I take it to the surface," Betty replied, splashing through the puddles behind him. "Anyway, I thought Ma had a bit more colour in her cheeks this morning, don't you? I reckon she's on the mend, Jack, and that's a cause for celebration. We'll get the rent paid even if I have to pawn something just to tide us over, and Ma will get better, you'll see."

"You're right," Jack said, returning to his usual

cheery self. "Our luck is on the turn...and about bloomin' time too."

SOMETIME LATER, Betty put her shoulder to the cart and heaved it towards the surface. For some reason, it felt harder to push than usual, and she wondered whether it was because the coal was wet. That would give Mr Crundell another reason to be in a bad mood, and she hoped he might be on break as she finally emerged from the shaft. Even though it was already well into the morning, it felt more like night. The trees in the wood beyond the colliery thrashed and heaved as the wind roared through them, scattering branches and debris in every direction. The rain was heavier than when she had gone below ground, and it smacked into her face with such force that it stung.

"Take the cart over there so Fred can tally up." Dai pointed to the open-sided shed where some of the other workers were queuing, and Betty pulled her shawl over her head, trying to keep the worst of the rain from her eyes. "It's taking him longer than usual." Even though Dai cupped his hands around his mouth, Betty could scarcely hear him as the wind snatched his words away.

"Hurry up, Fred, we ain't got all day." One of the women in front of Betty rolled her eyes, and soon, there was a chorus of complaints.

"Are you tallying me light, Fred Jenkins? I wouldn't put it past you."

"What sort of conditions is this for us to work in? It's shocking, that's what it is."

The line crept forward until it was Betty's turn, and as soon as Fred had examined her coal, she hurried over to the riddling line where Dai was helping one of the men to tip it out.

Betty shifted uncomfortably, wishing the day was over. Even standing outside for this short time had left her soaked to the skin and her dress stuck to her legs, making it hard to walk. Suddenly over the noise of the storm, there was a strange new noise. It was a rumbling that seemed to gather pace, like something careering towards them, getting louder and louder.

"Lookout…there's a flood coming!" Dai's face was grey with fear as he pointed to the hill behind the mine.

Betty looked up, and her stomach clenched with terror. Just as Dai had said, there was a torrent of water roaring down from the mountains, and it seemed to be getting deeper with every passing second as it tore everything up in its path. Branches from the trees snapped like matchsticks, and it gouged out mud and stones from the land on either side.

"Get back to work," Ezra Crundell bellowed. "It will just go down the hill into the river. It's nothing to worry about."

"Are you mad?" Dai hobbled across the yard as fast as his arthritic legs would carry him. "It's heading for the Blaeny shaft, you fool. If the shaft floods again, the men will be trapped."

Betty felt an icy hand of fear clutch her heart as she slithered through the mud to follow him. "We must go down and warn them," she shouted.

"You will do no such thing, Miss Jones." Mr Crundell drew himself up to his full height and glared around at all the workers who were milling around anxiously, torn between watching the floodwater and wanting to do something to help. "The shutter doors will do their job, and everyone will be perfectly safe. That's why they are there, as you well know."

The next few minutes passed by agonisingly slowly as Betty paced back and forth at the entrance. Even though she knew that Mr Crundell's words were true, she couldn't relax until she saw Jack above ground again, safe and sound. *What if one of the shutter doors wasn't closed properly?* The thought pulsed through her mind as she remembered what Jack had said about Wynn getting more careless lately. She knew she had double-checked each door as she passed through it that morning as she always did, but would Wynn have done the same? She could have sworn he was drunk earlier as well, which made her even more worried for Jack's safety.

Gradually some of the men of the village started to emerge from the dark mouth of the shaft, stumbling and shaking their heads in disbelief. "We heard a terrible noise…didn't know what it was," one of them cried.

"Have the pit props collapsed? Is it a fire? An explosion?" another man demanded of Mr Crundell. "Tell us what's going on? It makes no sense, but we knew we'd best get out as quickly as possible."

"It's a flood, just like I predicted," Dai said angrily. "They were supposed to dig proper channels to make sure the surface water couldn't go underground, but them penny-pinching toffs never did it, did they."

"Stop stirring up a load of old nonsense, Dai or

I'll have you taken away by the constable." Mr Crundell's face was puce with anger as he tried to stop the mutterings of protest that were starting to swell among the workers."

"Assemble over here, please." Fred Jenkins jumped up onto a cart and waved the men over. He had a ledger in his hand, and he scanned their faces. "Let me do a head count, and we can put our minds at rest."

"I can't see Jack. Did he come with you?" Betty shouted. She craned her neck, trying to see over the top of everyone, but it was impossible.

"It was only him and Wynn in the farthest part of the shaft, love. We were all working the new seam." One of the men patted her on her shoulder. "He'll be up in a minute, you'll see."

Fred started calling out all the names, and hands shot up in the crowd as each man was accounted for. "I think that's almost everyone," he said, shooing the women back to the riddling tables. "I expect the others will be waiting until they know it's safe to open the doors to come up so there's no need to worry.

"What about Jack?" Minnie cried. She ran to Betty's side, her face pale with worry.

"That's it...I'm going down to look for him."

Betty pushed past Mr Crundell and snatched up a shovel.

"You can't do that," Crundell said angrily, taking it back from her. "You know women aren't allowed down to the coalface. What if Lord Griffiths gets to hear about this?"

"I don't care one jot. Our brother is still underground and you're worried about Lord Griffiths?"

"Look...there they are." A shout went up and Betty felt relief sweep through her. She shoved her way through the workers just in time to see Wynn stumble from the entrance into the rain.

"Are you alright? Is Jack with you?" Betty darted forward and grabbed his arm but he shook her off.

"We were nearly killed, thanks to you, Betty Jones." His voice was loud and angry and the accusation ricocheted around the yard so everyone could hear it. "You left the shutter door open and the flood came into our section. I could have died."

"I...I didn't leave it open," Betty gasped. "Did you help Jack come up?"

"I couldn't see where he was...stupid boy...he was scrabbling on the floor trying to steal my coal, and I stepped away to have a mug of tea...next thing I know, I'm waist deep in water…I had no choice."

"Stand aside, Miss Jones. We're sending a rescue party down." Mr Crundell snapped his fingers and gestured to a gaggle of men who had already gathered ropes, lights and shovels and were hurrying towards the shaft entrance.

Betty stumbled backwards, her head spinning. "Please save him," she pleaded. Every part of her wanted to go with them, but Dai appeared by her side and put his hand on her arm.

"Let them do their job, maid. It's what they've practiced for and you'd only hinder them."

"I have to do something…what can I do?" Her voice was anguished and she pulled Minnie into a hug to comfort her.

"All we can do is pray," Dai said gently. "And hope they finally improve the safety of the mine once all this is over."

"You can think long and hard about your carelessness, too," Wynn hissed. "Leaving the shutter doors open in that way, it's unforgivable. Everyone knows how dangerous that is." He shoved past her, and Mr Crundell hurried after him, drawing him away to a quiet corner to talk.

"Is it true, Betty? Did you?" Minnie's face fell as she thought about the implications.

"I promise on Ma's life I didn't leave the shutter door open." Betty wanted to sob and rail against Wynn's callous lies, but she had to stay strong for Minnie. "Pa always told us to be extra careful, and I was."

"You have had a lot on your mind recently," Minnie murmured.

"Yes, but I've been doing this long enough not to make a stupid mistake like that, Minnie. If anyone's lying about this, it's Wynn. Which makes me wonder why."

Minnie nodded, her tears mingling with the rain on her cheeks. "I believe you, Betty. I'm sorry if you thought I doubted what you said." She shivered as the wind howled even louder and tightened her shawl.

The two sisters stood side by side, their gaze fixed on the shaft entrance. Each minute that dragged by felt longer than eternity. *How would we manage without Jack? Our family would be nothing if God took my brother as well.* The thought made Betty feel physically sick and she clung tighter to Minnie's arm, not daring to speak the words aloud in case doing so made them come true.

The sound of running footsteps snagged Betty's attention, and she turned to see Dylan running towards her from the entrance to the shaft where he worked. "We just heard about what happened," he said breathlessly. "I came up as quickly as I could." He knew from their stricken expressions that there was no good news yet. "Is there anything I can do to help? I'd go down with the search party, but Mr Crundell told me in no uncertain terms that they have all the men they need and I should get back to work." His mouth pinched with irritation at their manager's lack of heart.

Betty gave him a grateful smile. "You being here is comfort enough, Dylan. All we can do is wait, and hope for the best. Maybe Jack managed to climb into a passing place and stay above the water...I just...don't understand how Wynn could have come up without making sure Jack was with him. The two of them work side by side..." Her words trailed off as she saw Dylan's eyes cloud with conflicting emotions at the mention of his father.

As if their conversation had summoned him, Wynn strode around the corner, rubbing his eyes wearily. When he saw Dylan he came to an abrupt halt. "What are you doing above ground?" he demanded. "We can't afford to lose money with you idling your time away chatting to those two."

"Pa! How could you be so uncaring? I came to see if there was anything I could do to help. You know that's the miners' way, to look out for each other."

"The rescue team are taking care of things," Wynn said dismissively. "I'm sure Jack is fine and you're all making a fuss about nothing. Now get back down your shaft and get on with your work, boy, or you can explain to your mother why we don't have enough money for food this week."

"He's all heart," Minnie grumbled sarcastically as they watched Wynn marching Dylan back across the yard.

As the minutes turned to hours, Betty felt the fear in her chest solidify, as hard and black as the coal they pulled from the ground. The other workers darted looks of sympathy in their direction, laced with guilty relief that it wasn't their loved one they were waiting for. Meanwhile, Mr Crundell had managed to get everyone back to work now that the storm had abated, reminding them all that the inspection was due very soon and the Nantglas Colliery's reputation was at stake.

Twice there was a flurry of activity at the

mouth of the Blaeny shaft and Betty's heart leapt with hope. But both times, it was just the rescuers sending word that they were still searching and that conditions were difficult because of the amount of debris the flood had dragged into the tunnels and how much water remained, hampering their progress.

"The boss has said you should go home and wait there for news," Fred Jenkins said officiously after Betty's hopes had been dashed for a third time when there was still no word of how close the rescuers were to where Jack might have taken shelter. "You're distracting the other workers... making them grumble about safety and the like."

Betty nodded numbly. She had seen Mr Crundell looking in their direction several times, with a worried expression and she wondered whether his concern was for Jack or that Lord Griffiths might not look favourably on a disaster like this happening under Crundell's management.

"As you wish," she said. They walked quickly out of the yard in silence. Both of them had doubts and fears swirling through their minds but they didn't want to put them into words because it was too painful.

"What should we say to Ma?" Minnie eventually asked as they arrived home.

Betty paused at the gate. "We mustn't say anything yet. Ma's still so weak that a shock like this could worsen her condition. We'll say we were allowed home early because there was a problem with the machines." She gulped, wishing it was true. "We'll make her some nice soup, and maybe, by bedtime, everything will be alright." Her voice wobbled and she blinked, not wanting to cry.

Minnie dashed her hand across her face to wipe her tears away. "Maybe Pa is looking over Jack and keeping him safe?"

"I hope so, Minnie. I really do." Betty squared her shoulders and pushed the gate open. She had to believe Jack was alright because the alternative was simply unthinkable.

CHAPTER 8

*B*etty and Minnie reminisced about the past as they made the soup, avoiding the one topic that was uppermost on their minds. After they had helped Fay eat hers and she had gone back to sleep, the two sisters sat at the table, and Betty lit several candles even though it wasn't quite dark yet. Usually, she tried to eke it out as long as possible to save money, but there was something about the empty chairs around the kitchen table that tugged at her heartstrings. "This is to guide you home to us, Jack," she whispered quietly as she placed one of the candles in the window like sailors' wives did when their menfolk went out to sea.

"I'm going to get on with some mending,

Minnie. Would you fetch me Jack's shirt that needs the collar turning? Maybe you could read from one of ma's books. That would be a nice way to pass the time."

The clock ticked on the mantelshelf, and Betty wriggled her shoulders to ease the ache in them. Before long, two more hours had gone by, and Minnie was dozing in the wingbacked chair in front of the hearth. Betty yawned but knew there was no point in trying to sleep. *If I stay awake, I'll be ready for when they bring Jack back*, she told herself. She pulled the next shirt onto her lap and threaded her needle, stifling another yawn. It was going to be a long night.

A SHARP RAP at the door made Betty jerk awake from the fitful sleep which had claimed her, despite her intentions to stay awake. Her neck felt stiff, and the candles had both burned down, leaving the cottage in darkness. She hastily lit the lamp and held it in front of her as she opened the door.

"Is there news?" Minnie hovered behind her, and Betty lifted the lamp higher to reveal

Reverend Bowen, Doctor Cooper, and Ezra Crundell standing outside.

"Miss Jones...Minnie..." Ezra Crundell doffed his cap, looking awkwardly between both of them.

"What is it? Don't keep us in suspense, please." Betty's heart sank as she waited for the next devastating sentence to be spoken.

"By some miracle, the men have managed to rescue young Jack—" Reverend Bowen began.

"He's alive!" Minnie grabbed Betty's hand and hopped up and down with relief. "Where is he? Can we see him? The poor lad must be starving. It's way past dinnertime, and he does love his food."

Doctor Cooper held up a cautionary hand. "It's not that simple, I'm afraid. Your brother was badly injured, you see. From what we can gather, the flood water swept him off his feet and smashed him against the side of the tunnel. One side of his body is rather badly damaged." The three men stepped back slightly, and Betty gasped as she saw four of the villagers with a makeshift stretcher between them, on which Jack lay like a battered rag doll.

"Jack! You're alive...that's all that matters."

Betty ran outside and knelt next to the stretcher, taking his good hand in hers.

"Betty? Minnie?" Jack groaned as he turned his head towards the light, and he managed a weak smile. "Did I hear someone mention dinner?" He chuckled and winced again as pain shot through him.

"That's our boy," Minnie cried. "See...he'll be fine, won't he, Doctor Cooper?" She gave him a pleading look.

"One day at a time," the doctor said. "We'll get him inside, and then I'll tell you what you'll need to do to look after him."

"You won't be needing me anymore. I'll only get in the way, so I'll head for home," Mr Crundell said hastily. He jammed his hat back on and turned to leave. "I might need to ask you a few questions about why the shutter door was left open, Miss Jones," he added over his shoulder. "I will have to write a report for Lord Griffiths, but I'll let you have a couple of days off while you get Jack settled at home." He scurried away into the night before Betty had a chance to protest her innocence.

"Pay no heed to him," Minnie said as the men carried Jack into the house. "They can't pin the blame on you for something you didn't do."

The next hour passed in a blur of activity as they made Jack comfortable in his bed, and Doctor Cooper showed Betty how to change his dressings. He placed a bottle of laudanum on the kitchen table with instructions that Jack could have a few drops in water to help manage the pain.

Once everything was calm again, Betty made Doctor Cooper a cup of tea. As she tried to pour it out, her hands trembled violently, and the tea spilt on the table. "That's just the shock of everything that's happened," the doctor said kindly. "Jack's lucky to be alive from what the men said. The flood did terrible damage to the shaft, bringing down the pit props. He managed to cling onto a beam until the rescue team found him...he's a brave lad. You should be very proud of his plucky spirit."

"Us Jones's don't give up easily," Betty replied with a shaky smile. Her face grew suddenly serious. "I don't have any spare money to give you, Doctor Cooper. I'm already short on the rent, and now that it's just Minnie and me working..." Her words petered out as the full implications of their situation started to sink in.

"Don't worry about that, Betty. Let's call it my good deed of the day." The doctor drained his cup of tea and picked his bag up. "I don't want to be the bearer of bad news…not on today of all days…but I think you need to plan for the fact that it's unlikely Jack will be able to work down the pit again. I'm sorry, but his injuries are bad, and he might not recover fully."

Betty blinked back the sudden tears that threatened to roll down her cheeks. She gave him a smile and lifted her chin. "I'll think of something, Doctor. Pa raised us to look after one another, and that's what Minnie and I shall do. For now, we're just overjoyed that he's alive. Thank you for everything you've done today, and I will try and repay you one day, I promise."

A few minutes later, quietness descended on their home again, and Betty sat down at the kitchen table with her head in her hands. Despite her bold words, she felt as though she could scarcely breathe. *What should I do, Pa? What would you recommend if you were still here?* She wished she could look across the room and see Emrys's kind, weathered face looking back at her from his armchair and have the benefit of his wise counsel one more time, but the silence was deafening, and her shoulders slumped. Elis Jenkins had already shown that he was not the sort of man who cared about the plight of the tenants where the rent money was concerned. And even if Jack was fortunate enough to recover, she knew it would be weeks, if not months, before he would be able to work again. Betty knew she needed to come up with a plan if they were to survive. She decided to try and find Dylan at the earliest opportunity to see if he had any bright ideas, but first, she needed the blessed relief of a few hours' sleep where she could escape from the worries which crowded into her mind.

DESPITE DOCTOR COOPER'S dire words, Betty refused to give up hope that Jack might one day get completely better. Much to her relief, Elis Jenkins was nowhere to be seen for the next few days, and she wondered whether he had been told to give them a reprieve on the rent by Lord Griffiths. After a couple of nights of better sleep, Betty's head felt clearer than it had for a long time, and she told herself that maybe things would work out alright after all.

"Is that cake I can smell?" Jack's question drifted through to the kitchen from his small bedroom, and Minnie grinned at Betty. Even though it was late afternoon, he had only just woken up, and they heard him yawn loudly.

"I told you a poppy seed cake would soon perk him up." She took the cake out of the range and put it on the side to cool. "I'll bring you a slice shortly, Jack," she called back.

"I've decided it's time for me to get up and about again, girls." Fay's voice from the doorway made Betty jump, and she and Minnie spun around, both equally surprised.

"Ma! Are you sure? Minnie and I can take care of things…we don't want you to rush your convalescence. You know Doctor Cooper said you mustn't overdo things." Betty hurried over and offered her arm for Fay to lean on, helping her into the kitchen so she could sit at the table. Fay's shoulders felt bony beneath her nightgown, but the terrible grey pallor which had made her look so ill for weeks had improved. In the light from the window, Betty could see that their ma actually had a bit of colour in her cheeks again, and her eyes looked brighter than they had for a long time.

"I hate that all of this has had to fall on you, Betty," Fay said. She patted her eldest daughter's hand and gave her a grateful smile. "I might not be able to work on the riddling tables again, but I want to do my bit to bring in some money."

"Hush, Ma. We can talk about that later." Minnie cut a slice of cake and put it in front of Fay with a cup of tea to go with it.

"Minnie's right," Betty said hastily. "It's far too soon for you to be thinking about work. The two of us will work as many hours as Mr Crundell can give us, and we'll just have to see if we can tighten our purse strings in other ways. Maybe I could pawn a few things…" She glanced around the cottage, wondering what, if anything, might be worth enough to cover the rent before Elis came calling again. She felt a clench of anxiety when she realised their threadbare belongings were probably not worth much.

"I've had a lot of time to think while I was laid up in bed. Before your pa and I were married, I used to be quite good at sewing, you know. Not for money, of course. Papa never expected me to go out to work. But I was wondering if I could perhaps turn my hand to some dressmaking? It wouldn't bring in much, but at least it would be something."

"That would be perfect," Minnie said with a happy smile. It was so nice to have their ma up again that she would have agreed to anything. "Maybe I could help out as well in the evenings? You always said Betty was good at singing and I was better at needlework."

"It's certainly an idea, Ma." Betty bustled around the kitchen, her head spinning with everything that needed to be done before she started back at the colliery again tomorrow. Now that Fay was out of bed again, she would be able to give Jack some stew for his lunch while they were at work, which was one less thing for her to worry about. She pulled the last of their potatoes out of the cupboard and set about peeling them. She had spent a few pennies on a scrag end of mutton, and if she baked some bread to go with it, they would be able to stretch it out to last a few days before she got paid again.

Once the stew was bubbling gently on the range, Betty went and perched on the edge of Jack's bed. The gash on his head was already healing nicely, although he had a huge purple bruise around it. His arm was heavily bandaged, and his leg was in a splint. Doctor Cooper said the damage to his shin bone was a clean break, which meant that with a bit of care, he should be able to walk again, even though he might need a stick and would most likely have a limp for the rest of his life.

"Good news, Jack, Ma's up and looking a lot better," Betty said gently. She squeezed out a cloth and pressed it on his forehead. "How are you feeling now?"

"I'll be alright in no time, even if I have to hobble about on one leg and a crutch," Jack replied. He gave her a cheerful grin that eased some of her fears. "It's my arm I'm more cross about than anything. I'm worried I might not have a strong enough grip to hold my pick to dig out the coal." He lifted his bandaged arm and tried to flex his fingers, but they stayed stubbornly immobile.

"Let's just see how you get on, shall we?" Betty plumped up his pillows before handing him the plate of cake and placing a mug of tea next to his bedside candle. "Doctor Cooper said we must be very grateful that you're alive and that not everyone would recover fully from something like this…" She let her words hang between them, deciding it was too early to relay Doctor Cooper's exact prognosis. Jack had a stubborn streak under his sunny demeanour, which she hoped would serve him well in wanting to prove the doctor wrong. She didn't want to dishearten him before he'd even started.

"We'll soon see about that," Jack shot back, just as she'd hoped he would. "I'm going to be as fit as a fiddle again, so don't let the naysayers tell you otherwise, Betty."

"I thought you'd take that approach," Betty said, chuckling. "Now try not to misbehave tomorrow when Minnie and I go back to work at the pit. Who knows what sort of mischief you and Ma will get up to in our absence." She paused in the doorway, watching Jack fondly until he had finished his cake and the drops of laudanum she had put in his tea had started to take effect. Doctor Cooper had told her that rest would be the best medicine for Jack in the first week while the swelling in his arm and hand subsided, so she was determined to make sure he did exactly that.

Just as Betty sat down with a cup of tea for herself, there was a sharp knock on the door before it burst open. It was Dylan, and he looked flustered with his hair sticking up in every direction.

"Good afternoon, Mrs Jones. You're looking much better," he said hastily. "I'm sorry for all the commotion, Betty, but I thought you'd want to know. They've sent us home from work early today, and Mr Crundell is holding a meeting at The Red Dragon in a few minutes. It's about the possible investment for Nantglas Colliery from Lord Leyfield. I reckon you and Minnie should come…there might be some new jobs they're planning that could suit you better. Maybe bookkeeping or something like that?"

Betty jumped up, taking her apron off in one swift movement. "You don't mind us going, do you, Ma? I want to make sure we hear everything straight from the horse's mouth."

"Of course not." Fay handed Betty the bonnet that was hanging on the back of her chair and shooed them away. "You can tell me everything when you get home. Perhaps you could have a slice of Minnie's cake afterwards, Dylan? I feel like I haven't seen much of you while I was ill, and it will be nice to celebrate a new start for the colliery with you." She smiled when Dylan nodded, glad to see that he still seemed smitten with Betty.

The three of them hurried down the lane together. "Do you think Lord Griffiths might be at the meeting, Dylan?" Betty asked. "It could be a good opportunity to make sure he knows the flood was nothing to do with me instead of hoping that

Mr Crundell might put in a good word for me. I don't trust him. I've never known him to say a good word about our family. Even when they brought Jack home and he was at death's door, Mr Crundell was more worried about having to write a report."

"I'm not sure, Mr Crundell didn't say. All I know is what Pa told me...that Lord Griffiths and Lord Leyfield had a look around the colliery above ground for an hour or so. Pa said they both seemed decent sorts of fellows when he was chatting to them."

Betty glanced at Minnie. The fact that Wynn had managed to worm his way into the welcoming party at the mine inspection and talk directly with both Lord Griffiths and Lord Leyfield didn't bode well. She could only hope that Wynn had been bragging about how good the mine was rather than spreading untruths about her leaving the shutter door open.

"I doubt Lord Griffiths would want to be troubled with details of the day-to-day running of Nantglas," Dylan said, giving Betty a reassuring smile. "You know what those toffs are like...only interested in the money they can make from the place. That's what he has Mr Crundell for, to take care of all that boring stuff like the flood."

When they arrived at The Red Dragon, there was scarcely more than standing room only. Men, women, and children were crammed into every available space and Mr Gossop, the landlord, was bright red above his mutton-chop whiskers as he tried to serve enough beer to take advantage of the unexpected influx of visitors. It hadn't been this crowded since last Christmas Eve, and he grinned at the thought of the extra money he would earn.

"How's that brother of yours?" Dawn called from the corner when she saw Betty. "I'll send my Arthur round with a nice bit of ham in a few days when we kill our pig. That'll put some colour in his cheeks."

"He's coming along nicely, thank you," Betty replied.

"We shall include Jack in our prayers next week, my dear." Reverend Bowen squeezed past, looking slightly uncomfortable to be seen in the pub by so many people, but he didn't want to miss out on the announcement.

"I'll let him know, Reverend; thank you." Betty bobbed her head, suddenly wanting to giggle because he looked so out of place.

"It's nice to know that so many of the villagers are thinking of us," Minnie commented.

Dylan steered them towards the corner near the cavernous inglenook fireplace where there was a bit more space, and suddenly the chatter ebbed away to be replaced by an expectant hush as Mr Crundell strode into the pub.

"Give the boss some space," someone yelled. The villagers edged apart, leaving a pathway for Mr Crundell to make his way to the front of the room, where he clambered onto an upturned orange crate that Mr Gossop had put there as a makeshift platform. Fred Jenkins trotted along behind, clutching a ledger under his arm with an air of superiority.

"That looks promising. Hopefully, it's got details of our pay rise and all sorts of good things," Dylan whispered with a wry smile. His eyes widened with surprise. "I didn't know that Ma was coming," he added. "Pa usually likes her to stay at home in case people ask awkward questions about her bruises."

Betty followed his gaze to see Wynn elbowing his way to the front to stand next to Mr Crundell with Catherine trailing meekly behind him. She kept her eyes lowered other than to dart nervous glances in Wynn's direction, and Betty felt a wave of sympathy for the poor woman. She looked more downtrodden than ever, and Betty could tell by the way she kept gingerly lifting her shawl higher on her shoulder that she was probably nursing a new bruise from Wynn's latest drunken outburst. It was little wonder Dylan daydreamed about getting the two of them away from his father.

"Last chance to get a pint of ale before the meeting starts," Mr Glossop bellowed hastily while everyone was quiet. A few men hurried to the front to slap some coins down on the bar and grab one of the tankards he had already lined up.

"That'll do for now, Mr Glossop. This isn't the summer fayre." Mr Crundell threw the landlord an irritated look and then pulled himself up to his full height and twirled the points of his moustache, waiting until he had everyone's full attention.

"As you know, we had an inspection at Nantglas Colliery this morning by the owner, Lord Griffiths and his esteemed business associate, Lord Leyfield. They wanted to invest a considerable sum of money into coal mining because it's such a vital industry of this fine land of ours."

"Blimey...he likes the sound of his own voice, doesn't he?" Dawn whispered loudly, rolling her eyes. "Tell us when we're gettin' the money...and a pay rise; that's all we care about."

Mr Crundell ignored her and ploughed on. "I had a very interesting talk with Lord Leyfield because, as manager of the mine, I felt it was my duty to present the very best case for us getting the money instead of Ferncoed Colliery, which everyone knows does not benefit from having a manager of my vast experience."

"Sounds like Crundell's still upset that he didn't get that job," Dylan whispered in Betty's ear, making her smile.

"Lord Leyfield particularly wanted to know about what happened in the flood last week and the damage that was done to Blaeny shaft." Mr Crundell's face was hard to read, but Betty shifted slightly, ready to defend herself if she needed to.

"Maybe his money could make things a bit safer for us," Dai called out from the far corner of the pub. "It was lucky nobody was killed...I kept telling you about the great storm and how it could happen again."

Mr Crundell's face turned pink with irritation. "Now that you mention safety, Dai...I have to tell you all the bad news. It is with great regret that Lord Leyfield has decided to invest his money in Ferncoed Colliery after all. As you know, Lord Griffiths owns them both, so his business will still benefit overall. But they decided that because of the negligence of certain people and the storm damage, Nanglas will just have a modest amount spent on it to repair the Blaeny shaft—"

"You mean we're not getting a pay rise?" some interrupted.

"What about that roof we've been promised over the riddling tables?"

"How can that be fair? Ferncoed already had money spent on it a few years ago...what about us?"

The swell of angry questions sounded like a swarm of bees, getting louder and louder so that Mr Crundell could no longer make himself heard.

"I promised the family we could have a day to the seaside with the extra money we'd be getting."

"It ain't our fault there was a flood...if someone hadn't left that stupid door open, we would have got what we're owed..."

"Who was this negligent person anyway?" A woman Betty barely knew had jumped onto one of the tables and was looking angrily around the room. "Point them out, Mr Crundell. If it's one person's fault, it shouldn't be us who lose out, should it."

"You're right…"

"Who's to blame…"

"Give 'em the sack…"

The mood in the pub had changed in an instant. Gone was the jovial air as people anticipated having a few more coins in their pockets every week. Now the room crackled with indignation and outrage as more and more of the villagers looked for a scapegoat.

"Wynn…it was Wynn Parry, wasn't it?" a voice piped up from the back. Betty tried to see who it belonged to, but before she could, Wynn had suddenly jumped up onto a chair.

His face was dark with anger. "Silence!" he bellowed. His eyes raked across the villagers, and they fell quiet again, shuffling nervously under his menacing gaze. "I won't have such lies spread about me, not when I'm one of the village's best miners. Isn't that right, boss?"

Mr Crundell nodded hastily. "Mr Parry certainly made a very good impression with Lord Leyfield, but sadly it was not enough to sway him."

"There is only one person to blame for the damage to the Blaeny shaft," Wynn continued. He slowly lifted his hand and pointed towards Betty with a triumphant sneer. "Betty Jones left the shutter door open...I saw it with my own eyes. That is why her poor brother nearly lost his life... and that is why all of us will struggle to make ends meet without a pay rise or any investment in our colliery...just because of her careless behaviour."

Dark spots danced in Betty's vision, and she thought for one terrible moment she was going to faint as she saw all the enraged faces of the villagers turn towards her, edging closer like an angry mob intent on revenge.

"It's not true," she croaked. She took a deep breath and tried again. "What Mr Parry is saying is a lie. I didn't leave the shutter door open, and I never would. Pa taught us that, and I was always careful to double check—"

"Maybe you forgot...your family always fancied themselves a cut above us...what with your ma being better bred than us proper miners."

"As if a slip of a girl like you would know better than Mr Parry."

The venomous accusations from people in the crowd who Betty counted as friends and neighbours felt like darts going into her heart. She craned her neck, trying to see who was saying such terrible things, but everyone was so closely pressed together it was impossible to tell.

"I promise you, on Jack's life, that I didn't leave that door open," Betty cried. She could see from the corner of her eye that Minnie was looking at her with a horrified expression and decided she had nothing more to lose. "Jack told me that you have been drunk at work, Mr Parry. Perhaps it was you who left the door open instead?"

Mr Crundell's face turned red, and he spluttered into his handkerchief. "Be very careful what you are saying, Miss Jones. Are you implying that I would allow someone to work down the mine knowing they were drunk?"

"You mind your lip, young lady," Fred Jenkins added hastily. "Mr Parry is a well-respected member of our community. Someone must take the blame, and it's certainly not him."

"But you only have his word to take for it," Betty shot back.

"That's where you're wrong, Miss Jones," Wynn said smoothly. He drew himself up to his full height and cast a stern look down at his wife and then across at Dylan. "Tell everyone, Catherine. Tell them how I could not possibly have been drunk at work because I was at home with you, and not a drop of drink has passed my lips for weeks now since I gave it up."

Catherine's eyes widened slightly as she darted a glance up at Wynn, and she swallowed twice. "My...my husband is right..." she whispered.

"Speak up, dear. We need to make sure everyone can hear." Wynn placed a heavy hand on her shoulder and squeezed it slightly, making her wince.

"Yes...Mr Parry...my husband has not touched a drop of alcohol for three weeks at home as he has seen that it's not a godly way to behave. He told me when he got home after the storm that he was certain that...that..." Catherine's gaze flicked towards Betty for a second, and she swallowed again. "He told me that it could only have been Betty Jones who left the shutter door open," she finished in a breathless rush.

Betty's mouth gaped open, and she turned to look at Dylan. "I didn't do it," she muttered, pleading with him to say something in her defence.

Dylan looked between her and his mother, his eyes clouded with indecision. "I...I can vouch for Betty," he said to Mr Crundell, ignoring his father's furious look.

Wynn chuckled and shook his head, getting the

crowd on his side. "We have to remember that Dylan works in a different shaft. It was me who was down Blaeny, not him. I'm sure he's well-intentioned, but he doesn't know what we know, Catherine dear, does he?"

Catherine Parry shot an agonised look at her son as Wynn squeezed her shoulder again. "No, dear, you're right." She glanced at the villagers and gave them a nervous smile. "My husband tried very hard to get the money for our colliery…he's a good man, and you know he only has our best interests at heart."

Wynn puffed out his chest as several of the villagers nodded. "What Betty Jones has done to this village is nothing short of a scandal," he said firmly, looking around to make sure that everyone had heard. "A scandal that we might possibly never recover from."

Betty felt like she had been punched in the gut, and she stumbled backwards. "Come on, Minnie. We're not going to listen to these lies for a moment longer." She could see Wynn elbowing his way through everyone, coming towards them with Catherine firmly clamped to his side.

"Not so fast," he snarled as he stepped up to her. "I won't allow you to spread lies about me, Betty

Jones. You and your mother...you're nothing but trouble. The best thing you could do is confess to Mr Crundell and take the punishment you deserve."

"Never." Betty squared her shoulders and gave him a defiant look. "You might have everyone else fooled, but I'll never confess to something I didn't do."

"Our Pa taught us to check the shutter doors and to tell the truth," Minnie added, linking arms with Betty. "My sister isn't to blame for this, Mr Parry. I hope you can live with your conscience after doing this."

Wynn gave them both a lazy smile. "This won't be the end of it, trust me. Mr Crundell knows which horse to back in this particular race." He jerked his head. "You'd best get along home, Dylan. I don't want you mixing with the likes of them."

"Come on, we'd better go home too," Minnie whispered, tugging on Betty's arm. Some of the villagers still looked decidedly angry, and she didn't fancy having beer thrown over them.

"You should be ashamed of yourself," Betty said to Wynn as they turned to leave. "I won't rest until this is put right, you know. I owe it to Pa's memory."

Wynn shrugged, but a shadow of worry crossed his face. "Do what you like. My family will back me up regardless. It's your word against mine...do you honestly think anyone will believe you now after your carelessness lost our colliery the investment? Anyway, you've got bigger things than me to worry about," he added, looking across at Mr Crundell.

"What do you mean?" Betty demanded.

"I overheard Mr Crundell and Lord Griffiths talking earlier today about the incident. Lord Griffiths said that they can't rule out having to get the police involved...who knows, Betty, maybe you'll be thrown into prison for what you've done? How would your sister manage then? A crippled brother, a mother who's too feeble to work...and you in prison for causing this terrible accident... poor Minnie...who knows what might befall her? I doubt Mr Crundell will want you two working back at the pit anyway, even if you manage to stay out of jail."

Betty felt the blood drain from her face. She hadn't even considered that the constable might have to get involved, but now that Wynn had sown the seed of doubt, she realised that her situation could become even more perilous. Before she could say any more, Wynn gave her a triumphant smile and strode out of the pub, bundling Catherine and Dylan ahead of him.

"What are we going to do, Betty?" Minnie's eyes pooled with tears as they hurried home.

"I don't know, but we'll think of something. I'm not going to let him beat us." Betty paused for a moment in their tiny front garden to gather her thoughts. She trailed her hand over the rose blooms that tumbled over the front wall. Emrys had told her he had planted that rose the year she had been born, and every summer, he had picked her one perfect blossom, pinning it to her shawl. The rich damask scent in the evening air made her feel almost as though her pa was still with her in spirit. Drawing comfort from it, she knew that whatever happened, she would do her best for her family. It was what her pa would have wanted.

CHAPTER 9

*B*etty paced back and forth in the kitchen, unable to settle to her usual chores. She had lost her appetite and felt too anxious to even think that she might get a wink of sleep that night.

"I can't believe Wynn Parry is trying to blame you for the whole village's misfortunes." Fay picked at the fringe on her shawl, shaking her head. "He always was a sore loser, ever since I started courting your pa, but you'd think after all this time he would have got over it."

Minnie took the battered tin down from the top shelf of the dresser and emptied the coins onto the table. The meagre pile was nowhere near enough to pay the rent, and she could swear she had seen Elis Jenkins hob-nobbing with his brother as they'd left The Red Dragon, glancing in their direction as they did so. "What will we do when Elis comes for the rent, Betty? I don't think he'll show any more leniency after tonight's meeting, no matter that Jack is injured."

"I don't know...I need to think of something." Betty scratched her head and paced around the table again. "Perhaps I could team up with one of the other families and work underground again on the tubs. It pays better than being on the riddling tables."

"I don't think Mr Crundell will let you break the rules again, dear," Fay said gently. "Your pa always used to say that once a mine had come to the attention of the Mine Inspectors, the managers have to be on their best behaviour for a while. I'm sure with the damage down the Blaeny shaft after the storm, he won't dare do anything that might get him into more trouble."

"He didn't care about breaking the rules as long as he was getting a cut of our money," Betty sighed. Part of her wanted to feel bitter about the turn of events, but it wasn't her way and she preferred to try and think of a solution than dwell on things she couldn't change.

"Are you upset about Dylan not sticking up for you more?" Minnie asked. She added a pinch of tea leaves to the pot and poured boiling water over them. Even if Betty was too upset to eat, a sweet cup of tea might help settle her nerves.

The question brought Betty to a stop. It was what had been scratching away at the back of her mind as well. "I don't think Dylan had any choice but to go along with what his pa was saying," she said sadly. "You could see how terrified Catherine was. Dylan has to look after his ma, and that's how it should be." She felt a wash of regret that Wynn would probably always try to drive a wedge between her and Dylan. "It wouldn't be fair of me to expect Dylan to put his ma in danger by angering his pa. Catherine looks so frail and it's all because of that bully of a husband of hers."

Fay shot her daughter a sympathetic look. She could tell that Betty and Dylan loved each other and would be well-suited to marry, but the chance of that happening after tonight was less likely than ever, and her heart went out to her daughter. It was cruel of Wynn to come between them, but that was the sort of man he was. She had underestimated just how much Wynn hated her family because of the past but she wouldn't make the same mistake again. Dylan was nothing like his father and she could only pray that fate might find a way for him and Betty to be together one day.

SUDDENLY THERE WAS a knock on the door. The sun was just starting to set and Betty could hear the squeak of bats overhead as she cautiously opened it, terrified that it might be the constable on the doorstep, coming to drag her away.

"Hello, maid. I hope you don't mind me calling?" Dai Llewelyn took his cap off and clutched it in his hands.

"Of course not." Betty felt momentarily relieved. "It's nice that at least one person in the village isn't looking at me as though I'm some sort of monster." She stepped back and ushered him in.

"Good evening, Mrs Jones." Dai bobbed his head at Fay and twisted his cap, unsure of what sort of reception he might receive.

Fay's eyes lit up, and she pulled a chair out for him. "Welcome, Dai. How lovely to see you. Minnie will pour you a cup of tea. Would you like a slice of cake to go with it?"

Dai looked slightly taken aback by Fay's gracious greeting and he nodded. "That would be grand, thank you. I...I'm sorry about the times at the pit when I might have been a bit short with you in the past. It took me a bit of time to get used to having women working on the riddling tables. Mrs Llewelyn, my wife, always says I can come across as a bit cantankerous when my knees are sore. How she puts up with me I'll never know, but she's a wonderful woman."

"I never took offence, Dai," Fay said, patting his arm with a gentle smile. She could tell that the old man was nervous and wanted to put him at his ease. "Emrys always spoke very highly of you and I know it was a big change when Mr Crundell put Minnie and me to work as tip girls, but we never wanted to do you out of work."

"Aye, well, there was plenty for everyone, as it turned out, and I could see you're a hard-working family." He took a sip of his tea and looked around at the homely kitchen, starting to relax. "I like to see that in the youngsters," he added. Mrs Llewelyn and I were never blessed with children of our own, but I like to think that if we'd had them, they would have been like your three, Mrs Jones. Upstanding and hard working. My sister, Mary said your Betty was very polite when she called the other day."

Betty and Minnie exchanged glances, grateful for Dai's kind words. "I hope Mary's hand is healing well?" Betty asked. She sat down at the table and poured herself a cup of tea. Having a visitor had taken her mind off their dilemma for a few minutes, and she realised how hungry she was.

"Her eyesight isn't as good as it used to be. In fact, that's why I've come to visit you. I have a proposition for you all."

Betty's eyes widened with curiosity. "Go ahead. After tonight's meeting, I think we're open to hearing anything."

Dai hesitated, choosing his words carefully. "I don't want to cause offence, so I'll say my piece and then let you think about it." He looked at Fay and Betty, waiting for their agreement, before continuing. "I think what happened at the meeting tonight was very unfair. Everyone knows that Wynn Parry drinks too much, and it wouldn't surprise me one bit if he was responsible for leaving the shutter door open. He has Mr Crundell wrapped around his little finger, and that poor wife of his is as timid as a mouse."

Fay nodded. "That's what I think too, but it's Betty's word against his and Mr Crundell would always side with Wynn rather than someone as inconsequential as Betty." She gave her daughter an apologetic look. "What I'm trying to say is that a young girl is expendable, but Wynn can make life difficult for Mr Crundell."

Betty shrugged. "I know. The women are held in the lowest regard, and I'm sure they've all been in cahoots to cover their own wrongdoings."

Dai looked pointedly at the tin, which was still open, from where Minnie had returned the coins. "I expect you must be short of money too, what with only two of you able to work at the moment. I hope you'll forgive me for asking, but are you able to pay your rent? I heard a rumour that Elis Jenkins has been hounding you for money?"

"You heard right," Betty said. She pulled the tin towards her. "You may as well know that Elis has told us his brother Fred wants to live in this house, and unless I can come up with some sort of miracle in the next few days, we will probably be evicted."

Dai shook his head. "It's shocking how they treat folks when they're down on their luck. If anything, they should be helping you out until Jack recovers, but I doubt the men in charge see it that way. Fred and Elis Jenkins always take what they want." He sniffed disapprovingly and took another gulp of his tea.

"Even if I pawn our furniture, it could be months before Jack can work again," Betty said quietly, glancing towards Jack's bedroom to make sure he was still asleep. "And Doctor Cooper said you need to live away from the damp, Ma, so we're not going to move somewhere that puts your health at risk." She hesitated for a moment, and Fay gave her a worried look.

"What is it, dear? Is there more that you haven't told me?"

"No...it's nothing," Betty said hastily. She ignored Minnie's raised eyebrows. "Maybe you have an idea of how we might be able to earn more, Dai? If I can tell Elis that I'll have the money soon, it might keep him off our backs for a few more weeks."

"I think I might have an answer to your rent problems," Dai said, smiling. "As I said, my sister, Mary's eyesight isn't what it used to be, and I do worry about her living in that cottage all alone. My dear wife Emily considered asking her to live with us, but Mary loves that cottage with all her heart. I...we...we wondered whether you might like to move in with her? It's away from the worst of the smog, being on the edge of the village, and she would like the company. Also, I wouldn't have to worry about her having another accident like when she spilt the boiling water on her hand."

"Move into Mary's home?" Fay blinked, not quite understanding.

Dai nodded. "It would help us as much as it could help you. You'd have a roof over your heads, and Mary would have people I can trust looking after her."

"It could work," Betty said slowly, her mind whirling with possibilities. "Are you sure Mary wouldn't mind? We would pay her some rent, of course, whatever we could manage."

"It was actually her idea," Dai said with a grin. "I went around to see her after the meeting at the pub. Everyone thinks that because she lives alone and doesn't work anymore, she has no idea what's happening in the village, but not much gets past Mary. She knew about Elis bothering you for the rent, and she doesn't believe for one minute that the accident was your fault, Betty."

"If we moved to Mary's cottage, it would mean we wouldn't need to worry about earning so much," Minnie said. "Do you think Mr Crundell is going to let us go back to work? What about if the constable comes?" she blurted out.

"What do you mean if the constable comes?" Fay gave her daughters a firm look. "I know you're trying to protect me by not telling me everything, but I'm not as delicate as you think. I need to know what's happening."

Betty sighed and got to her feet again to light the lamps. "We didn't want to worry you, but Wynn said that Lord Griffiths might get the police involved about the accident in the Blaeny shaft."

"He told Betty she could end up in jail," Minnie cried indignantly.

"I've never heard anything so preposterous." Dai's folded his arm and puffed his cheeks out with outrage. "He's a wrong 'un that Wynn Parry. The trouble is he's just as likely to lie to the constable to save his own skin, and you'll never get work back at the mine again."

"There must be something we can do instead." Fay's eyes were bright with determination. "I was thinking about taking up dressmaking, and Minnie would make a good seamstress with a bit of guidance." She turned to Dai. "Mary used to sew dresses for all the wealthy folk before her eyesight got bad. Maybe she could teach us what to do and introduce us to some of her old customers? Do you think that could work?"

Dai nodded enthusiastically. "I think she'd be tickled pink to do that. It would give her something to take her mind off the past."

"That's a wonderful idea, Ma." Minnie sat up straighter and clapped her hands, suddenly invigorated. "If we keep out of Mr Crundell's way, perhaps he'll forget all about everything that's happened. I've always wanted to do something away from the colliery, and learning to be a seamstress from Mrs Lloyd could be a fresh start for us."

"Mind you, it still doesn't solve the problem of Betty worrying about the constable calling," Dai said cautiously.

"I'm no seamstress," Betty admitted. "Working at the mine is all I've ever known and all I've ever expected to do. Without that, I have no idea what I could turn my hand to instead? Maybe I should just throw myself on Mr Crundell's mercy and beg him for work on the riddling table again." Even to her own ears, the idea sounded hollow. It was unlikely the villagers would ever accept her working alongside them again, not when they blamed her for losing out on the chance of getting more money.

"I think I might have a better idea," Fay said hesitantly. In the shadowy light of the lamp, her expression was suddenly serious. "It's time for me to tell you about my brother, Ralph, because he could be the key to your future, Betty."

BETTY AND MINNIE both gasped with surprise. "We didn't know you had a brother, Ma. Why have you never told us about him before?"

Dai Llewelyn struggled to his feet and put his cap back on. "I think this is my cue to leave, Mrs Jones. You all need time to think about my suggestion and Betty's future, too, by the sound of things." He bobbed his head and hobbled to the door. As he went to let himself out, he gave Betty a shrewd look. "I remember your Uncle Ralph... mind you listen to your ma's ideas with an open mind...she's got more gumption than most folks give her credit for. Good evening to you." With that, he bobbed his head again and vanished into the night.

Betty shot the lock across the door and closed the curtains before hurrying back to sit at the table. "So who is Uncle Ralph, and where is he now?" She eyed her mother curiously.

Fay placed a gentle hand on both of her daughters' arms and took a deep breath. "I should have told you about my brother years ago, but the longer I left it, the harder it became. Ralph is two years older than me, and we were inseparable when we were growing up." Her eyes misted over for a moment as she thought fondly about her childhood. "Papa wanted him to follow him into the business, but Ralph was never that way inclined."

"So what did he do instead?" Minnie's eyes were round with intrigue.

"He became a singer. That's where you get your talent from, Betty."

"I'm not sure I'd call humming a few tunes a talent, Ma," Betty said hastily.

Fay shook her head firmly. "Don't say that. Ralph was good enough that he had an opportunity to sing on stage in London. Unbeknown to Papa, he visited some of the theatres and auditioned. When he told Papa that he was going on stage, Papa cut him out of our lives completely. We never spoke of him again." Her face was etched with sadness. "I missed him so much, but then I fell in love with your pa, and my life changed as well."

"Grandfather sounds very unkind," Minnie said hotly. "Just because you and Uncle Ralph didn't do what he wanted."

"It was just his way, dear. What saddened me the most was that I lost touch with Ralph for many years until I received a letter from him last year, in fact." Fay suddenly smiled, all traces of her former sadness gone. "The strangest thing is that he left London some time ago, and he has been managing a theatre on the coast, not very far from here at Abertarron."

"Really? You mean he's close enough for us to visit, Ma? This could be your chance to make up for all those years you were apart." Betty's eyes lit up at the thought of something to bring happiness to her mother again. "If we worked really hard and saved up, we could send you on a day trip. The sea air would be good for you."

Fay shook her head with a chuckle. "Trust you to think of me before yourself, Betty. No, what I mean is that you could go and work for him for a while—"

"I can't leave you all behind," Betty cried, cutting across Fay's suggestion. "I have to look after you all. How can I do that if I'm miles away? No, that wouldn't work at all." She pushed down the tiny flame of hope that had blossomed in her mind for a second. It would have been thrilling to work in a theatre, even if it was just as a stage sweeper, but she wouldn't dream of leaving her family, not when they needed her.

"Hush, Betty. Let me finish, will you." Fay gestured for her to sit down again. "When Ralph wrote to me, he said that he felt terrible for leaving so abruptly and not being in touch with me for all these years. He also mentioned that if he could ever do anything to make it up to me, I only had to ask."

"I'll find some sort of work locally, Ma. We don't need to worry about the rent if we move in with Mary Lloyd." Betty was determined that her family would not be left to fend for themselves against Wynn's accusations.

"What if the constable comes, though. I'd feel much happier knowing that you were safely working somewhere else, and it's not as if you'd be all alone. I can send a letter with you, explaining everything to Ralph. Just until the dust settles here, Betty. Won't you at least consider it?"

"You always said you'd like to sing on the stage,"

Minnie said. She pouted slightly. "You'll be having all sorts of fun while I'm learning how to sew."

"Don't be silly. Uncle Ralph is hardly likely to have me on stage, Minnie." Betty rolled her eyes. "I've had no training. If anything, I'll be running errands or doing whatever jobs nobody else wants to do…that's if he doesn't send me on the first train home again." She looked at her mother, feeling the first glimmer of hope for a way out of her terrible dilemma. "He might have just been being kind, Ma. I doubt he ever expected you to take him up on his offer. He's going to be very shocked to see me."

"You don't know my brother," Fay said, beaming. "He has the sort of artistic temperament that thrives on unexpected ideas like this. So do you agree?" she added.

"Well…I…I'm not sure." Betty murmured, swinging between outright shock and a surge of excitement.

A sudden scuffling sound behind them made everyone turn around. Jack was standing in the doorway, using the broom Minnie had left next to his bed as a makeshift crutch. He swayed slightly, and Betty leapt up and darted to his side.

"What on earth are you doing out of bed so

soon?" she scolded. "Doctor Cooper said you needed bed rest for three weeks at least."

"I woke up and overheard Ma's story and what you said about being thrown in jail." Jack leaned heavily on Betty as she helped him shuffle to the nearest chair. He sat down heavily with a thump. "You must go to the coast, Betty," he said urgently. "We can't take the risk of you being sent to prison for something that wasn't your fault. Please...do as Ma is suggesting," he pleaded.

"I suppose I could send money home to help you out. But don't you think running away will make me look even guiltier?"

Jack shook his head, as did Fay and Minnie. "We'll keep your whereabouts a secret. If anyone asks, we'll just say the strain was too much, and you've gone away to convalesce. And I'm determined to do whatever I can to clear your name, Betty. Now that I'm up and about, I can tell Mr Crundell my side of the story. You don't need to go away forever, and you might even enjoy it."

Betty closed her eyes for a moment and then opened them again, looking slowly around the cosy cottage which had been her home for all her life and at the people she loved so dearly. It would be a wrench to leave them, but Jack was right. She didn't really have much choice, not if she wanted to earn enough money to support her family while they got back on their feet. Blinking back her tears, she nodded. "You'd better write the letter for Uncle Ralph, Ma. I'll help you move down to Mary Lloyd's cottage tomorrow, and there should just be enough money left for me to take the train to Abertarron."

CHAPTER 10

"We'll be alright, children, I'm sure of it. I don't know where we would have ended up if it weren't for Mary's generosity." Fay's words were as much to comfort herself as her family, and she brushed the unexpected tears from her cheeks with a lace handkerchief as Minnie unpacked the last of their boxes into the cupboard under the dresser that Mary had cleared for them. Seeing her best china cup that she had been given to her by her mama when she was a child in its new setting had felt very final, and she couldn't help but feel a bit emotional about the change in their circumstance. It had taken Dai several trips and almost a whole day with his pony and cart to move all their belongings from Limetree Lane through the cobbled streets to Hollyhock Cottage, amidst many curious glances from the villagers who weren't at work.

Mary had hobbled between the rooms of her home, showing them where they could put things, and there had been a jovial air of anticipation about the fresh start for all of them that eased any lingering qualms Betty had had about the move.

Once they had cleared all their personal possessions from their old home, Dai and Betty returned to Limetree Lane and helped Jack onto the back of the cart, lying him flat on their old patchwork quilts for the last journey down the hill. Betty had expected to feel overcome with sadness at leaving their cottage, but she was surprised to find that without their belongings in it and with the embers of the fire now cold and grey in the hearth, there was only the echo of old memories. *It's the people who make a home, not the four walls.* The thought comforted her, which was a good job because just at the last minute, Elis and Fred Jenkins had strolled down the lane towards them.

"Said your goodbyes, have you, Miss Jones?" Elis had the swagger of a man who was pleased with having won. "Fred's looking forward to enjoying the view from up here," he sniggered.

"I hope your brother has as many happy years in here as we did," Betty said airily. She was determined not to let the two of them spoil her day. She turned to Fred and smiled. "You might want to have a word with the landlord about the leaky roof...and I think there's a family of rats living behind the chimney."

Fred's face fell, and he glared at Elis. "A rat infestation? You said this was a nice house. I'm not paying full rent if the roof isn't sound, and you know my Gladys hates rats. She's not going to be very pleased about this, and it'll be me who has to listen to her nagging."

"I would have mentioned it before if you'd asked me, but you were in such a hurry to move in," Betty continued. "Never mind, I'm sure you'll soon get used to it." She shrugged and gave them a cheery wave as she climbed up on the cart seat next to Dai, who was coughing to cover his laughter.

"That'll serve them right," Jack chuckled. Betty turned around, and they smiled as the sound of the two brothers squabbling drifted after them as the horse clopped away.

Once Jack was lifted from the cart at Hollyhock Cottage, Betty could finally relax a little bit. No matter what happened to her, she knew now that the rest of her family was safe. Mary patted her on her arm as she bustled past with some sheets for Jack's bed. "We'll be fine, dear, don't you worry about a thing. I'm looking forward to passing on my dressmaking skills to your ma and Minnie." She reminded Betty of a little mouse, the way her mobcap perched on her grey curls and her dark eyes twinkled in her wizened face. It was as if she had a whole new lease of life now that the Jones family had filled the cottage and Betty's heart swelled with gratitude at Mary's kindness. "I reckon your brother might be a dab hand in the garden once he's better, too," Mary added.

Betty followed Mary's gaze. Jack had been shuffling up the garden path on a new pair of crutches that Dai had made for him as a surprise, but now the two of them were deep in conversation next to the vegetable beds. She watched as Jack's face lit up with enthusiasm as Dai pointed to various plants. "Our pa was a keen gardener, Mary. I never thought Jack was very interested, but perhaps it was just that he never had the chance."

"A young man could make a decent living as a

gardener," Mary said thoughtfully. "I always thought if I'd had a son, I would encourage him to follow that path...'tis a nicer way to earn a wage than being down the pit."

"You might be onto something there. I just hope his leg heals well enough not to leave him crippled. Doctor Cooper wasn't very optimistic about it."

Mary handed the sheets to Betty. "He's can be a gloomy old codger, that doctor. All Jack needs is some good country air and something to get better for. I reckon Dai and I will give the lad a few little gardening jobs to make sure he doesn't get down-hearted. And if he's anything like your pa, he'll be determined enough to prove the doctor wrong."

Betty hurried away and shook out the sheets to make Jack's bed, marvelling at how Mary Lloyd seemed to have the measure of her family already. The villagers might think the old lady was a strange recluse, but nothing was further from the truth. All she had been was lonely, and she seemed to know exactly what was going on in the village, even though she rarely ventured out. Betty could only assume it was Dai's daily visits which kept her informed.

A few moments later, she saw that Dai was

about to leave, and she hurried after him. "I don't know how we can ever thank you enough," Betty said. She patted the pony's neck as Dai climbed up into his cart.

"Think nothing of it, maid. If there's one thing I can't abide, it's injustice. You and your family work hard, and Emrys was a good man. It's not right for you to lose your home and be accused of something you didn't do. Mary and I were raised to know right from wrong and stick up for folks who are down on their luck. And my wife agrees as well."

"I'm worried that Mr Crundell might make life difficult for you at work," Betty said hesitantly. "I mean, people might treat you badly because you've helped up. Everyone saw us moving into Hollyhock Cottage today. Aren't you scared it will paint you as guilty by association?"

Dai picked up the reins and gave her a shrewd look. "You're a kindhearted girl, Betty, always thinking about others. But you have to make sure you don't forget to look after yourself as well. If anyone gives me any bother, I'll remind them that Reverend Bowen tells us every Sunday to be kind to one another." He clicked his tongue against his teeth, and the cart rolled forward.

"Thank you, Dai. I'll make you all proud one day." Betty waved, feeling sad to see him go.

"I don't doubt that for one moment, maid," he called back over his shoulder. "Good luck for the future, and don't worry about Jack. I'll have him up and about in no time...he's got the makings of a gardener in him, and I happen to know somewhere he might be able to get work." He doffed his cap and urged the pony into a trot, keen to get home for his dinner.

THE SUN HAD BARELY RISEN the following morning when a tentative knock at the door sent Mary's terrier darting across the flagstones, yapping loudly. Betty was up early, packing her few belongings into a carpetbag for her journey, so she hurried to open it.

"Pa has forbidden me from seeing you, but I couldn't let that happen," Dylan blurted out as soon as the door swung open. He threw a defiant look over his shoulder, and a shaft of sunlight revealed the swollen, purple bruise on the side of his face, making Betty gasp out loud.

"I can't bear what he's doing to you and your ma, Dylan. It's breaking my heart." She stepped outside and reached up to gently stroke his face. The scent of the honeysuckle in the garden enveloped them in its sweet fragrance, and Betty wished they could stay in the moment forever.

Dylan grasped her hand and held it, looking into her eyes. "Please don't think badly of me. I know Pa's making up lies about you, and I'll do whatever I can to clear your name. It's just…"

"I know, Dylan. You have to look after your ma, it's no different from me looking after my family."

"I want you to understand that I'm not like my father," he said vehemently. "I hate the way he treats Ma. I used to wish I had a father like yours, Betty, someone kind, who I could look up to. But instead, we have to put up with his bad tempers and drunken rages."

"I'm going away for a little while, Dylan," Betty said softly. "I hope that my family will be safe now that they're living with Mary, but I'm worried that if I stay in the village and the police don't believe me…" Her words petered out. "At least if I go away, people might eventually forget about the flood and the investment going to Ferncoed instead of us."

"I'll miss you so much." Dylan stepped closer and looked intently at her. "Don't forget about me, will you?" His mouth lifted into the lopsided smile

Betty was so familiar with, and she felt the breath catch in her throat.

"I'll never forget about you, silly," she whispered. Her heart skipped a beat as he tucked a curl of her hair behind her ear, suddenly looking bashful.

"I wish I had a keepsake I could give you to take." He rummaged in his coat pocket and pulled out an iridescent blue jay feather which he had been planning to use to make a fly for fishing. "This is all I have," he said, looking apologetic. He threaded it into Betty's shawl and stood back, glancing nervously over his shoulder again. "Pa was asleep when I left, but he'll be up any minute and in a bad mood, no doubt."

"You must go," Betty said hastily. She blinked back the tears that pricked the back of her eyes. If she allowed herself to cry, it would make leaving even harder. "I'll send word to my family about where I am, but it will have to be our secret, Dylan. You won't tell your Pa, will you?"

"Was that someone at the door?" Minnie's voice floated through from the kitchen, and the sound of clattering dishes followed as everyone started to get up.

"I'd never tell him anything to put you in

danger, Betty." He nodded at the feather. "Think of me every time you see a jay, won't you?"

Betty nodded. The lump in her throat made it almost impossible to speak. "Look after yourself... goodbye..." Two loud blares of the horn at the pit split the air making Dylan step backwards. It was the sound she had heard every morning for as long as she could remember, announcing the first shift at the colliery.

"It's not goodbye forever, Betty," Dylan cried. Throwing caution to the wind, he seized her hand again and brushed a kiss on her cheek, making her blush. "We'll be together again one day, I promise." With that, he turned on his heel and ran down the dusty lane, vanishing from her view.

"Please don't forget me," Betty whispered. A future without Dylan was almost unimaginable, but she had to face up to the fact that she had no idea how long it might be until she would see him again.

"Come and have some porridge," Minnie called. "You can't travel all the way to Abertarron on an empty stomach, and if you don't eat it quickly, Jack will."

Betty smiled and turned back into the cottage.

She would miss Minnie and the easy camaraderie of family life, but she couldn't deny that she was also feeling a little bit excited at the thought of travelling to a new town to work in a theatre with her mysterious uncle. Never in her wildest dreams had she imagined she might leave their little village for such an adventure. But today, life would be changing irrevocably. The train was leaving in two hours, and Fay had already given her her old beaded reticule with some money in it to pay for her fare plus enough for a few meals in case she needed it.

"I hope you've saved me a spoonful of sugar?" Betty asked her sister cheerfully. She sat down at the scrubbed wooden table and nudged Minnie. "I might be commissioning you for a new gown one day if I make my fortune."

"I'll see if I can fit you in," Minnie shot back with a giggle. "Mary's already told me the names of three well-to-do ladies who like to have their dresses altered to keep up with the latest fashion. She's going to introduce me as her new apprentice."

The two sisters ate in companionable silence as the clock ticked on the mantelshelf, each of them thinking about what the future might hold for them.

"We'll be alright, Minnie," Betty murmured. "You'll see." They shared a smile, and Betty poured them both a cup of tea.

CHAPTER 11

*a*s the steam train chugged through the lush green countryside, Betty looked out at the patchwork of fields and tried not to think of everything she was leaving behind. The carriage was quiet. Sitting opposite her, there were two elderly sisters who told her they were visiting their brother, and on the next seat over, a tired-looking governess was taking her charges to the seaside while their parents travelled abroad. At the first glimpse of the sea, the children leapt up and pointed excitedly, and Betty couldn't help but feel a surge of excitement too. She had heard tales of the colliery occasionally sending their workers for a day trip to the coast, but the last year it had happened had been a lean time for the family and they hadn't been able to afford the time away from work.

"I wish you could see this, Minnie and Jack," Betty murmured under her breath. The sea gradually revealed itself between the billowing clouds of steam coming from the train's engine. At first, it was just the odd glimpse of a blue sparkle away in the distance, but as the train wound its way through the last few hills, suddenly the view opened up and Betty's eyes widened with wonder. The town of Abertarron was mainly clustered along the seafront with another part that spread further inland on either side of the river that the train was following. Beyond the town, Betty could see the white-tipped waves of the sea dancing as far as the soft blur of the horizon. As the clouds scudded over the sky, Betty realised that the sea was not just one colour as she had always believed. Rather it was an ever-changing palette of green, blue and grey depending on how the light fell on it. She could see boats bobbing in the harbour and a long sweep of golden sand edged by cliffs at either end where the sea met the land. It was quite the most charming place she had ever seen and she smiled as she caught the eye of the two sisters.

"Are you meeting family as well, dear?" One of

the old ladies leaned towards Betty and gave her an inquisitive look. "We love visiting our brother Cedric in Abertarron, it's such a quaint town. It used to be very quiet, but it's getting more popular every time we visit. The gentry like to come for holidays, and it's seen as quite the place to be, by all accounts."

Betty nodded. "I'm meeting my uncle. I've never been here before. It certainly looks lovely." She suddenly felt self-conscious about the black lines on her hands that marked her out as a pit girl. Although she had scrubbed them vigorously the night before, Fay had told her it would most likely take a good week or more for them to look properly clean again. In the village, it was normal for everyone to have the telltale black ingrained in their skin, but she needed to leave that world behind now. She pulled on the lace gloves that her ma had given her and hoped her hands wouldn't stain them too much.

"Very nice, dear. Well, I hope you have a lovely time." The two sisters nodded in unison and sat primly with their reticules on their knees as the train's screeching brakes and juddering carriage indicated that they had almost arrived at Abertarron station. It was so loud that Betty was spared from having to think of anything else to say, and she hastily put her carpetbag over her arm and perched on the edge of the seat, ready to disembark.

A few minutes later, Betty found herself standing on the platform. Pigeons strutted boldly around her feet and clattered overhead in the ornately vaulted roof, and all around her, porters hurried past with handcarts laden with luggage. A train from London had just arrived on the other platform, dwarfing the small one she had been on.

"...Freddie, darling, do stop running around, will you. Amelia, don't touch that, or you'll get oil on your dress."

"Put our cases over there, please, and for goodness sake, don't hurl them around like sacks of potatoes...they're worth more than you'd earn in a year..."

The brusque instructions from several well-to-do families drifted over to Betty, and she stood for a moment watching them. The ladies wore delicate sprigged muslin gowns and large feathered hats, and the gentlemen's suits were finely fitted, with all of them looking so elegant and fashionable that Betty felt as dowdy as a tramp by comparison. She had never seen so much luggage in her life.

Mounds of banded trunks and hatboxes teetered next to the flustered porter who was in charge of helping them, and several maids hovered anxiously nearby, awaiting their orders. It was the first time Betty had seen such wealth on display, and all she could do was stare in amazement, marvelling that they had more luggage for their holiday than her family had moved from their entire cottage.

"Are yer goin' to stand there gawping all day, love? It'd be 'elpful if you could move out of my way," another porter grumbled, bumping into her as he struggled past laden down with boxes. He rolled his eyes as the red-faced matronly woman following him complained loudly about him being slow.

"Sorry…I didn't mean to get in your way." Betty came to her senses and hastily moved to the side of the platform. There was such a cacophony of sights and sounds she had never experienced before that it was almost overwhelming. She felt a pang of worry that she was all alone in a strange place where anything could happen to her and nobody would be any the wiser. *Ma put her trust in me…I have to make this work for the sake of the family.* The firm thought gave Betty an injection of courage, and she squared her shoulders, deter-

mined not to look too much like a country bump-
kin. As if to spur her on, there was a loud whirring
sound followed by the deep chimes of the clock
hanging at the end of the platform. Time was
getting on, and it reminded her she wasn't here for
a leisurely day out but to find work. All she had
was an address written on a scrap of paper and her
ma's letter of introduction, and she had no idea
how long it might take to walk to her destination.

She scurried up to one of the porters who had
pulled out his pocketwatch and was surveying the
platform. "Can you tell me the way to the theatre,
please?"

"Take the exit at the end, turn right, and then
head towards the main town square. It's a little
way beyond it on the far side of town." He eyed her
suspiciously. "They don't let any old riff-raff in the
theatre, mind. It's a high-class establishment...one
of the big draws of Abertarron for all the toffs
visiting from London."

"Thank you, Sir, but I'm meeting my Uncle
Ralph, who manages the theatre, as it happens."
Betty gave him a brief smile as she saw the look of
surprise on his face. Clearly, he had underestimated her as just a pit girl who had fallen on hard
times. "I might even be on the stage performing,"

she added with a toss of her curls. She grasped her carpetbag tightly over her arm and emerged from the station into the bustling streets of Abertarron, hoping that what she had just said would not end up being just a fanciful dream.

The town was a pleasing mix of buildings. Some streets were of elegant, symmetrical Georgian houses behind ornate iron railings, and others contained tall redbrick houses that jostled cheek by jowl with shops and taverns, as well as more traditional whitewashed cottages with fishing nets draped outside. Seagulls screeched and squabbled for scraps in the gutters, and in the background, Betty could smell the pervasive salty tang of seaweed and fish from the harbour where boats landed their catches. Above all, Betty couldn't get over how busy the town felt to her. After the gentle pace of life in Pencastle village, where she knew every home and the families who lived within them, Abertarron felt like an assault on her senses.

"Mind how you go," a costermonger yelled as she almost tripped over his display of vegetables at the edge of the large town square.

"Coffee and a ham roll, Miss? You look like you could do with a square meal in yer belly." A gap-toothed old crone thrust the food in her direction and then gestured to her husband, who was pouring out thick, black coffee into battered tin mugs on their stall. "It's the tastiest coffee in town, dear."

Betty hesitated and then shook her head, ignoring the rumbling in her stomach. It had been a long time since breakfast, but she didn't want to spend any money until she had met her uncle in case he wasn't as welcoming as her ma said he would be.

"Go on, love. It's only a penny, and I'll throw in one of yesterday's currant buns for yer." The old woman sensed Betty's hesitation, and she whipped a stale-looking bun from the depths of her apron pocket and darted out to stand in front of her. "You don't want to try and find yer way around town on an empty stomach, Miss. Eat this, and then we'll help you on yer way."

"Alright then," Betty said, knowing she was beaten. She dug a penny out of her reticule and handed it over before taking a welcome bite of the ham roll. The bread tasted slightly musty, but she was beyond caring. "How can you be so sure I don't know my way around?" she asked curiously.

"My missus has a nose for new arrivals," the old

man piped up, giving Betty a shrewd look. "Come from the valleys and lookin' to make your fortune, are you? There are more opportunities here than down in them wretched pits."

"We used to work at one of the collieries until it about finished us off," the old woman explained. "I can always recognise a fellow worker from down the pits. It's a hard way of life, but we were lucky to save enough money to come and set up our little stall here rather than end up buried six feet under before our time."

Betty's eyes watered as she gulped a mouthful of the scalding, bitter coffee. "You've got me about right," she said casually. "I'm looking for Mr Hughes at The Glan Mor Theatre. Am I correct in thinking it's on the other side of the square, near the big church?"

"Mr Hughes, is it?" The couple looked at her with slightly more respect. "Yes, follow yer nose... you can't miss it. The big white building with columns out the front and all sorts of reprobates hanging around the stage door. How exactly do you know Mr Hughes then?"

"Just someone I've been told to speak to about work," Betty said, keeping the details vague. Dylan had once mentioned that his pa had relations who lived somewhere in this area, and she decided she would have to be careful about describing herself until she knew who she could trust.

The food quickly revived her, and Betty set off across the cobbled square with a spring in her step. Amid the throng of shoppers and costermongers, a group of children dressed in rags strolled out from a side alley. The eldest boys were taller than her and hung back slightly, watching the younger ones who had two wooden hoops that they were rolling between each other.

"Send it my way, Reggie." The smallest girl had dimpled cheeks, and she giggled as she scampered in front of Betty chasing the hoop. "Look, I can make it go faster than you," she cried. She tried to send the hoop back to the boy, but it was almost as big as her, and she stumbled, tripping over it and losing her balance. She sprawled onto the cobbles, landing hard on her knees. Immediately, her big blue eyes filled with tears, and she wailed loudly.

"Are you alright? Don't cry. It's probably just a little scrape." Betty took her handkerchief out of her sleeve and bent down to examine the girl's skinny legs. One of her knees was grazed, and droplets of blood started to ooze from it onto the hem of her tattered dress.

"I don't feel right...I think I'm going to faint." Fat tears tracked down the girl's grubby cheeks, reminding Betty of when Minnie had been younger. She had always been equally as prone to sob loudly every time she hurt herself, and Betty knew she couldn't walk away. The other children swarmed around her, crowding in from behind, and she waved them away. "Just give her a bit of air. She'll be fine in a minute or two."

"Look at all that blood on my knee, Miss. It hurts somethin' rotten." The girl grabbed Betty's arm as she struggled to her feet, hopping up and down and sobbing even louder.

"Can one of your friends take you home?" Betty glanced around, looking for the other children who had been with her, but much to her surprise, they had all vanished. "Where do you live? Maybe I could take you."

"I'm an orphan...I don't have a home or anyone who loves me." The girl looked furtively over her shoulder as though expecting to see someone. "I'm all alone..." She sighed, and her mouth trembled with emotion as she clung to Betty's hand.

Before Betty could say another word, a shadow suddenly fell over them. She looked up, and her mouth went dry as she realised a thickset constable was blocking their way. His face was red with anger, and his small eyes darted suspiciously between the two of them.

"Well, if it isn't young Annie Poulter...up to her thieving ways again." The constable grabbed the girl by the shoulder and held her in a vice-like grip. He turned to Betty. "And who might you be?"

Betty swallowed, feeling shame and terror wash over her in equal measures as she saw all the other shoppers turning to stare. Several of them pointed and sniggered, and her cheeks flushed guiltily. She wondered whether Wynn had somehow tipped off the police about her escape already.

"I...my name is Elizabeth, Sir...Constable." Betty swallowed again and stood up taller.

"Constable Booth to you. Turn out your reticule, please," he barked.

Betty opened her beaded bag with trembling hands and held it between them. Out of the corner of her eye, she could see the little girl had turned chalky white, and she really did look as though she was about to faint.

"Are all your belongings still there?" The constable poked a stubby finger into the bag and flicked the contents around. "Is anything missing?"

Betty waited and then looked into the bag herself. She pulled out the spare tortoiseshell comb and handkerchief that her ma had given her as a gift, as well as the letter for her uncle. But then her fingers met emptiness. All her money had gone, and her heart sank as she realised she'd been taken for a fool. The group of children were pickpockets, no doubt all working together while the girl had distracted her.

"I don't believe it. I've been—" Just as she was about to say she'd been robbed, the girl sobbed again and looked up at Betty with pleading eyes. "I'm not sure..." Betty muttered, trying again.

She saw Constable Booth's hand tighten on the girl's shoulder and a triumphant smile starting to spread on his face. "I knew it...we'll have this little toe rag in the orphanage where she belongs," he crowed. "She's a blot on society, just like her wretched, drunken parents used to be before they drank themselves into an early grave." His lip curled with contempt. "Better still, she might lead us to the gang leader, and I can get the whole lot of 'em thrown into jail."

Tears rolled silently down the girl's face, and she started to tremble violently. "Please take pity, Sir...I didn't mean any harm...I just fell over."

The constable's face hardened as he looked at Betty, but all she could feel was pity for the young girl who was still looking up at her with a beseeching expression. Wynn's recent threats to get her thrown in prison had given her a new appreciation of how easy it could be to end up on the wrong side of the law, even if you were innocent. She came to a sudden decision.

"What I was going to say, Constable Booth, is that I'm sure everything is here." Betty placed the items back in her reticule one by one. "Handkerchief...comb...letter...and yes, a twist of mint humbugs. All present and correct, thank you very much." She beamed up at him. "You can let her go now. I was just helping her up after she fell over, and I shall make sure she comes with me, so she doesn't get into any more trouble.

"Are you sure, Miss?" The constable scowled. He had been looking forward to reporting that he had singlehandedly broken up the gang of street pickpockets which had been plaguing Abertarron for months. He leaned closer to Betty and lowered his voice. "It would help me if we could make an example of her, you see. Make those other rapscallions think twice about robbing innocent people."

Betty hesitated and then remembered how

disheartening it had felt when she'd thought that nobody was on her side. She glanced down at the girl who was still shaking like a leaf. "I shall take responsibility for her, Constable Booth. You have my word. I have a job at the theatre and a roof over my head. I would like to give her a chance to reform her ways, and I think it would reflect very generously on you too. You seem like the sort of man who believes in giving people a chance to improve themselves." She gave him a persuasive smile, and his expression softened slightly.

"Just don't go spreading it around that I let her go," he harrumphed.

"Oh, thank you, Sir, thank you." Annie threw her arms around his waist. "You're the kindest gentleman in all of Abertarron, Constable."

"Alright, alright, that's quite enough of that." He peeled Annie's arms off him and stepped backwards. "Don't make me regret this," he added, wagging his finger before striding away.

"Am I really going to come and live with you, Miss Elizabeth? I can hardly remember what it's like to have a family of my own, let alone to live somewhere as grand as the theatre." Annie took Betty's hand and pulled her across the cobbles. "Come on then, it's this way."

"Hold on a minute." Betty squatted down in front of Annie and gave her a stern look. "Do you know how I can get my money back? Just because I didn't tell Constable Booth you and that band of rag-tag children robbed me blind doesn't mean I'm going to let you off the hook, you know."

Annie rubbed her sleeve across her cheeks, wiping away the last of her tears. "I'm sorry but you won't see your money again. Old Mr Westbrook who runs our gang will have already squirrelled it away, I expect."

Betty sighed. She had suspected as much, but it didn't hurt to ask. "Will he be worried if you don't go home or wherever it is that you live?"

"Bert Westwood, worried?" Annie shook her head as though Betty was simple. "The only thing he'll be worried about is that I almost got his pickpocket gang caught. That's why I can't go back there ever again. He'd have my guts for garters." She glanced nervously around the streets as though expecting him to leap out of the shadows.

"I suppose I'll have to make good on my promise to the constable then," Betty said. "And my name's Betty, by the way. I just said it was Elizabeth to the constable, but that can be our secret, alright?" She stood up, and they walked across the rest of the square. Annie was still hanging onto her hand, and she skipped alongside her, suddenly quite cheerful.

"It ain't far to go. I'm very excited to see inside the theatre. It's a good place to work because there are lots of toffs who are easy to steal from when they arrive for a performance," she added with a giggle.

"Annie! This will only work if I have your solemn promise that you won't steal things anymore." Betty bit her lip, trying not to laugh. The girl was fearless, and she wondered if she would end up with her hands full trying to stop her from reverting back to her law-breaking ways.

Annie stopped and gave her a shy smile. "I'll try and be good, Betty. You can be like my big sister, and we can look out for each other. I reckon you need a friend who can help you settle in. Country folks like you are always easy targets, but I'll look after you, don't you worry." She reached into her grubby apron pocket and held out a handful of coins. "I'm sorry the boys stole your money. But look, I pinched this off the constable when I hugged him. You have it, so you know I mean it when I say I'll look after you."

Betty shook her head and burst out laughing.

"You're incorrigible, Annie Poulter. We'll have to agree to start with a clean slate. No more stealing! Now, let's go and find my uncle, who I've never even met, by the way. Let me introduce myself first, and you'd better be on your best behaviour, otherwise we might both be homeless by nightfall."

CHAPTER 12

*B*etty felt a ripple of nerves as they rounded the corner of Bridge Street, and she had her first view of Glan Mor Theatre. It was an imposing three-story building with wide steps leading up to the main entrance flanked by white columns. On either side of the central section was a long, ornate cast-iron veranda in front of the first-floor windows where guests could stroll and enjoy the sea view before the performance and during the interval. She could see several young girls up there busily sweeping and polishing, and the tall windows glinted in the sun.

"Ain't it grand." Annie hopped up and down and pointed to the row of smaller windows up in the roof. "Do you think we'll have a room up there?"

"I hope so." Betty clutched her carpetbag tightly and took a deep breath, reminding herself that her ma had assured her that Uncle Ralph was a kind-hearted man. *But she hasn't seen him for years.* The worrying thought made her pause.

"Come on. The stage door is round the back." Annie tugged at Betty's hand with no such qualms about their reception.

A moment later, Betty found herself standing in front of a rather ordinary-looking wooden door at the end of the alley that ran down the side of the theatre. She lifted her hand to knock, but before she could, it flew open, and an elegant young woman swept out, coming to a halt in front of her.

"No beggars allowed. Get on your way." She looked Betty and Annie up and down and wrinkled her nose delicately.

"We ain't beggars," Annie said hotly. "We're related to Mr Hughes, so mind your manners."

Betty squeezed her hand and shushed her. "I'm sorry, my...my friend can be a bit outspoken. Could you tell me where I can find Mr Ralph Hughes, please? I've been told he's the manager here. He's my uncle," she added.

"Oh, sorry, duckie." The woman grinned. "We get all sorts hanging around the back door…can't be too careful. If it's Ralph you want, his office is at the end of the corridor." She gave Betty an appraising look. "Now you come to mention it, you do look very like him. I'm Felicity, one of the chorus singers." She shook Betty's hand enthusiastically. "I hope you're good at pitching in and helping…we don't have any airs and graces…apart from Camilla Covington, of course. Anyway, I've got to dash. See you later."

Annie's eyes were as round as saucers as she watched Felicity hurry away. "Blimey, Betty. That could be you soon." She giggled and did a pirouette. "I'm going to be a chorus singer when I grow up and have a posh gown, just like Felicity."

Betty chuckled. "Let's not get ahead of ourselves, Annie." They stepped into the dark corridor and followed it to the end. "Remember what I said. You be quiet and let me speak to Mr Hughes first, alright?"

"Did someone say my name?" A deep voice behind them made Betty jump, and she spun around to see who it was. The man striding towards them wore a flamboyantly chequered suit with a dark blue cravat at his neck. As soon as he saw Betty, his stride faltered. "Are my eyes deceiving me?" His mouth gaped open. "If you're not Fay's daughter, I'll eat my hat. I've been wondering if I might ever get to meet any of her family, and it looks like the day has finally come."

After a flurry of brief introductions, Ralph took them into his office and gestured for them to sit on the chairs in front of his large desk. Betty's first impression was that his office and the furniture looked as though they had seen better days. The horsehair sofa was worn, and the Persian rug in front of the hearth had small holes from where someone had allowed embers to fall out of the fire at some point. A half-smoked cigar sat in an over-flowing ashtray perched carelessly on top of a stack of ledgers, and the wall behind the desk was covered with overlapping gaudily coloured posters from previous performances. "I'm not the tidiest man as you can see, but the punters never see this part of the theatre." Ralph waved his arm to take in the room and gave Betty a rueful smile. "It's spot-less out the front and in the auditorium, though. You can be sure of that."

"It looks very nice to me," Annie piped up. She clamped her lips together hastily, remembering Betty's warning.

Ralph leaned back in his chair and folded his hands across his ample stomach. "So, Betty. Why are you here…and who is this urchin with you?"

Betty handed him the letter from her reticule and sat quietly while he read it with an impassive expression. After reading it again, he finally looked up again. "Poor Fay. I'm sorry to hear you've all been through such hard times. Losing your pa, then Fay getting ill, and Jack's accident." He shook his head. "I did tell Fay to let me know if I could ever help her, but I have to be honest, I didn't expect her to reply. Things were strained when I left, but from her letter, it sounds as though she's forgiven me, which I'm pleased about. I'm only sorry it's taken this long, but I suppose we can't turn back the clock."

"I don't know what Ma has put in the letter about why I had to leave?" Betty said hesitantly.

"She said you were accused of something you didn't do." Ralph shrugged. "Fay was always as honest as the day is long, so her word is good enough for me. You don't need to tell me anymore if you don't wish to. Do you want me to offer you some work then? And her too?" He raised his eyebrows and glanced at Annie.

"Yes please," Betty said quickly. "I'm happy to

do whatever you want...I can cook, clean, help the...the actors and singers..." Her words petered out as she realised how little she knew about the workings of a theatre. "And it's a long story, but I promised Constable Booth I would take care of little Annie too. She's escaped from the clutches of a gang of pickpockets, and if she goes back, she'll probably be beaten black and blue. In all good conscience, I can't allow that, Uncle Ralph. It would be terrible for her, and she's an orphan."

Ralph held up his hands, and his eyes twinkled with amusement. "You can certainly be as persuasive as my sister used to be."

"So you'll take us on?" Annie sat up straighter and swung her skinny legs under the chair, hardly able to contain her excitement. "I can turn my hand to anything, mister. You just tell me what needs doing...and I won't get in anybody's way. You won't even know I'm here."

"We'll see," Ralph said slowly. "If anything goes missing or any of the audience is pickpocketed, I won't hesitate to get the constable involved. I can't afford any sort of scandal here at the theatre, otherwise our wealthy patrons might stop coming." He gave Annie a stern look, and she nodded rapidly. "How old are you anyway?"

"I'm nine, Mr Hughes," Annie said proudly. "Almost ten, I think, although I can't remember exactly when my birthday is."

Betty gave her a startled look, and Annie grinned back at her.

"I know, you were thinking I was younger, weren't you? That's why old Mr Westwood said I was so useful because the people we were robbing thought I was just a nipper, and they used to feel sorry for me. The boys used to use me as the decoy, and the toffs fell for it every time." She realised what she'd just said and clapped her hand over her mouth again. "Sorry. I won't talk about stealing again, Betty. It just popped out."

Ralph shook his head briskly. "Let's have no more talk about your past, Annie. Consider this a fresh start, alright? You can start by helping behind the scenes," he continued, turning to Betty. "Fay says you have a good voice, but it's help backstage that I need more than anything. Besides, I don't want to ruffle any feathers by showing favouritism. You'll soon see that performers can be sensitive creatures. They hate to think of anyone else stealing their limelight." Ralph sighed wearily. "I will listen to your audition one day, but for now, keep your head down and work hard. You can share a room in the attic. It's nothing grand, but it's that or nothing."

"Thank you, Uncle Ralph. I promise you won't regret it." Betty felt as though a huge weight had been lifted from her shoulders as she stood up.

"It's probably best you call me Mr Hughes for now," Ralph added. He jumped up and took them back out to the hallway. "Go up the back stairs and find an empty bedroom for yourselves, then come back down and ask for Felicity. She's one of my best girls, and she'll help you settle in."

BETTY WOKE with a start at the sound of urgent tapping. Her heart was pounding, and she felt disoriented. She turned her head and gasped as a pair of beady yellow eyes observed her through the window. There was another staccato tapping sound, and she heaved a sigh of relief as she realised it was just a large herring gull on their windowsill. The bird's bill was sharp and hooked at the end, and it tilted its head to one side, giving her a bold stare before pecking at the window pane again. As soon as Betty slid out of bed, the bird flapped lazily away, and she watched as dozens more flew up from the town's rooftops where they had roosted for the night. The air filled with the sound of mewling as the flock of seagulls glided towards the harbour to scavenge on the fish guts that littered the quayside, and the thought of being so close to the sea made her smile again.

"Is it time to get up?" Annie emerged from under the blanket on the small wooden pallet bed in the corner and rubbed her eyes.

"I reckon it is. It's early, but we want to make a good impression." Betty wriggled into her grey cotton dress and hastily tied an apron around her waist. As Ralph had said, their bedroom was nothing grand, but it was perfectly serviceable for what the two of them needed. Her bed was narrow but comfortable, and Annie had been more than happy to curl up on the makeshift pallet, which Felicity had covered with some old blankets she found in the bottom of the laundry cupboard. There was a set of drawers for their belongings and a table with a jug and bowl of water for them to wash in.

The best thing about their room was that it was tucked away high up in the theatre's eaves with a small window which overlooked the seafront promenade below them. Betty had discovered that if she leaned out of the window, she could see the harbour off to one side and the rest of the town to the other. The waves were lapping on the beach, and Betty threw the window open and took a deep lungful of the sharp, salty air that was so different from home. A surge of homesickness engulfed her, and she turned back to the room feeling unexpectedly emotional. Even though Minnie would probably have been green with envy at Betty's adventure, she couldn't help but wish she still had the people she loved around her. She pictured Dylan and touched her cheek, where he had brushed the kiss which had set her heart racing. *Will I ever see him again? Is he missing me?* The questions filled her mind, and she sighed.

"Cheer up, Betty. I expect you're missing your family, ain't you?" Annie dragged Betty's comb through her knotty hair, but it didn't make much difference, and she gave up with a shrug. "I always say a little prayer to my ma before I go to sleep, so I don't forget about her. Maybe that would help you too?"

"That's a good idea," Betty replied, surprised that the little girl was so astute. "Now then, we'd better go down and join everyone for breakfast and introduce ourselves. And after that, I'll see if

Felicity can find you a better dress so you don't look like a ragged orphan anymore." She eyed Annie's tangled hair. "And I think a wash under the pump could be in order too."

Annie wrinkled her nose and then brightened. "As long as it's you and Felicity doing it, I don't mind. And if I have a posh new frock, the children from the gang won't even recognise me if we bump into them in town."

"I think we should avoid going out around town for a little while," Betty said as they clattered down the stairs. "Hopefully, Mr Westwood won't come looking for you, and we can just get on with our new work." She shivered slightly. It wasn't only Annie who needed to hope that the people from her past wouldn't come looking for her, and she wondered whether she would ever be free from the worry of Wynn's lies catching up with her again.

"WELL, WHO DO WE HAVE HERE?" The drawled question came from a statuesque woman in an elaborately embroidered morning gown who swept into the dining room and sailed past the long scrubbed table where everyone was eating.

She was followed by a young man who looked to be about the same age as Betty. He bore a strong resemblance to the woman, and Betty wondered if they were mother and son. His velvet waistcoat strained over his rotund middle, and the two of them sat at a separate table which had been laid for two, away from everyone else.

The hum of chatter in the room dwindled away to nothing, and Betty glanced up from her bowl of porridge to see the woman looking directly at her as she settled herself into her chair. "I'm Betty Jones, and this is Annie," she said quietly. She saw Felicity glance at the woman before rolling her eyes and shaking her head slightly.

"I see," the woman said frostily. "I am Camilla Covington, and this is my son, Tarquin. I expect the others have already told you that I'm the principal singer at the theatre...the star of the show in every sense," she added with a tinkling laugh.

"What would you like for breakfast today, Mama?" The lad clicked his fingers, and one of the young girls Betty had seen cleaning windows the day before scurried over to the table. Tarquin gave her an imperious look. "I shouldn't need to call you over, Bertha. You know Mr Hughes said Mama and I should be treated like royalty."

"I'm sorry, Master Covington." The maid gulped nervously. "Cook had trouble with the range this morning, shall I get you both some porridge like the rest of them are having?"

"Porridge?" Camilla's face blanched. "Good grief, girl, you cannot expect me to rehearse for hours on a bowl of that muck. Tell Cook I would like two softly boiled eggs with toast and a cup of Darjeeling tea. And Tarquin will have eggs and bacon. You know it's his favourite breakfast, and the dear boy works so hard he needs building up." She pinched her son's pudgy cheek fondly and waved the maid away before turning back to examine Betty. "I hear you're Ralph's niece," she said bluntly.

Betty felt the blood rising to her cheeks. Even though the other performers and members of the theatre who lived in had been pleasant during the ten minutes they had been eating, she hadn't yet told anyone other than Felicity who she was. "Yes...Mr Hughes is my uncle. I'll be helping out backstage for the time being."

"He mentioned you fancy yourself as having a good voice?" The incredulous tone of Camilla's question made it clear she thought the idea was ridiculous.

"Betty can sing like an angel," Annie said, leaping to Betty's defence. She glared at Tarquin, challenging him to disagree. "She ain't done an audition yet, but when she does, and Mr Hughes puts her on stage, the crowds will come flocking. Just you wait and see."

Camilla raised her eyebrows in disbelief, and her lip curled with contempt just as Betty kicked Annie under the table. "Annie's just being kind," she murmured hastily. "Mr Hughes has already told me that you're the best singer they've ever had." She nudged Annie, who looked as though she was about to say something else and nodded for her to eat her porridge instead. The last thing she wanted to do was to make an enemy of the theatre's star performer.

"Quite right too," Tarquin said firmly. "Your uncle is lucky that Mama is even here. She was in great demand in London, you know. It's only because the sea air is better for her health that we agreed to work at Abertarron."

A muffled snort from Felicity caught Betty's attention, and she noticed several of the other performers smirking with amusement at the conversation. Before anything more could be said, the maid appeared with a pot of tea, and two fine bone china cups on a tray and Betty was relieved the attention was no longer on her and Annie.

"In demand in London, my foot. She only washed up here because nobody else would have her and that spoilt brat of a son of hers," Felicity whispered behind her hand. She winked at Betty. "I'm looking forward to hearing you sing, dearie. I hope you're good. It's about time somebody knocked Lady Muck off her perch."

The next ten minutes passed without any further upset, and Annie kept glancing at Betty, hardly able to believe that she was allowed porridge and then a slice of bread and butter as well. She curved her arm around her plate as though expecting someone to snatch it off her at any moment until Betty whispered that there was no need to.

"I'll introduce you to everyone later," Felicity said quietly, leaning closer to them. "Most of them aren't very talkative at this time of day anyway, you'll find. Too many late-night performances. They'll start to wake up properly and be friendlier as the day progresses. If you've finished your breakfast, you can go and find Abe Lucas, Annie. He'll give you some cleaning jobs to be getting on with."

Annie jumped up, eager to get started. "Miss Betty said you might have something better for me to wear?" she asked, looking self-consciously at the ragged dress that barely came below her knees.

"Of course. Mrs Snape, our dressmaker will be able to find you something suitable." Felicity took Annie's hand and led her away, leaving Betty to finish her food.

A moment later, the sound of more footsteps made Betty look up, and she felt her stomach lurch as another young man came striding into the dining room. He had dark hair that flopped over his forehead and the lithe physique of someone who never sat still for long. But what took her breath away was not that he was handsome in a rakish sort of way. It was the fact that she could have sworn he was one of the older boys in the pickpocket gang who had stood in the shadows the day before, watching as Annie's fate had hung in the balance with Constable Booth.

"Elizabeth Jones?" He flopped down in the chair next to Betty and grinned at her. "How nice to meet you again. You managed to evade the police then?"

"*I* managed to evade the police?" she whispered in disbelief. "You and your friends stole all my money. *You're* the one who's wanted by Constable Booth for being a pickpocket!" She shook her head, wondering whether her day could get any stranger. "What on earth are you doing in my uncle's theatre?"

CHAPTER 13

The young man tucked Betty's hand in the crook of his arm and, after nodding a brief greeting towards Camilla and Tarquin, propelled her through the door to the relative privacy of the hallway beyond. "That's a mighty rude accusation to be levelling at me," he said. His mouth twitched with amusement again.

"But it's true, isn't it?" Betty snatched her hand back and folded her arms, determined not to be fobbed off by his charming manner. "You've scrubbed up well, but I know it was you dressed in rags with the other children. And I saw you hanging around after Annie fell over. What sort of double life are you leading? Perhaps you're planning to rob the theatre too?" Her voice rose as all the different possibilities swirled through her mind.

"Yet when you were with Constable Booth in the town square, unless I'm much mistaken, you had the terrified look of someone who was expecting to be arrested...never mind young Annie," he shot back. He gave her a long stare and then nodded as Betty was stunned into silence. "I knew it. You're in some sort of trouble with the law, aren't you?" he exclaimed.

"I...it wasn't my fault...someone spread lies about me, that's all, and I have to try and put it right." Betty sighed, feeling defeated. It looked as though her time at the theatre might be over before it had even started. "I suppose you'll want to tell everyone," she said gloomily. "I was genuine in wanting to help Annie, for what it's worth."

"Alas, that you should think so badly of me." The young man extended his hand and pumped Betty's enthusiastically. "I'm Tom Thornton, aspiring illusionist and magician." He waited for a moment, assuming that she would understand. "You know...the great Gerry Thornton's son? He's the magician here at the theatre, and I'm following in his footsteps. And you're Ralph's niece, I believe?"

Betty nodded cautiously. "I still don't under-stand why you would be in a gang of known pick-pockets if you work here?"

Tom lowered his voice and glanced up and down the hallway. "Could we keep that little secret between us? My Pa will probably take his belt to me if he finds out. I managed to gain the trust of the notorious Mr Westwood because I thought if I learned how to pick pockets, it would be a useful skill for an illusionist to have." He gave an embar-rassed chuckle. "I only intended to do it for a few days, just learning off the younger boys. Being light-fingered is good for sleight of hand, but the old codger said I was so good he wanted me to be one of the gang leaders...so now I'm in a bit of a pickle."

"So your pa doesn't know you're embroiled with a pickpocket gang, and Mr Westwood thinks you're a poor orphan like Annie, and he's taken you under his wing?" Betty's eyes widened incred-ulously, and then she stifled a burst of laughter. "I thought my life was complicated. I don't suppose my uncle, Mr Hughes, knows any of this either?"

Tom shook his head guiltily. "I'd be very grateful if you didn't tell him. My pa has worked hard to earn his place at Glan Mor. It's only the two of us since my ma died, and I only did it because I wanted to help make his act even better."

"I'm not sure...how would it look if Uncle Ralph thinks I've been keeping secrets from him when I've only just joined." Betty followed Tom towards the dressing rooms, grappling with her conscience. He seemed like a genuine fellow, but the fact that he could fool Mr Westwood so easily gave her cause for concern. *Can I really trust him? What might he do if I don't agree?*

As if reading her thoughts, Tom paused outside a door which had *Gerry Thornton Magician and Illusionist* painted on it in a slanting font. "I think you and I could be good pals, Betty," he said quietly. "The way I see it, you have your secrets, and I have mine. If you take a leap of faith and trust me, maybe I can help you clear your name somehow? Why don't you tell me all about it later this afternoon? We usually have half an hour off before the show starts, and I'll even treat you to a cup of coffee."

Betty gave him a steady look, weighing him up. "I suppose so," she said slowly. If nothing else, it would be nice to have a few more friends and give her a chance to try and learn a bit more about the people she would be working and living with.

"Perfect." His face lit up with a sudden smile. "Bring Annie too. She's a good 'un, and I need to explain to her who I really am. It was kind of you to bring her here and get her away from Mr Westwood. His type only looks after the children for as long as they're useful, but we'll have to be careful that he doesn't find out. I heard from one of the other boys he was spitting feathers when she didn't go back to their digs last night."

"Betty, if you come with me, I'll give you the grand tour." Felicity came bustling towards them. "I hope you're not leading her astray already, Tom." She beckoned for Betty to follow her. "You'll want to check you still have all your ribbons and hair combs if you've been standing next to him," she said with a wink. "You should see how the toffs in the audience react when they realise he's taken their expensive pocket watches without them even noticing."

"Don't forget to tell her I always give them back, Felicity," Tom called after them. "It's all part of the act...of course, I would never steal something for real."

. . .

221

THE NEXT FEW hours passed in a whirl of activity as Felicity helped Annie and Betty settle in. They were introduced to so many different people that Betty could barely remember their names or who did what, but everyone was friendly, and by the time they sat down for some bread, cold meat and pickles for lunch, her homesickness was starting to ease.

"I know some folks would say we're a strange group of misfits, but the thing about theatre performers is that we're like a family, and we look out for each other. It can be a lonely life for the ones who travel all around the countryside to be in different shows. At least here at Glan Mor, we're fairly settled because the ladies and gentlemen come here all year round for their holidays, so Ralphie can keep us employed all the time."

Annie eyed a second piece of bread hungrily, and Felicity nodded for her to help herself. "I ain't never had a proper family," Annie said wistfully. "Do we have Christmas together and everything? With a goose and plum pudding and presents?"

"Some of the performers travel home to be with their families once the Christmas shows are over, but the rest of us stay here. It's all very festive, you'll have a wonderful time, Annie."

Annie beamed at them and took a huge bite of her bread, chewing it happily.

"So what jobs do you think we'll be best suited for, Felicity? I think my uncle was happy for you to decide."

Felicity nodded. "He asked for Annie to carry on helping Abe Lucas. He's been here for years and does all the odd jobs, sweeping up on stage, cleaning the seats where the audience sits, that sort of thing. His knees are getting arthritic, but Ralph has promised he'll always have work here, so Annie will be ideal for getting down under the seats and clearing up any rubbish for him."

"I'm quick too," Annie said stoutly. "Mr Lucas already said I was going to be a godsend because I can crawl under all the seats and get into the spaces he can't reach with his broom. He told me I might even find a penny under the seats sometimes, or a dropped handkerchief. Finders keepers, he told me, so I'll have all sorts of treasures to call my own soon."

"I asked Ralph if we could have you with us in the dressing rooms, Betty. We need help doing our costume changes and making sure the props are in the right place for when we switch between acts. It's all very exciting, and it means you get to peek out at the audience and hear all the performances too."

Betty felt her spirits lift. What Felicity was describing sounded positively frivolous compared to the backbreaking work down the pit. "I feel slightly guilty at the thought of being paid to do something so easy compared to hauling the coal tubs," she confided.

"Don't assume it's all fun," Felicity warned. "We have a show on six evenings a week, and you'll have to deal with some of the more demanding performers who will want you at their beck and call, I expect."

"Like that lady with her horrid son this morning?" Annie said quickly. "Abe told me some of them call her Crabby Camilla because she's so bad-tempered."

Felicity spluttered into her cup of tea. "He shouldn't be saying that, Annie. But yes, Camilla is known for being rather demanding. Rumour has it that the theatre director in London sent her packing because she upset so many of the other performers. You'd both be wise to steer clear of her as much as you can."

No sooner had the words left Felicity's mouth than Camilla appeared in the doorway. Her cheeks were flushed, and her good looks were spoilt by the thin set of her lips and frosty expression. "I heard what you just said, Felicity, and I'll have you know it was nothing of the sort. I chose to leave The Royale because they didn't appreciate my talent." She sniffed with disdain. "Not that I'd expect a common chorus girl like you to under- stand the challenges a star performer must suffer."

"That's a bit rude—" Annie coughed on a bread- crumb which had gone down the wrong way as Betty jabbed her sharply with her elbow.

"Just saying what I heard, Camilla. You know theatre life is a small world," Felicity said airily.

Camilla glared at the three of them, her gaze finally resting on Betty. "Shouldn't you be making yourself useful instead of listening to unfounded gossip? I have a gown that needs mending. Come to my dressing room in ten minutes, and you can take it to the seamstress for me." Without saying please or thank you, Camilla turned her nose up in the air and glided away.

"Remember what I said," Felicity whispered. "Just watch out that she doesn't start thinking of you as her own personal lackey. She ran the last girl ragged until the poor thing couldn't take it anymore. And to top it all, Camilla never had a good word to say about her."

Betty gulped her tea down even though it was still too hot. "I'm sure she won't be too bad with me, especially with my uncle being the theatre manager? Not that I want to trade on that," she added hastily. "Besides, I'll tell her that I'm expected to help all the performers, not just her."

Betty quickly finished her meal and patted her hair, making sure that she looked neat and tidy. She had no illusions that her voice was good enough to be on stage and was sure that once Camilla realised Betty just wanted to fit in and work hard, she would soon become more pleasant towards her. *If I managed to keep in Ezra Crundell's good books for as long as I did, I'm sure Mrs Covington and her spoilt son won't be any bother.* The thought of how she had survived for longer than many might have done in the harsh colliery environment gave her a burst of confidence, and a few minutes later, she knocked sharply on Camilla's dressing room door, ready to start working in earnest.

"Come." The word was barked in a tone that expected obedience.

"I'm here to collect your dress, Mrs Covington." Betty opened the door slowly and tried not to let her surprise show on her face. The dressing rooms Felicity had shown her that morning had been functional, with cluttered dressing tables, rails of costumes in various states of repair, and the hum of good-natured chatter between the performers who shared them. But Camilla's was like stepping into a grand drawing room. There were tall sash windows along the far side of the spacious room, edged with swagged curtains that pooled on the polished floorboards below. A large chaise longue upholstered in ruby satin was angled next to the hearth, and there was an inlaid walnut desk next to it, littered with perfumed writing paper and several gilt-edged invitations. One wall was dominated by the largest mirror Betty had ever seen, and there was a rail of gowns in every colour imaginable, with a table full of jewellery and decorative hair combs and ribbons to match.

"Mama won't be long?" Betty turned to see Tarquin lounging in an armchair in a small alcove to one side. He had a plate of pastries on his knee and popped a mouthful into his mouth before wiping his fingers carelessly on his trousers.

"I told Mrs Snape not to make the corset so tight, but did she listen?" Camilla appeared from behind a large screen in the corner of the room, wearing a tightly laced, ruched dress that accentuated her ample chest. "How am I supposed to sing if I can hardly breathe?" she demanded, giving Betty an irritated look as though it was somehow her fault.

"Do you want me to tell Mr Hughes she should be sacked, Mama?" Tarquin's small eyes gleamed with anticipation at the thought, and he struggled to his feet. "This is the second time Mama has been let down by that wretched woman. It's not good enough.

"Why don't I take the dress for you now and ask Mrs Snape to let it out? Felicity said she's the best seamstress they've ever had. I'm sure it won't take her long to adjust it to your liking."

Camilla struck a pose and lifted her arm theatrically before hitting a high note that was so loud it made Betty jump with surprise. The note ended in a squawk, and Camilla scowled. "You see? That woman will ruin my career unless I take her to task." Her face was bright red, and Betty feared for one moment that she might keel over in a faint.

"The dress is very flattering, though. I could ask her to prioritise your alteration over everything else."

Tarquin strutted to the door and flung it open.

"Mrs Snape should prioritise Mama's costumes anyway," he scoffed. "You clearly don't understand how important we are to the theatre, Betty. Without Mama being the star of the show, this place would probably barely last a season. And as her appointed manager, I'm determined that she shall have nothing but the best. Now run along and tell Mrs Snape to come here immediately."

"If she can work quickly and adjust my gown before tonight's show, I might just overlook her mistake this once." Camilla collapsed back onto the chaise longue and rested the back of her hand on her brow with a pained expression. "I really don't know how I would cope without darling Tarquin. I swear all the other performers and workers are ungrateful fools who don't appreciate how a talent like mine should be treated with the utmost respect."

Tarquin jerked his head towards the hallway and gave Betty a thin smile as she squeezed past him.

"Lawks, no sooner have I got away from Wynn Parry than I come across another bully," Betty muttered to herself as she scurried away. It seemed that Felicity's warning was right and she would have to watch her back. Tarquin Covington seemed like exactly the sort of person who would delight in seeing her get into trouble, or worse, thrown into jail. She decided to tell Annie and Tom they would all have to be careful to protect their secrets otherwise, they might all end up out of work and with nowhere to live.

CHAPTER 14

"How are my two favourite theatre friends?" Tom swirled a long black velvet cloak over his shoulders and doffed his top hat towards Betty and Annie, making them laugh. "What do you think? Does this make me look mysterious enough?"

Annie nodded enthusiastically. "Mysterious and a bit scary," she said with a dramatic shiver.

"Wonderful. That's just what I was hoping you would say. Now that Pa and Ralph have agreed that I can do mind reading as part of our act, I need the audience to feel as though I can see right into their innermost thoughts." He let out a spooky chuckle and waggled his eyebrows, drawing the cloak across the bottom half of his face so that only his eyes were showing.

"What's mind reading, Tom?" Annie leaned on her broom, which was practically taller than her and paused from her task of sweeping up the dust at the back of the stage.

"Yes, come on, you can tell us," Betty added. She had been quietly singing one of Felicity's chorus girl songs to herself, but now she put her paintbrush down and stood back to look at the backdrop she was creating for Camilla's new repertoire. The picture was of castle turrets amongst woodland, and although she wouldn't go as far as to say she was naturally artistic, she was pleased with the effect.

Tom swirled his cloak again and strode to the front of the stage. He turned to face them and pointed at Betty. "I sense that there is music in your life...you yearn to sing more, but so far, it has only been for your own pleasure and those closest to you..." He closed his eyes and pressed his hand to his forehead for a long moment as Annie's eyes grew wider. "Wait...it's coming to me in a vision..." His eyes flew open again and gleamed with conviction. "You hope to sing on the stage...and one day, very soon, your wish will come true. All you need is the courage of your convictions."

Betty's cheeks flushed pink. Although she had never said as much, now that she had been at the Glan Mor theatre for well over a month, she had been secretly hoping that Ralph would remember his promise to give her an audition. But as the days turned into weeks, she could only conclude he must have forgotten as he hadn't mentioned it again. Betty had told herself she was just grateful to have a job she enjoyed and a group of new friends for company, but she couldn't help being a tiny bit disappointed, although she didn't want to admit it to anyone.

"Yes," Tom continued, "the vision is becoming clearer...I see an audience clapping and cheering because they are so delighted...they're saying your voice is as sweet as a nightingale's."

"Your acting is very good," Betty said with a self-deprecating shrug. "But I'm sure there are more than enough singers in the cast already for what Uncle Ralph needs. Besides, I'm happier working behind the scenes."

Annie resumed her sweeping, bending down to get into the corners behind the props. "I think you should be on stage," she said stoutly. "I've heard you singing when you think nobody's listening and you're just as good as all the others."

"It's not my opinion, Betty," Tom said, strolling back towards them. "When a vision comes to me, it must not be ignored."

"Oh, stop it." Betty laughed and swatted him with the old rag she used to mop up drips of paint. "You can save that sort of talk for the audience. I'm not falling for that old flannel. Anyway, how do you read their minds? You still haven't said."

"Aha, a great magician and illusionist never tells." Tom perched on the edge of a wicker basket that was stuffed full of old curtains. "But, seeing as it's you two and I can trust you, it's simple. I just go out into the foyer before the show begins and mingle with the audience as they arrive. You'll be surprised what I can learn by listening and watching. People give away their secrets and dreams all the time. Take Felicity, for example. She's sweet on Miles in the orchestra. How do I know? Because she makes a point of never looking at him directly when they're in the dining room together."

"No, surely not?" Annie's mouth gaped open, and she darted a look at Betty, who looked equally as surprised.

Tom tapped the side of his nose and grinned.

"I'm right, you'll see. And not only that, I think they will be married within a year, as long as Miles can get over his shyness and ask her to go courting. Anyway, I'd better go. I have to help Pa with his new card tricks. See you at lunch, and remember, don't reveal my secrets to anyone else." With another flourish of his cape, he hurried away.

"I'm going to help Abe stick up some new posters at the front of the theatre." Annie quickly swept up the pile of dust into her dustpan. "Have you got much more painting to do?"

Betty walked to the front of the stage and looked at the backdrop with a critical eye, trying to see it from the audience's view. Camilla would no doubt come and inspect it later, and she wanted to make sure it would meet with her approval. "I think I'll stay for a while longer and make the trees a bit darker," she replied. Camilla had recently decided to perform some new songs, casting herself as a woodland nymph yearning for love, and her costume was a diaphanous concoction of lace and sequins that glittered under the gaslights. She had already insisted that whatever Betty painted must be done in such a way to make her stand out more clearly so that her adoring public would focus on her and her alone.

She was soon absorbed in her task again, and the repetitive work allowed her mind to drift freely over the last few weeks. She thought about how much her life had changed. After initially being hesitant about whether Tom was trustworthy, Betty had let her guard down, and now she considered him to be a good friend. With a bit of gentle persuasion, Betty had even confided in him about the storm and Jack's accident, as well as the terrible lies Wynn Parry had spread about her being the reason Lord Leyfield had taken his money elsewhere. Tom had been most indignant on her behalf, declaring he could tell she wasn't the sort of person who would do such a thing. And likewise, he had taken Betty and Annie into his confidence, explaining that he had managed to convince Mr Westwood that he wasn't really a pickpocket. Annie had looked alarmed when the subject came up, but Tom had reassured her that she had soon been replaced in the gang, so they could both put their thieving days behind them.

Felicity had also proven to be a kindhearted friend who had helped her settle into theatre life, never tiring of Betty's questions or making her feel silly if there was something she didn't understand. Betty realised that she was fortunate to have been taken into the Glan Mor family so readily, and what pleased her even more was that Annie was blossoming too. It had quickly become evident that Annie was a bright girl and that with the right sort of guidance and the security of a place to call home, she would have a good future ahead of her at the theatre.

As Betty dabbed some dark green paint on the canvas, her thoughts turned to the letter she had received from her ma a few days earlier. It had been filled with news about the village and how well Minnie's dressmaking skills were improving under Mary's tutelage. Jack was taking a keen interest in the garden, and he and Dai were already planning to grow some different vegetables the following year. His leg was healing better than expected, and she hoped it wouldn't be too long until he would be able to walk more easily. Fay had also passed on a message from Dylan, saying how much he was missing her and hoping she was thinking fondly of them all.

Betty sighed and felt a tug of yearning to see Dylan's face again and hear his easy laugh. Although her new friends helped fill the gap, her heart still belonged to Dylan, and it was hard not knowing when she might see him again. When she had told Felicity about him, she had squeezed Betty's arm with understanding, telling her to send him a letter. Then a few days later, she gave Betty some violet-scented notepaper, explaining that one of her admirers gave it to her as a gift, but she wanted Betty to have it instead.

Will Dylan think I've moved on and that I'm forgetting about him? Betty tried to put herself in his shoes, imagining what it might feel like if he'd left the village and their old life and she had stayed behind. She knew that she was rather naive in matters of the heart, but Felicity had reassured her, reminding her that she had only left Pencastle village out of necessity, not because she disliked her old life. Betty decided she would write a letter to Dylan over the next few nights after the shows were finished. There was so much she wanted to tell him, and she smiled as her head filled with tidbits of gossip and how she would describe all the different characters of the performers she now lived with.

"I hope that backdrop is going to be finished in time?" The abrupt question from Tarquin snatched Betty from her pleasant reverie. "I don't want Mama's songs ruined by the smell of paint. It might catch in her throat and spoil her voice." He strode closer and swiped his finger on the canvas, looking at the wet paint that smeared on his fingertip with annoyance.

"I've just finished now, and if I prop the stage door open, it should be dry in no time." Betty swished her paintbrush in a jar of water and wiped her hands on a rag. "Maybe Camilla would like to come and see it after lunch to check that it's to her liking?"

Tarquin shook his head. "How many times do I have to tell you, Betty? I manage all of Mama's affairs. She needs to keep her mind clear of inconsequential details like this." He gestured at the backdrop with a disappointed sigh. "It's a bit garish, but I suppose it will have to do for now."

"Well, if that's all you need, I'll get on with something else. I need to take some dresses to Mrs Snape's room for mending." Betty tidied up her painting supplies, determined not to rise to Tarquin's churlish comments about her work. He never missed an opportunity to put her down, but most of the time, she managed to ignore it and go about her chores.

"I fancy you've had a rather easy time of things here at the theatre simply because you're Mr Hughes's niece. What do the others think of that then?" Tarquin stood in Betty's way and smirked. "From what I've heard, they're annoyed that you get all the best jobs even though you've only been here a matter of weeks."

"Everyone has been very welcoming, actually," Betty shot back. "Well, most people," she added pointedly.

Tarquin glanced over his shoulder to make sure they were alone. "You don't need to be so prickly with me, Betty. I just want to point out that not everyone might be as pleasant to you as Mama and I have been." He placed his hand on her arm and squeezed it as though suddenly sympathetic to her plight. "The thing is...maybe they've realised you're not the innocent young girl from the valleys you claim to be. There are whispers about town that imply you left your home under something of a cloud?

"Certainly not," Betty muttered. She wanted to pull back from him, but his grasp was surprisingly strong. She decided to try a different approach, giving him a brief smile. "You know how rumours get around in the theatre. Most of the time there's no truth to them."

He nodded, looking down at her with a thoughtful expression as though she was a puzzle to be solved. "If you have secrets from your past, Betty, they're safe with me."

Betty chuckled. "I don't have any secrets. I'm just here to work hard and help my uncle. Much like you helping your mama, Tarquin. Now I really must go, and I expect Camilla will need to start rehearsing soon."

"Now that you mention your uncle, there is a little something you could help me with." Tarquin's voice was silky smooth, but his eyes were cold, and he edged closer again, forcing her to step back into the corner. "Mama says I have a very fine voice, and I think the theatre could benefit greatly from having me on the stage performing. With the repu-tation of the Covington name, I'm sure to be a huge draw for the audience, just like Mama is."

"You? A singer?" Betty blinked rapidly, unable to hide her surprise.

"Of course," Tarquin snapped, looking offended. "Mama is never wrong about such things, and she believes Glan Mor is crying out for a man of my talent. The other male singers are very mediocre."

"Oh…so what do you need my help with?" Betty realised that there was no point expecting Tarquin to show any degree of modesty. Camilla had brought him up to be a pampered young man who expected to get his own way.

"Mama will make the suggestion to Ralph very soon, and I'd like you to put in a good word for me. Can I count on your support, Betty? Otherwise, I might have to find out a bit more about your brush with Constable Booth and your mysterious past…" He let his words hang between them, enjoying the sudden look of alarm in Betty's eyes.

"Of course," Betty stuttered. "As long as you understand that Uncle Ralph makes his own decisions. I mean, I'm just a backstage helper, Tarquin. I don't have any influence over who my uncle decides to include in the performances."

"You underestimate yourself, my sweet." Tarquin gave her a predatory smile and suddenly lunged forward and wrapped his arms around Betty, pulling her into a clumsy embrace.

"What are you doing?" she demanded. She managed the push him away so that his moist lips only brushed against her hair instead of the kiss he had intended to force on her. "Get off me this instant." Betty stumbled backwards and folded her arms across her chest defensively. "I said I would speak to Uncle Ralph, but I…I'm already courting. Your behaviour is very ungallant."

"Pah, I suppose you think holding a flame for some oafish boy from home counts as courting? You're deluded if that's the case." Tarquin's cheeks had two bright spots of colour on them, and his eyes glittered with anger. "Anyway, I've seen how you flirt with Tom Thornton, even though he's a nobody. You should be please I picked you out for my attention, Betty. There are plenty of other women who would be thankful."

"Tom and I are just friends," Betty said hotly. She grabbed her paintbrushes and scurried away before he could try and embrace her again.

"Don't forget to put in a good word for me," Tarquin called after her. "I'd hate to have to rake up your past and get you into trouble, but I do have plenty of contacts in Abertarron who aren't as honourable. Who knows what they might find out in return for a few coins to spend on ale?"

As Betty hurried away, she could still hear him chuckling, but there was no humour in it. She realised she had underestimated him, and her stomach clenched with anxiety at the thought that now he had a hold over her. *Maybe I should just speak to Constable Booth myself and explain that I didn't cause the scandal in the village. It was just a terrible accident...I didn't leave the shutter door open and cause the flood in the Blaeny shaft.* The idea slid through her mind, but she dismissed it immediately. For all she knew, the gossip and accusations had died down back at home, and Wynn had decided to let bygones be bygones. All she could hope for now was that Tarquin would get the singing part his heart was set on and that he would forget about being rebuffed in his attempt to kiss her. She shuddered at the memory. Even if her heart wasn't already given to Dylan, Tarquin was the last person she would ever feel attracted to, but he was so thick-skinned he probably thought he was a marvellous catch.

BETTY BARELY SLEPT a wink that night. She tossed and turned in bed and picked through all the conversations she had ever had with Tarquin, trying to pinpoint how he might have caught wind of what had happened at Nantglas Colliery. Tom, Annie, and Felicity were the only people she had confided in, and she knew that they all disliked Tarquin so much that they would never have blabbed to him. Finally, as the darkness gradually gave way to sunrise, she drifted into a shallow, troubled sleep in which she dreamt she was being chased through the cobbled streets of Abertarron by Ezra Crundell and Constable Booth, both of them intent on throwing her into jail.

"Betty, wake up!" Annie's face loomed over her, and Betty woke up with a start. Her heart was thudding in her chest, and she realised she had overslept.

"I heard you thrashing about earlier. What's troubling you?"

"Oh, it's nothing much." Betty yawned and quickly slipped out of her nightgown and into her grey cotton dress. She twisted her long hair into a bun and secured it with several hairpins. "Tarquin wants me to persuade Uncle Ralph to let him have his own singing act."

Annie's eyes widened. "Surely not? Abe and I saw him strutting around the stage the other day when we were sweeping the seats up in the gods. Camilla was giving him direction, and then when he struck up a song, it sounded like two alley cats fighting." She stifled a giggle and shook her head. "Mr Hughes won't want Tarquin on the bill."

"That's what I'm worried about, but I don't have any choice. I'll just have to mention it to Uncle Ralph, and then they can sort it out between themselves. Hopefully, that will be the end of my involvement."

Betty put Tarquin's request out of her mind for the next few hours as she bustled between all the dressing rooms collecting various items from all the performers' costumes for the washerwoman. Maggie White came twice a week to spend the day toiling in the laundry, swathed in clouds of billowing steam from the old copper pots, and it was Betty's job to keep her supplied with clothes and then peg everything out on the washing lines. Just as she went to fetch the flannels the actors used to wipe their greasepaint and makeup off with, she saw Camilla and Tarquin deep in conversation outside Ralph's study.

"Did you do what I asked?" Tarquin demanded when he caught sight of her.

Betty's heart sank. "I haven't had a chance to speak to Uncle Ralph yet," she said hastily. "I was going to do it after I finished all my chores."

Camilla's expression hardened. "Your chores can wait. This is far more important." She raised a bejewelled hand and rapped sharply on Ralph's door. "You may as well come and do it now instead."

Tarquin smirked as Betty hurried to join

them. "Remember what we talked about, dear Betty," he whispered as Ralph threw his door open.

"Goodness me, I don't usually get so many visitors at this time of the day." Ralph looked rather distracted and ran a hand through his hair. "I was just in the middle of tallying the accounts. Can't it wait, whatever you need me for?"

"Dear Ralph, you're simply marvellous the way you work so hard keeping Glan Mor going," Camilla purred. "We won't take much of your time." She swept into the study and stood with her back to the window, always careful to place herself in the most flattering light. Tarquin followed and jerked his head slightly, indicating that Betty should join them.

"Is there a problem? Please don't tell me you need time off because your voice is suffering?" Ralph paced back and forth with a worried frown. He darted a look at the stack of bills on his desk and sighed. There never seemed to be enough money to cover them, and he wondered absent-mindedly whether Camilla would consider waiting a couple of weeks longer to be paid. The fee she demanded was far in excess of what he paid any of the other performers, but he had to admit that she did attract an audience, and the theatre couldn't do without her.

"Quite the opposite, Ralph. Not a problem but an opportunity." Camilla followed his gaze towards the bills and smiled to herself. "I think it's time you gave Tarquin a place on the stage with his own singing act. He has such a splendid voice. I'm certain it will attract an even bigger audience, especially when they know he's my son."

Tarquin stood a little taller and nodded graciously, agreeing with the compliment. "I've long known that I have Mama's talent, Ralph. It's a waste having me only as Mama's manager when I could be singing." He nudged Betty with his elbow and twitched one eyebrow expectantly.

"Y…yes," she stuttered. "I heard Tarquin singing just last week, and he certainly has a very…memorable voice, Uncle Ralph. I know it's not my place to say, but it might be a wonderful addition to the show."

Ralph looked between the three of them with a puzzled expression. "Are you sure about this, Camilla? You've never mentioned Tarquin's singing before, and I'm not sure that we need another male singer. The Burton brothers were both professionally trained in London and Paris and they're very happy to stay on at Glan Mor for as long as I need them."

Camilla snapped her fan open and fluttered it in front of her face. "It's only modesty which has prevented me from bringing Tarquin's talent to your attention, Ralph." She gave him a tremulous smile and then dabbed a lace handkerchief delicately on her eyes. "Since I lost my dear late husband, I have to think of our futures. It would be a terrible shame if I had to return to London in order to give Tarquin the opportunities he deserves..."

Ralph strode over to the sideboard and reached for his whisky decanter, splashing some into a glass as he considered her words. Camilla had begged him for a place at Glan Mor when they first arrived two years ago, but since then, she had built something of a name for herself. He knew she might be bluffing but didn't want to take the risk. "If you put it like that, I don't suppose it would harm for him to have an audition." He raised his glass in a toast and gulped the whisky back, hoping he wouldn't regret giving in to her thinly veiled threat.

"Oh, he scarcely needs an audition," Camilla

cooed happily. "You'll be delighted, I can assure you."

"I can't be seen to be favouring Tarquin over the other performers," Ralph said hastily. He sat down behind his desk again and closed the ledger, not wanting to see the debts that kept him awake at night. Suddenly his face brightened as he remembered something. "I promised Betty an audition when she came here, and it completely slipped my mind. "You can both sing for me tomorrow morning. If it goes well, I might even put you in an act together."

Camilla pursed her lips with displeasure, looking down her nose at Betty's drab work dress. "You know best, Ralph, although I wouldn't want her to detract from Tarquin. I'm sure once you've heard him, you'll want him to have equal billing as the star of the show with me, not be paired with someone who looks and behaves like nothing more than a glorified maid."

"Please remember this is my niece we're talking about, Camilla. My mind is made up. We'll do it at ten o'clock tomorrow morning while the orchestra is rehearsing." Ralph leaned back in his chair and put his hands behind his head, looking happier.

"Very well. Come along, Tarquin; you need to

rest before your big moment. Don't let us keep you from the dirty laundry, Betty." Camilla linked arms with her son, and they swept out of the room. "I hope you won't be too disappointed when it doesn't go well for you," she added spitefully as she gave Betty one final glare.

"Thank you, Uncle Ralph. I'm terribly nervous, but I'll do my best. And I want you to know that I'm very grateful to have a place at the theatre, even if I never get to sing a note."

Ralph chuckled and picked up his ledger again. "I trust Fay's judgement about you more than Camilla's about Tarquin, that's for sure. If Fay says you can sing, you deserve an audition. Anyway, it's about time Camilla realised that I'm in charge around here. Maybe having a bit of competition from you might keep her on her toes."

CHAPTER 15

"*H*ow do I look?" Betty's hands trembled slightly as she patted her hair. She had swept her flowing locks back with two tortoiseshell combs, leaving some tendrils to curl softly around her face, and she looked at her reflection, feeling rather shocked at the stranger who looked back at her. Felicity had insisted that she should wear one of the elegant silk gowns she performed in so that she would feel the part, and it was the first time Betty had ever worn anything so grand.

"I can hardly recognise you," Annie declared. She darted around her to make sure the ruffles at the back were falling correctly and stood back again, beaming with admiration. "You look like a proper lady now, Betty."

"It fits you like a glove," Felicity said happily. She fastened a velvet choker around Betty's neck to complete the look and chuckled. "Camilla's nose will be put right out of joint when you come out on stage, you look beautiful."

"That's because Betty's kind," Annie said firmly. "Camilla is always grumpy and ungrateful, even when she's all dressed up, which is why she's not pretty."

"Goodness me...what a transformation." Tom's eyes widened with surprise as he poked his head around the dressing room door. "Ralph sent me to fetch you. The orchestra have finished rehearsing, and we're all waiting for the auditions. Can I escort you, my lady?" He grinned and offered his arm for her to take.

"What do you mean, you're all waiting? I thought it was just going to be Ralph listening."

"Ah yes...I meant to tell you that," Felicity said, bustling behind them with Annie. "It's theatre tradition that all the performers come and watch auditions. We'll be sitting in the seats as though we're the audience."

Betty stopped in her tracks. "Everyone?" Her

cheeks went pale, and suddenly the gown felt too tight as she gasped for breath.

"You'll be fine," Tom said hastily. "We didn't want you to worry about it; that's why we didn't say anything before. Anyway, when you're on stage with the gaslights on, you can't really see the audience very clearly. Just pretend you're singing on your own, the same as when I overheard you the other day when you were in the laundry with Maggie."

"I didn't know you were listening?" Betty rolled her eyes at his mischievous grin and then took a deep breath to steady her nerves. "Don't expect too much. I know my ma says I have a nice voice, but I expect she was just saying it to be kind."

"Just enjoy yourself," Felicity advised. "You might just surprise yourself and enjoy it, and when everyone claps at the end, there's no other feeling like it."

Camilla's shrill instructions to the orchestra drifted down the hallway just as Betty arrived backstage.

"I must insist you play at the tempo I told you to use. Tarquin is used to singing this song in moderato, but you keep playing it too fast." She had her hands on her hips and tapped her foot firmly, ignoring the violinists who exchanged annoyed glances with each other. "That's better," she said eventually as the orchestra finally played it to her liking.

"You're looking nervous, Betty." Tarquin was leaning casually on a box at the back of the stage as though he didn't have a care in the world. "I think I should go first...you won't mind waiting, I'm sure."

"No...of course not," she stuttered.

"Lawks, what on earth is he wearing?" Annie whispered loudly. She nudged Felicity as they looked at the brightly coloured ruffled satin shirt that strained over his stomach above short breeches and buckled shoes. His hair was swept into a quiff held in place with pomade, and he carried a red cloak over his arm.

"I think he must be doing some songs from a Spanish opera," Felicity said behind her hand. "It's a matador's costume. You'd think his ma would have put him in something a bit more flattering."

Annie giggled, and they scurried away with Tom to take their place in the audience. Betty hovered in the wings and peeked around the curtain. Even though Tom had told her she wouldn't notice everyone, there seemed to be an alarming number of faces gazing up expectantly, waiting for the auditions to begin. From the other performers to the maids, and even Abe, the hum of whispers from beyond the gaslights at the front of the stage suddenly made Betty wonder why she had ever thought she might be able to sing in public. It was a far cry from the Sunday evenings when her family had encouraged her to entertain them in their cottage.

"Are you ready, Tarquin, dear?" Camilla bustled over and made a few last-minute adjustments to his costume. "Your Papa would have been so proud of you." Her eyes glistened with unshed tears, and she dabbed them daintily with a lace handkerchief. "I can picture it now...all the high society ladies and gentlemen coming from London to watch you perform. Maybe we shall be invited to sing together in Paris and beyond. A grand tour of Europe." She sighed happily and ushered Tarquin to the centre of the stage.

"I'm looking forward to this," Ralph called from his front row seat. He nodded to the conductor, and the orchestra struck up the dramatic introduction to the piece of music Tarquin had chosen.

Suddenly Tarquin held up his hand, and the music fizzled out as the musicians looked at each other with confusion. "I think that as Betty is the amateur, she should go first after all. I'm sure it must feel very strange for her to be on stage after working down a coal mine, so I shall do the honourable thing and go second."

A ripple of shocked whispers went through the onlookers, and Betty felt the blood rush to her cheeks. Although she wasn't ashamed of her upbringing, not many of the theatre performers knew she had worked down the pit, and she felt the weight of their curious stares on her.

"That's a wonderful idea," Tom shouted from his seat. He stood up and opened both his arms wide. "I'm lucky enough to have heard Betty sing. She might be from a humble background, but so are many of us, and today, ladies and gentlemen, you are about to witness our very own Nightingale From The Valleys. Let's give her a warm welcome." He clapped his hands, and soon everyone was clapping enthusiastically along with him after his rousing introduction.

"Let's hear you, girl," Abe called.

"Come on, Betty. Sing us a tune." Felicity and Annie both stood up and beckoned her forward.

Tarquin sidled away to the edge of the stage, and Betty walked to where he had been standing.

Clasping her hands in front of her, she blinked and cleared her throat several times.

"Are you ready for us to play?" the conductor asked.

Betty closed her eyes for a moment, trying to recall the song she had thought would most impress her uncle, but her mind had gone blank. "I...I...can't remember the song," she whispered.

"Do the one you said made you think of home," Tom hissed.

"Yes...yes...do you know 'The Winding Road Home' by any chance?" Once the conductor had nodded, Betty closed her eyes to shut out the faces of everyone staring at her and took a deep breath. As the first haunting notes of the sentimental song washed over her, she started to sing and immediately felt all her worries melt away. Her soprano voice rang out, clear and sweet, filling the vast auditorium in a way she had never experienced. The music rose and fell as the heartfelt words spoke of missing her true love and then travelling home to marry him. As the last note ended like a songbird falling silent at dusk, there was a moment of stunned silence in the audience before they erupted into rapturous applause and cheers.

Betty looked up shyly and saw Abe wiping tears

away and Annie and Tom hugging each other with excitement.

"More...more...sing us another one." The Burton brothers, themselves both accomplished tenors, were looking at her in amazement and nodding for her to continue.

"Are you sure?" She leaned over and whispered something to the conductor. Moments later, the elegant strains of 'My Love, Her Heart Is True' from her favourite opera rang out, and Betty launched into the song about unrequited love between a soldier and his sweetheart who had died before he got home from battle. At the end, there was another silence before everyone stood up and started clapping and cheering again.

"We must give Betty a part in the show, Ralph," Alex Burton cried. "She could sing with us...we would bring the house down."

Ralph stood up and nodded, hushing everyone. "Thank you, Betty. I could see that you were nervous, but that was a wonderful audition. Let's hear Tarquin now, and then I can decide the best way to have you in the show."

Betty felt as though she was walking on air as she took her place back in the wings. After all this time of thinking her voice was nothing special, she

could hardly believe the genuine words of appreciation from the other performers, and now she
understood why Felicity had been so excited about
this chance to prove herself.

"You did alright," Tarquin said gruffly as he
strode out to the centre of the stage, swirling his
cloak with a flourish. He nodded curtly at the
conductor, and the musicians started playing for
him.

Betty had expected Tarquin to have a rich
baritone, but as he started singing, she was
surprised to hear a modest tenor that sounded
slightly flat. Strutting back and forth across the
front of the stage, Tarquin raised his arms with
every dramatic moment in the matador's song.
His expression was, by turn, serious, then aston-
ished as he acted out the emotions and swished
the cloak for added effect. The orchestra tried to
keep up as he sang faster with each new verse.
Tarquin forced his voice higher and higher,
ending the final verse in a breathless rush that
barely reached the first few rows, let alone filled
the large auditorium.

As the last note ended, Camilla rushed to his
side with her hands clasped to her ample bosom.
Tears were streaming down her face. "Oh, Tarquin,

that was quite the most exquisite thing I've ever heard," she gushed.

"Exquisite? More like a cat being dragged out of a dustbin," someone in the audience shouted, setting off a ripple of nervous laughter.

"I ain't never heard anything so bad…it's worse than ol' Nancy outside the pub when she's been on the gin," another person called from up in the gods.

Tarquin's face darkened with anger, and Camilla glared at the audience. "Ralph, how can you let them say such terrible things?" she spluttered. "It's that girl's fault, singing those common ditties as if we were in a back-street pub." She shot Betty a malevolent stare. "Tarquin had a cold last week which has gone to his chest, and the musicians were distracted by playing her stupid songs first."

Ralph stood up hastily. "I expect Tarquin just needs a little more time to practice," he said diplomatically. The last thing he wanted was to upset his leading lady. "Why don't you give him a few more lessons, Camilla. I certainly think you might be able to have a part in a show…next year perhaps, Tarquin."

Before Camilla could reply, several people

booed from the shadows. "He could be a comedy act," someone yelled.

"Don't let him…it will make us all a laughing stock. He hasn't got what it takes."

Tarquin threw his mother's arm off and stormed off stage, his face like thunder. "I suppose you think this is funny?" he spat at Betty as he barged over to where she had been standing quietly watching.

"No…I'm sorry, Tarquin. Like Uncle Ralph said…your mama will be able to help you improve, I'm sure."

"Who are you to say I need to improve?" Tarquin gripped her arm tightly, making Betty yelp from the pain. "You're nothing but a skivvy, Betty Jones. You'll never make a success of being on the stage. People will see you for the common pit girl that you are." His lip curled with contempt, and he pushed her away. "You made a fool of me today. You might think you've got away with it, but I'm going to make sure you live to regret this." With that, he strode off, leaving Betty ashen-faced in his wake.

.   .   .

"You were so good today." Annie hadn't stopped smiling since the audition, and she did a pirouette as she carried a teapot towards Betty, making the lid rattle alarmingly.

"Let me pour us all a cup of tea. I think we've earned it." Felicity took the teapot from Annie, and the young girl yawned loudly. "Tom, you'll have one with us, will you?"

The four of them sat companionably in the dining room. The evening show had finished an hour ago, but Annie had declared she was far too excited to sleep and had chattered nonstop as they tidied away the costumes until Felicity suggested a cup of tea to help them relax.

"I'm delighted your uncle has agreed you can start on the stage next week." Tom crossed his long legs and took a sip of his tea. "What did Tarquin say to you after his appalling audition? I've never seen him looking so angry."

Betty sighed. It had been a day of high emotions, but even though she was thrilled she would soon be a theatre performer, Tarquin's words had taken the edge off her happiness. "He cornered me a couple of days ago, demanding I should put in a good word with Uncle Ralph, and then…and then he tried to force a kiss on me."

"What an odious man," Felicity said, looking shocked. "I know he has a reputation for being spoilt, but that's going too far." She patted Betty's hand with concern. "Should we tell Ralph? I'll back you up if you want to."

"Or maybe I should take him into the alley, and we can sort it out like men." Tom's fists were bunched, and he looked as though he was about to leap up and find Tarquin.

"No, please...you'll just make it worse." Betty felt the familiar worry return and decided to confide in her friends. "The thing is, I think Wynn Parry has a cousin who lives somewhere near here, or possibly even in Abertarron. And Tarquin threatened to rake up my past and tell everyone that I caused the accident down the pit. He implied that he has contacts in the town who know all about my past...not that I have any secrets to hide."

"That ain't fair," Annie burst out. "Just because he can't sing doesn't mean he should ruin your chances, Betty. I've got a good mind to go and tell Mr Westwood. He knows some nasty types who will give him what for."

Betty smiled weakly and shook her head. "It's very kind of you all to defend me, but I fear that Tarquin is like a hornets' nest, best left well alone.

If you get involved, he might turn his meddling ways to try and make trouble for you too, and I don't think I could bear that."

"But we can't just ignore what you've told us, Betty." Felicity's brow was furrowed with distress.

"If he does find out about Wynn and tries to spread lies about me here, I'll just have to take the consequences," Betty said firmly. She stifled a yawn, the day's events catching up with her. "Come along, Annie. We'd better get some sleep now, otherwise we'll be exhausted tomorrow."

The four of them stood up, and Felicity tidied away their teacups. "You only have to say the word, and we'll stick up for you."

Tom nodded, looking thoughtful. "I've had an idea. I'll play Tarquin at his own game. He's known for frequenting the card tables in some rather down-at-heel pubs in town, and I made a few contacts of my own back when I was studying the art of pickpocketing." He shot Betty a mischievous smile. "The best way to beat a bully is to have something to use against them, just in case. I'll ask around and see what I can come up with." Seeing Betty's look of alarm, he held his hands up. "We'll only use it if we ever need to, Betty. I'm not malicious, but it's good to know your enemy."

"As long as you're careful, Tom. I don't want you getting embroiled with that gang again, or you, Annie." Betty felt a ripple of unease as they wearily trudged up the narrow stairs to their room under the eaves. She hadn't told her friends quite how venomous Tarquin's words had been, but the memory of the anger in his eyes after being humiliated on stage was etched on her mind. She wondered how far he would go to ruin her reputation, just as her dream of singing on stage was about to come true.

CHAPTER 16

*B*etty blinked back her unexpected tears as she pinned a soft yellow primrose on the collar of her gown. The arrival of the lightly scented spring flowers in Abertarron's parks was a welcome end to the long, cold winter, but they were also a poignant reminder of how much she missed her family.

"Would you like a primrose as well, Annie?" Betty held another flower to her nose and breathed in the slightly citrusy scent, remembering that day so long ago when her dear pa had picked one on the way home from church for her mother.

Annie quickly hung up the last few costumes on the long rail in the dressing room Betty shared with Felicity. "Nobody's ever given me flowers before." She smiled proudly as Betty tucked it into her shawl.

"You're a good girl, Annie, and almost like a sister to me. My Pa always used to pick them from the hedgerows where they grew wild and give them to us, so I'm carrying on his tradition."

"I feel as though I've known you all my life. I can't believe we've been at the theatre for over six months," Annie remarked, admiring her reflection in the large mirror over the dressing table. She dabbed a puff of face powder on her nose and grinned. Helping Betty and Felicity get ready for their nightly performance was her favourite part of the day.

"I know. When I think that this time last year I was still lugging those tubs of coal from underground for twelve hours a day and now I'm singing on stage instead, I can hardly believe it either. I sometimes wonder whether it's all a dream and I'll wake up back in our cottage in Limetree Lane with the colliery horn going off to wake us up."

Betty gave Annie a fond look. The scrawny girl with tangled hair and a grimy face who had sprawled on the cobbles in front of her was long gone. Under Betty's care, Annie had filled out, and her blonde hair was tucked neatly under a mob cap. She was loved by all the members of the theatre for her willing attitude, and Abe had taken her under his wing and was teaching her to read and write for an hour each afternoon which Ralph had happily agreed to.

"Are you looking forward to the new show, Annie?" Felicity bustled into the dressing room with a rustle of silk. Ralph had promoted her to be the head of the chorus girls, and it was the grand opening of their new season, so there was a palpable air of excitement backstage.

"I can't wait. Abe promised I could sit in the wings and watch because I got up extra early to finish all my jobs in time."

Felicity paused to look at her reflection next to Betty, turning this way and that. She smoothed her hands down the tightly corsetted gown and adjusted the bodice to reveal just the right amount of décolletage. "Poor Mrs Snape's hands are getting so arthritic she struggled to get all our costumes done in time. I think we might have to suggest that she gets some help when we do the new programme for autumn and winter."

"Maybe I should suggest it for Minnie," Betty replied, looking thoughtful. Her ma's latest letter had mentioned that they had so many ladies on their books having new dresses made that they could scarcely keep up, but Betty knew that Minnie would jump at the chance to create the beautiful costumes they wore on stage.

"Ten minutes until the show starts," Tom called. "Good luck, everyone." Tom hurried along the corridor, knocking on each dressing room door, and Annie darted after him to join in.

"Our adoring public awaits." Felicity and Betty hugged, and Betty felt the familiar sense of butter-flies in her stomach that she always had just before a show started. Even though Felicity told her often that she was now a professional singer with almost a whole season under her belt, Betty still struggled with feeling like an imposter.

"Look, there's your name on the poster." The day before, Tom and Felicity had dragged her to the steps outside the Glan Mor and pointed at the huge painted poster which had been pinned up by the entrance for the last few weeks. Sure enough, Betty was listed amongst the other acts that included comic songs, magic and illusion, acrobats, performing animals and more. "'Betty Jones, The Nightingale of the Valleys' and this time you're second on the billing too, right beneath Camilla," Tom had said proudly.

"Here's to a good first night." Betty touched the primrose as though it was a talisman, and then they hurried to the area backstage, where the performers waited until it was their turn to go on.

"See you later," Felicity whispered before gathering her chorus girls together. She put her finger to her lips, miming for them to be quiet.

"Ladies and gentlemen…it gives me great pleasure to welcome you to the Glan Mor Theatre on this, the first night of our new show." Ralph's deep voice boomed out from where he was standing in front of the curtains, and Betty felt a shiver of anticipation as the crowd clapped and stamped their feet.

"Out of our way." Tarquin pushed Betty roughly aside, and Camilla sailed past with a toss of her tightly curled ringlets. "Mama needs to have a quiet space to gather her thoughts away from the less talented acts," he muttered with a sour expression.

"Thank you, dear." Camilla gave her son a doting look and drew herself up to her full height. Under the harsh glare of the backstage gaslights, the thick rouge on her cheeks accentuated the fine lines of her skin and the way her good looks were starting to fade like a rose losing the lustre of its first flush of beauty. "You might think you're popular because Ralph has put you higher up the billing, but it's only favouritism for a family member, not because you have any *real* talent." Camilla wrinkled her nose and looked Betty up and down. "You do look rather common in that gown as well."

"What more would one would expect from a pit girl," Tarquin added. He turned his back on Betty and took Camilla's elbow. "Follow me, Mama. It's up to you to give the audience what they really want instead of her tawdry ballads."

Annie scowled and nudged Betty. "How can you let them be so mean without saying anything back?" she whispered. "It ain't as if Tarquin has any talent," she added slightly louder, making sure he heard.

"Hush, Annie." Betty edged back slightly into the shadows of the wings as the rousing music from the orchestra filled the theatre. With a squeak of the pulleys, the red velvet curtains whisked apart to reveal the Burton Brothers, who were singing a comical ditty about sailing on the high seas. "I've decided just to ignore Tarquin, and you must too," she whispered next to Annie's ear. "We have to get along, and I know Ralph wouldn't like it if bad feelings were festering between his performers. I'm sure Tarquin will get bored of goading me soon enough."

The next hour sped past as Betty watched all the other acts in the show. Hidden in the wings, she could see how much everyone in the audience was enjoying the new performance, laughing at the comic timing of the Burton Brothers, gasping with astonishment as they watched Tom and his father perform seemingly impossible magic tricks, and cheering as the acrobats hung from gossamer thin wires and flew high above the rows of onlookers, holding on with effortless grace.

Camilla had two appearances. One was strategically placed just before the interval, at her request, so that the audience would already have relaxed but would not be getting fidgety from sitting for too long, and the second was the final act of the evening so that she would be the person everyone remembered as they left. Her new songs were all from Italian operas, which she had assured Ralph would lend an air of sophistication to Glan Mor. At first, Ralph had been hesitant to agree, saying that it might be too high-brow, but during the rehearsals, Camilla had won him around, and

Betty had to admit, her rich mezzo-soprano voice suited the music.

"You're on next, Betty, and then you afterwards to close the show, Camilla." Ralph gave Betty's arm a quick squeeze in a show of support. "Be confident and remember that many of the people in the audience have come especially to see you. In fact, you're becoming so popular I've had a few asking me to give you a longer time on stage than you had before."

Betty nodded and took a sip of water from the cup she kept backstage to keep her voice in good condition. The orchestra changed tempo as the acrobats exited the stage on the far side to loud cheers and started playing the opening strains of her first song as she stepped out into the dazzling glare of the gaslights.

Taking a deep breath, Betty lifted her arms and gave a gracious nod to the audience before launching into one of her favourite songs that she hoped would tug on everyone's heartstrings, Molly Under The Apple Tree'. No sooner had she finished that one than she followed it in quick succession with a lively sea shanty, 'The Jolly Boatman' and then a rousing ballad about a fair maiden being courted by a handsome lord. Betty sang five songs in total, enjoying each one more than the last. By the end, she had all but forgotten there were hundreds of people watching her and all she could feel was the sheer joy of doing something that she loved. Her sweet soprano voice echoed high into the rafters, and as the final chords of her last song gently finished, she saw the rapt expressions of the people in the front rows as they listened to her spellbound.

"More...more..."

"Sing us another song, Betty!"

"Don't stop now..."

The applause and cheering, with shouts for her to carry on, grew louder and louder, and Betty bowed her head, feeling a wave of gratitude for such appreciation. She darted a glance into the wings, looking for Ralph, but under the glare of the lights, she couldn't spot him.

"Thank you...you're very kind," Betty said humbly. Out of the corner of her eye, she could see Camilla preparing to come on for the closing act of the show, but suddenly a red rose landed by her feet, thrown by someone from the audience, followed by several more.

"Oh...thank you. But now, please welcome the great Camilla Covington back on stage." Betty stepped aside as Camilla swept past her with her arms thrown wide in a theatrical flourish.

Another rose landed at Betty's feet, so she hastily picked the flowers up before hurrying into the wings.

"Boo...get 'er off. We want the Nightingale of the Valleys back on again." The strident shout from the back of the auditorium could clearly be heard by everyone, and there was a moment of stunned silence as Camilla flushed with annoyance.

"Bring back Betty...encore...encore!" Another voice joined in, and a ripple of slow, rhythmical clapping started, quickly drowning out the orchestra who were playing the first few bars of Camilla's opening song.

"What's going on?" Ralph suddenly appeared by Betty's side, looking alarmed. "Why are they booing?"

"I'm sorry, Uncle Ralph. I tried to introduce Camilla, but the audience kept shouting for me to sing again." Betty wrung her hands as she caught sight of Camilla's furious expression.

"Do something, Ralph. You can't let Mama be humiliated like this." Tarquin strode out on stage, pulling Ralph with him and thrusting him into the spotlight.

"Ladies and gentlemen, please...have some consideration for the star of our show," Ralph said hastily. "As you know, our principal singer and leading lady, Camilla, has sung in some of the grandest theatres in Europe. I'm glad you enjoyed our other acts...and I'm sure you'll be delighted with Camilla's final songs that will live on in your memory to make it one of the best nights you've ever enjoyed at the Glan Mor."

Tarquin ushered Camilla to the front of the stage and gave a loud cheer, raising his arms to whip the audience up into a frenzy of appreciation.

"Thank you...thank you...my adoring public... so kind..." Camilla fanned herself with her hand-kerchief and blew a coquettish kiss at the gentlemen in the front row. "I shall now sing my finest songs for you, much loved by the aristocracy of Paris and Rome..." She launched into her last few songs, trying to ignore the disgruntled mutterings from the people who had wanted Betty to return for an encore.

By the time the final curtain fell, Camilla seemed to have been appeased by the handful of roses which had been thrown at her feet and the cheers from the older gentlemen who had followed her singing career for the last several years. Her face was wreathed in smiles, and she waved graciously until the last person had left the auditorium, lapping up the attention.

"WELL DONE, that was a wonderful opening night, and I'm sure the newspapers will report how well it went in their society pages." Ralph raised a glass of port and gestured for Bertha, the maid, to pour a glass for everyone else, as was their tradition at the end of the first night of a new show. He mingled between everyone, slapping the men on their backs and bowing gallantly over the ladies' hands.

"A fine show, Ralph. And you have some charming new acts, I must say." The bewhiskered bank manager, one of their most supportive patrons, shook hands with Ralph, congratulating him loudly.

After Ralph had ushered away the last of the patrons, he thanked everyone again and then yawned extravagantly. "I must turn in now. Don't stay up too late; we have another busy day tomorrow." Ralph strolled off, heading for his study to count the takings, then put his feet up. The first night of a new show was always nerve-wracking, but he was happy with how this one had gone.

"Looks like Betty might get star billing soon," Alex Burton said a few minutes later, with an admiring grin in Betty's direction. He was generous enough to want to acknowledge her rise to success, especially as he had seen how nervous she was before the show. "It's been a long time since we've had so many requests for an encore," he added, tipping his hat.

"Certainly not," Tarquin shot back. "I shall have to insist that Mama must retain her rightful place at the top of the bill. Without her fame, the Glan Mor would soon revert back to the dusty little music hall it was before we made it a place worth visiting." He drained his glass of port and grabbed another one from Bertha's tray, gulping it back just as fast. Emboldened by the drink, he jabbed a finger in Alex's chest. "You'd better give Mama the respect she deserves as well. Your act is scarcely better than a couple of performing monkeys at the circus, and I can tell you're only praising Betty because she's Ralph's niece." With that, he marched off, muttering loudly about how he might contact the London theatres and get work for Camilla there instead.

"Does that man's rudeness have no limits?" Felicity linked arms with Betty with a roll of her eyes. "If I don't take this costume off and put my feet up soon, I'll be hobbling like an old woman tomorrow. Come on, Annie, let's leave them to it."

By the time they had changed out of their show outfits, Annie could hardly keep her eyes open, but Betty's nerves were still fizzing with all the high emotions of the evening. She bade Annie good-night and decided to make herself a cup of hot chocolate in the kitchen and take it to the bench in the courtyard at the back of the theatre.

Even though the spring nights were still chilly, Betty was glad to be in the fresh air after the heat of the gaslights on stage. She tightened her shawl and leaned back, sipping the milky drink and gazing up at the stars, which looked like a thousand pinpricks in the inky sky. She could hear the faint lapping of the waves from the seafront and the occasional burst of laughter from men stumbling home from the pub.

Suddenly she heard the scraping rasp of a window opening nearby, and the sound of familiar voices reached her. It was Camilla and Tarquin. The light from Camilla's dressing room pooled out onto the flagstones between Betty and the back door of the kitchen, and she realised that if she tried to leave, they would see her. After Camilla's upset earlier in the evening, the last thing Betty wanted was for them to catch her, thinking she was eavesdropping, but she was trapped. She shrank back into the shadows and hoped they would shut the window again, remembering that Camilla often said the cold air played havoc with her throat.

"It's not good enough, Tarquin. I've told you before that we will be ruined if you keep losing money at cards." Camilla's voice was petulant, and she sounded close to tears.

"You worry too much, Mama. I wish you would stop treating me like a child."

Betty heard Tarquin sigh loudly. His shadow crossed the ground just in front of her feet as he paced back and forth.

"I'll have to ask Ralph to pay me more. If your papa was still alive, he would have taken care of everything, but I suppose I must do it now...it really is very demeaning having to go cap in hand to Ralph."

"It's not for much longer, Mama. I've just had a run of bad luck lately, that's all. In fact, I wouldn't be surprised if the other men have been cheating, but I'll be back on a winning streak in no time."

"It feels as though everything is conspiring against us," Camilla said bitterly. "Ever since that wretched girl, Betty Jones arrived, nothing has gone right. Ralph used to idolise me, but now he constantly drops hints about how good Betty's voice is...and how young she is, with her whole singing career ahead of her."

Tarquin harrumphed in agreement. "It's down to her that my chances of being on stage were ruined, as well. She's hungry for attention, Mama, and Ralph is blinded by family loyalty. Perhaps it's time we returned to London? Or how about Paris?"

"I'm not sure, dear. People in our circles have long memories, and you know how upsetting those rumours at The Royale Theatre were for me. As if I would have done anything so sordid...and certainly not with a man as decrepit as the Duke."

Betty's ears pricked up at Camilla's words but before she could hear anything more, Tarquin's shadow loomed larger as he came to the window. Her heart pounded with fear. He only had to lean out, and he would see her.

"This cold night air won't do you any good,

Mama. I'm going to the gentlemen's club to play cards now and win back all of my money. Don't worry, I won't let those cheating ne'er-do-wells get one over me again." Tarquin reached up and closed the tall sash window, and the courtyard was plunged into darkness again as he drew the curtains closed a moment later.

CHAPTER 17

"*A* letter came for you, Betty." Annie's cheeks were pink from the unseasonably warm May weather as she burst into the dressing room. She flopped down on a chair and fanned herself vigorously with her apron. "Do you think Mr Hughes would let us have a paddle in the sea before tonight's show? I think I might melt sweeping out the gods, it's so hot up there."

"I don't see why not, as long as you've done your chores. I wouldn't mind dipping my toes in the sea myself too."

"Is it from Dylan?" Felicity peered over to look at the letter and winked at Betty. "Maybe he's going to propose to you soon." Since she had recently started courting Miles Duggen, the lead violinist in the orchestra, her mind was full of romance, and she was desperate for Betty to be courting too.

Betty was happy for her friend but couldn't help feeling sad that it had been so long since she had seen Dylan. With each passing week at the theatre, her old life felt ever more distant and lately, she had started to wonder whether Dylan would give up on their childhood promises of getting married one day.

"Aren't you going to open it?" Annie nudged the letter closer and smiled. She enjoyed hearing all the news from Betty's family and often asked when she might be able to meet them.

"It won't be anything romantic, I'm sure. Dylan's not that way inclined." Betty put down the socks she was darning and pulled the letter from its envelope, feeling her spirits lift. She skimmed the contents quickly, and a range of different emotions chased across her face.

"What? Is it bad news? Read it to us, Betty, don't keep us in suspense. I want to know whether Jack's leg is better and who Minnie is sewing a gown for."

Betty chewed her lip and nodded slowly.

"Alright...you two are my best friends, and I know I can trust you not to repeat any of this."

Annie and Felicity leaned closer and gave Betty their full attention as she read the letter out loud.

Dear Betty,

I'm sorry it has been a while since I last wrote to you. Ma's health has been getting worse. She rarely leaves the house now, and I think the coal dust has settled on her lungs, much like it did for your pa. I do what I can to make things a little easier for her, and your family has been very kind. Fay brings her beef broth with fresh vegetables that Jack and Dai have grown, and Minnie has made her a lovely woollen shawl as Ma can never seem to get warm.

Work at the pit is just the same as it ever was. The repairs to the Blaeny shaft still haven't been carried out yet, and Ezra Crundell is convinced that Lord Griffiths is refusing to give him a promotion to become manager of Ferncoed Colliery because of the flood damage. There is still a lot of bad feeling about what happened, even though I tell everyone that it was not your fault.

Pa goes drinking in the Red Dragon almost every night, which I don't mind. At least it gives Ma some welcome relief from his bad tempers, although he barely seems to notice her other than when she hasn't cooked dinner to his liking. He never stops talking about how your pa stole the woman he should have married and how he's determined to get his revenge by pinning the blame for the pit losing out on Lord Leyfield's investment on you. I don't want you to worry, though, Betty. Pa mumbles about getting in touch with his cousin, Andrew Waverly, who lives in Abertarron, to tell the police about you, but it's just the drink talking and empty threats. Besides, none of us has told Pa that you're at the Glan Mor theatre. He's nothing more than a bully who didn't get his own way, and Ma and I just ignore it.

We all miss you very much. I hope you don't consider it too forward, but I have saved up enough money to pay for a train ticket to Abertarron and one of the cheap seats at the theatre. Your ma is so proud of you being on stage, and she suggested that maybe Minnie and I could come and see the show. Ezra has agreed that I can take the first Saturday of June off work in lieu of my bonus payment, and Mary has said that Minnie could have a day off as well.

It would be lovely to see you perform. I remember the day you sang for us in your kitchen when we were children. I'll keep our visit secret from Pa. I've already told him Dai is taking me and Jack fishing for the day, and I'll leave some money on the table, so I'm sure Pa *will take it for the pub and be too drunk to notice if I'm home late.*

With best wishes,

Your friend,

Dylan Parry

Felicity clasped her hands to her chest, and her eyes shimmered with tears. "Oh, Betty. Poor Dylan and his ma having to put up with his father. He sounds awful."

"You're right about that; Wynn Parry is a horrible man." Betty sniffed with emotion and slipped the letter under her hairbrush for safe-keeping.

"But Dylan sounds nothing like him. And to think, he's going to come and see you in a show. He must still be sweet on you."

"And Minnie's coming too." Annie jumped up and clapped her hands. "Do you think she'll like me, Betty? I hope she does…what if she doesn't? I'll be so disappointed."

Betty chuckled and stood up, glancing at the clock on the mantelshelf. "Minnie and Dylan will both be delighted to meet you, Annie. They already feel as if they know you from my letters. In fact, I shall ask Uncle Ralph if you can look after them and show them to their seats for the show. How about that? He's been saying for some time that he would like to meet more of the family, so it should be a very jolly affair, even if only Minnie can come."

"And Dylan," Felicity added with a mischievous smile. "Maybe Ralph will want to check if he'd make a suitable husband for his rising star performer."

"You're incorrigible," Betty laughed. "I'd better go and arrange everything with Uncle Ralph. Their visit is only a couple of weeks away."

"Why don't we ask Ralph if we can also have a picnic in the park as a bit of a celebration?" Felicity's eyes gleamed at the thought of something exciting to organise, especially if it helped nudge Betty and Dylan towards a romance. "That day will mark the middle of our summer season, and the weather is bound to be nice. We could have a walk along the seafront and then a picnic to follow."

"Don't forget it's the town's summer fête that week too," Annie piped up. "They have stalls all along the promenade and a band on the seafront in the afternoon. We could all go to that in the afternoon, and then they can come to the show afterwards. It's going to be the most wonderful day ever."

The three of them hurried out of the dressing room to go and tell Ralph the good news, chattering loudly about Dylan's letter and the forthcoming visit, not noticing Tarquin, who was loitering nearby in the shadows. He watched them with narrowed eyes and edged forward, nudging the dressing room door open. His eyes fell on the letter that was still under Betty's hairbrush.

"Are you looking for Felicity and Betty?" Abe hobbled past, sweeping a pile of dust ahead of himself, heading for the store room where he was planning to rest his aching feet for a moment.

"It's alright, thank you, Abe. I just wanted to congratulate Betty on her performance last night, but it can wait." Tarquin made a show of pulling a note from his pocket and reading it, leaning casually against the wall. Annie skipped along behind Felicity and Betty at the end of the corridor, and their high-spirited chatter was still in full flow.

"Dylan sounds like the perfect gentleman, Betty. He's kindhearted and chivalrous, as well, the way he defends your honour to the villagers...nothing like that odious toad, Tarquin. You had a lucky escape there...I hope Dylan manages to help you clear your name and marries you soon...I can't even believe his father told those lies that could have got you arrested..."

Felicity's words drifted back to Tarquin, growing fainter as they turned past the kitchen. His expression darkened. Darting a look up and down the hallway to make sure that Abe had gone and nobody else was around, he carefully opened the ladies' dressing room door again and slipped inside, snatching up the letter and reading it intently. A moment later, he strode away with a smug smile on his face. He hummed a lively tune as he thought about what he had just discovered... happy that he was armed with all the information he needed to ensure that he and Camilla would finally regain their family's rightful place as the stars of Glan Mor Theatre. Better still, he would be able to bring about the downfall of the person who had caused all their misfortune.

THE DAY of Abertarron's summer fête dawned bright and warm. It was the perfect weather for a celebration, with clear blue skies and a gentle breeze that rippled the sea's surface into white-tipped waves. "A good drying day, Ma would say."

Betty flung the window open and leaned out to breathe in great lungfuls of the salty air, sending the gulls flapping and mewling into the sky above.

"Budge up, will you." Annie clambered onto the chair next to her and poked her head through their rooftop window as well. "Look at all the bunting and flags along the seafront. Minnie and Dylan are going to love it, Betty. We'll be able to stroll along to the park, just like the toffs down from London do on their holidays." She jumped off the chair and whisked a brush through her hair, eager to get started on the day's chores.

After much cajoling, Ralph had agreed that everyone could attend the festivities in the park as long as they were all back in the theatre in good time for the show, and there was a buzz of excitement in the dining room over breakfast.

"What time does the train get in, Betty?"

"Dylan's letter said it was eleven o'clock this morning, and then they can get the last train home at nine o'clock, which will give them ample time to enjoy our early evening show without having to rush."

Felicity nodded and sipped her tea thoughtfully. She eyed Betty's grey dress; it was the serviceable one she wore most days, and although it was pleasant enough, it did little to bring out Betty's peaches and cream complexion. "I'm going to lend you my green silk tea gown. It should fit you well, and I want Dylan to be bowled over when he sees you."

Betty blushed. "I couldn't possibly, Felicity, it's your favourite dress. What if I spill something on it or damage it. My blue Sunday dress is perfectly good enough. Besides, if you realised what Dylan used to see me wearing down the pit, you'd understand that he's not the sort of person who cares about such things."

"Nonsense," Felicity said firmly. "I know you've been sending every spare penny back home to take care of your family instead of ever treating yourself. You're a good friend, and I want to do this for you." She glanced across at Annie. "I haven't forgotten about you either, Annie. Mrs Snape has used one of my old show gowns to make you a new dress...it's a little surprise Ralph and I came up with because you've worked so hard, and it's almost a year since you came here."

Annie threw her arms around Felicity. "Thank you so much. You and Betty are the best friends I ever could have asked for." She brushed the back of her hand across her eyes and sniffed loudly, overcome with emotion.

"All ready for the big day?" Tom flopped down in the spare seat next to them. "I hope you're going to introduce me to your sister and your beau, Betty."

"Of course…but Dylan and I aren't courting. I'm sure he's far too busy with looking after his ma even to consider such a thing." Betty sounded slightly wistful, which didn't escape Felicity's notice.

"May I remind you that I was correct about predicting that Felicity and Miles would start courting within the year if you remember," Tom said, shrugging nonchalantly. "Who's to say I haven't had another vision about a happy courtship ahead for you too."

"When he sees you in that green gown and then hears you singing on stage, I don't think he'll be able to resist," Felicity added, smiling conspiratorially across the table with Tom.

Betty could feel her excitement mounting as she hurried back to the dressing room to get everything laid out ready for the evening performance. Even though she and Dylan had corresponded frequently enough that she felt as though they hadn't grown apart, her excitement was tinged with worry.

"What if he doesn't like me anymore?" she blurted out as Felicity buttoned her into the dress a couple of hours later. "Maybe it was just a childish daydream. I honestly can't see how we could ever be together anyway. His pa would never allow it."

Felicity draped a cream fringed shawl over Betty's shoulders and stood back, nodding happily with how pretty she looked. "True love will find a way, Betty," she said sagely.

A moment later, there was a sharp knock on their dressing room door. "Your guests are here, Miss Betty." Abe's rumbling voice and his announcement made the breath catch in Betty's throat. She had longed for this moment for so many nights as she fell asleep under the eaves, and now it was finally here. She opened the door, feeling a jumble of mixed emotions, and the next moment found herself engulfed in a hug from Minnie.

"I can't believe we're here…at a real theatre… you look so different…like a proper lady…ma and Jack would be tickled pink…" Minnie's exclamations grew louder and louder until she suddenly released Betty again. "I'm sorry, I'm forgetting my manners." She looked shyly at Felicity and bobbed her head.

"Felicity, this is Minnie, my sister." Betty looked beyond Minnie and felt her pulse quicken as she saw Dylan standing uncertainly in the hallway. "And this is my best friend, Dylan," she added.

Dylan stepped into the room and shook hands with Felicity, giving Betty a chance to see him better now that he was in the light. He seemed to have grown from being a boy into a man in the months they had been apart. His broad shoulders filled his jacket and his eyes still crinkled at the corners when he smiled, making her heart skip a beat. "Hello Felicity, it's nice to meet you. And hello, Betty. I swear I hardly recognise you...you look so grand."

The sound of running footsteps made everyone look around. "I ain't too late, am I? Are they here already? Why didn't you tell me, Abe?" Annie's shout echoed down the hallway, and she came tearing through the doorway, her curls springing out from under her mob cap.

"Minnie, Dylan...this is Annie," Betty said with a wry chuckle.

"Oh my...you never told me Dylan was so

handsome...and Minnie so pretty too," Annie blurted out, looking between them. She hopped from one foot to the other. "I've been awake since it was still dark, we're that excited about your visit...we've got the summer fête to go to...and then stalls with all sorts of fancy things to look at...and then the band play and we're having a picnic...and then you'll see Betty on stage...she sings like a proper nightingale...that's why they call her The Nightingale of the Valleys...this is going to be the best day I've ever had, I can already tell..."

Betty and Minnie exchanged glances over Annie's head and burst out laughing at her breathless chatter. "Now you can understand why I told you Annie reminds me of you, Minnie." Betty put her arm around Annie's shoulder and gave her a hug. "Annie and Felicity have been wonderful friends to me...they helped me settle in and stopped me feeling quite so homesick."

"Let's give you the guided tour, and then it will be time to walk along the seafront to the park." Felicity linked arms with Minnie and swept her out of the room. "Your Uncle Ralph is looking forward to meeting you before the performance," she added as Annie scurried after them, leaving Betty and Dylan alone.

"You look wonderful—"

"I've missed everyone from home so much—"

Dylan and Betty's words tumbled over each other, and they both smiled. After a brief moment of awkwardness, it felt as though the last months had melted away, and their easy friendship was restored instantly, as though they'd never been apart. Dylan offered his arm to Betty, and she happily tucked her hand in the crook of his elbow, enjoying his reassuring solidness by her side again.

"I've got so much to show you and tell you about, Dylan…let's follow the others, we must make the most of this precious time together."

CHAPTER 18

he first hour of their visit flew by as Betty proudly showed them every part of the Glan Mor Theatre, from the dressing rooms and costumes to the seats where the wealthiest customers sat, and the living quarters where they ate and socialised. As she introduced them to all the performers, Betty realised just how fond she had become of this group of quirky characters who had become her surrogate family.

"We're very lucky to have Betty as part of the show," Mrs Snape said as she welcomed Minnie into her sewing room.

Minnie's eyes lit up as she saw all the rails of costumes and gowns awaiting repairs and the bright bolts of fabric and lace that would soon be turned into costumes for the winter show. "I feel like I've fallen asleep and woken up in the most perfect place," Minnie breathed, turning to Betty. "Imagine creating all these beautiful clothes and seeing them on stage."

Mrs Snape nodded, delighting in Minnie's enthusiasm for her craft. "You're quite right, my dear. When I used to work as a dressmaker in town, I rarely saw the ladies wearing the dresses I made for them because they moved in very grand circles. But now, if the mood takes me, I can sit backstage and see everything I've made while I watch the show."

"You're very talented, Mrs Snape. I'm learning dressmaking from Mary, who we live with, but I'd give anything to sew like you." She gently touched one of Camilla's luxurious silk gowns that looked as light as a cloud, shot through with silver, and then held up a smart red soldier's costume, studded with gold buttons next to it, admiring the neat stitching that was barely visible to the untrained eye.

"That's kind of you to say so." Mrs Snape held up her hands and looked at the swollen joints ruefully. "I can't sew as fast as I used to, what with my arthritis. But Ralph is very generous and has said I'll always have a home at the theatre...and an apprentice soon as well, I hope."

"Maybe we could ask Uncle Ralph if you could come and visit for a few weeks, Minnie, if Mary and ma can spare you?"

"Oh, yes, please do," Minnie exclaimed.

"So this is where you've all got to." Tom came striding into the room, looking very dashing in his long cloak. "I've got a small tear in the lining, Mrs Snape. Could you mend it for me if you have time? I don't want one of our doves making an appearance during the show before it's meant to." He swept the cloak off and gave Minnie a mischievous smile. "I hope you can keep a magician's secret? The audience doesn't know our cloaks have hidden pockets."

Minnie flushed, and Betty noticed her eyes sparkling even brighter as she looked up at Tom. "My lips are sealed," she said.

Tom bowed. "Betty didn't tell me her sister was quite so beautiful. I'm Tom...magician and illusionist." He shook hands with Minnie and Dylan. "Are we going to take them to the park for our picnic now, Betty...I'm starving."

Minnie chuckled. "You sound just like our

brother, Jack." With one last lingering look around Mrs Snape's sewing room, Minnie bade her goodbye.

"You must tell me all about yourself," Tom said, falling into step next to Minnie. "It's just a short walk along the promenade to the park."

Abertarron had never looked so jolly with the bunting draped around the railings along the seafront and the boats bobbing in the harbour. "Imagine the fish I could catch here if I had a little boat of my own." Dylan's eyes were wide with possibility as he pictured being happily married to Betty in a quaint cottage of their own, on the outskirts of town. "This sea air would be so good for Ma," he added, looking slightly forlorn.

As if by unspoken agreement, Betty and Dylan hadn't talked about Wynn, but she felt she couldn't let the moment pass. "I'm sorry she's been so unwell, Dylan. I wish there was something I could do to make your pa leave you both alone."

Dylan sighed. "Ma's too afraid to stand up to him, and if I do, he only takes it out on Ma. He'll never change…maybe the drink will take him before his time and leave us in peace." He gave Betty an apologetic look. "I'm sorry, I know I should think more kindly of him, but I've had to watch him reduce Ma to little more than a shadow. Maybe one day…"

"Don't give up hope," Betty said, squeezing his arm sympathetically. "Let's just enjoy our day and pray that something will change for the better soon."

The picnic was a jovial affair. Bertha and the other maids had laid out rugs under the trees and Cook had provided baskets groaning with pies, sandwiches, pickles, and cake, as well as several bottles of her delicious lemonade.

"I don't think I'll be able to move after eating this much food, let alone go on stage." Tom patted his belly and groaned as he finished the final mouthful of his slice of fruitcake.

"Aren't you going to introduce us?" Their pleasant gathering was suddenly interrupted by Tarquin's well-spoken tones, and everyone fell silent. "I meant to tell you how good your performance was last night, Betty. Mama said you sang beautifully, which I'm sure means a lot from someone of her talent."

Betty almost choked on her lemonade at the unexpected compliment. "Th…thank you," she stuttered. "This is my friend Dylan Parry and my sister, Minnie. They're watching the show tonight before catching the train home again. This is Tarquin Covington...his mother is the principal singer at the theatre," she added, by way of explanation.

"Enchanted, my dear." Tarquin bent over and took Minnie's hand and brushed a kiss on the back of it, and then doffed his hat to Dylan. "I hope you have a very enjoyable visit, and perhaps you will come again another time." With that, he strolled away, leaving Betty looking startled.

"I don't think I've ever heard him be so friendly, what's got into him?" Annie muttered suspiciously.

"Maybe he finally won at cards," Tom said with a chuckle. "Anyway, let's hope it lasts."

"More like he's finally realised that Betty's an excellent singer and an important part of Glan Mor." Felicity watched Tarquin's retreating back and shook her head slightly. "Perhaps he'll be more respectful towards you now, Betty. Especially if Ralph does give you equal billing with Camilla next season." She clapped her hand over her mouth guiltily as Betty gasped with astonishment.

"Equal billing? Surely you're mistaken?"

"I wasn't meat to say anything yet…don't let on," Felicity said hastily. "Ralph was discussing ideas for the autumn and winter shows, and he told me the audience rate you just as highly as Camilla now."

Betty shook her head. "I'm very flattered, and I promise I won't say anything, but I recognise that Camilla is far more talented than I am."

"Talent isn't everything," Tom interjected. He stood up and brushed the crumbs from his trousers. "You have a way with the audience…you make them feel involved, especially when you ask them to request songs for you to sing. They like it, and it's making the Glan Mor even more popular. Why shouldn't Ralph reward you with equal billing?"

Dylan looked at Betty with open admiration. "I'm so proud of everything you've achieved, he whispered. "Wait until Minnie and I tell your ma. We'll have to find a way of bringing her down to watch one of your shows next time."

The deep chimes of the church clock rang out across the town. "We'd better get back to the theatre, it's time to get ready for the show," Annie said, jumping up. "You're in for a treat now, Minnie. Ralph has agreed that you and Dylan can have two of the best spots on the balcony, and I'm allowed to show you to your seats."

* * *

BETTY FELT an extra frisson of excitement as she stepped out onto the stage, knowing that the man she loved was in the audience. Every note seemed to come from her heart, and every word of the lovesongs that left her lips was infused with longing mingled with happiness. Despite the long months of being apart, she knew without a doubt that Dylan was still the man she yearned to be with for the rest of her life.

At the end of the show, after Camilla had come off, Ralph acknowledged the wave of shouted requests from the audience, demanding an encore from Betty, and for the first time, he beckoned her back on stage to close the show, ignoring Camilla's sour looks from the wings.

Betty accepted graciously and glided to the front of the stage, choosing a song that described how two starcrossed lovers overcame adversity to be together. She imbued it with such passion there was scarcely a dry eye in the theatre as her pure, soprano voice effortlessly tugged on everyone's heartstrings. As the last notes died away, the audience erupted into rapturous applause, and she hoped that Dylan would know that she had been singing it for him, to send him a message from the depths of her heart.

"Now do you see why we're so proud of your sister," Ralph said jovially to Minnie half an hour later as the performers mingled backstage.

Minnie nodded, starstruck. "It was the most beautiful thing I've ever heard," she murmured, giving Betty admiring glances. "If only Ma and Jack could have come too."

Ralph patted Minnie's shoulder. "Leave it with me. I know Fay isn't in the best of health, but perhaps if I could arrange for you all to stay in a boarding house for a few days, the sea air might do her good. I'll find a way to pay for it," he added hastily, seeing Minnie's worried expression. "It's high time I saw my sister again, it's been far too long since we were together, and I'd like to meet Jack as well."

Betty freed herself from the cluster of theatre patrons who Ralph had invited to meet the performers after the show and bustled over. "Did you enjoy it? I bet you couldn't believe Tom's magic tricks? And how about the acrobats?"

"You're too modest," Dylan said. He drew Betty aside as Ralph chatted to Minnie about her dressmaking skills. "I always knew your voice sounded lovely, but to hear it in a setting like this grand theatre, Betty, it was…I can hardly describe how wonderful."

Betty blushed. "I'm still just me, though, Dylan. The girl who used to go fishing in the Aberglas river with you and cook chestnuts on the fire in the winter…you won't forget about that, will you?" she asked, suddenly feeling shy.

Dylan hesitated and put his hand in his pocket. His fingers closed around the small leather pouch with the gift inside that he had made for Betty. It was a tiny polished pebble from the riverbed, set in a brooch that he had carved to look like a primrose. He glanced around, wondering whether this was the moment to ask the question which had been on the tip of his tongue all day.

"Of course I'll never forget," he said softly. He gazed into Betty's warm brown eyes and thought back to all the times they had innocently held hands together as children and how they could always make each other laugh, even during the worst of times. "Betty…there's something I want to ask you…before I have to leave…" He took a deep breath, wanting to pick exactly the right words to declare his love for her.

"Betty! Have you met Mr and Mrs Washbrook? They are the theatre's longest patrons, and I'm sure they would love to speak to you. Sorry, Dylan…do you mind if I whisk her away for a moment?" Ralph beamed at both of them. "Didn't she treat us to a marvellous performance tonight? You must be very proud of her…"

Betty gave Dylan an apologetic smile. "I'll be back in a moment. We have to keep the patrons happy because they donate money to the theatre," she whispered.

Dylan dropped the pouch back into the depths of his pocket and nodded. "Of course. I'm not surprised they'd want to meet you." He watched proudly as Ralph introduced Betty, smiling to himself as she glanced in his direction as often as she could. He had been worried that Betty might have become too grand to want to be with him anymore, but the time they had spent together had banished any fears immediately. She was still the same girl who had stolen his heart all those years ago, and he was determined to tell her how much he loved her.

"She's a remarkable young lady, isn't she." Tarquin sidled up to Dylan, following his gaze to where Mrs Washbrook was gushing with praise for Betty's singing, and Mr Washbrook was congratulating Ralph for his fine choice of performers.

"She is," Dylan said quietly. "Although we're still just Betty and Dylan to each other. We've been friends for as long as I can remember," he added, by way of explanation.

"It's rare for a singer to have that level of talent without professional training," Tarquin continued. He shot Dylan a friendly smile and chuckled. "She's better than my mama…but don't say I said so."

Dylan wondered whether Betty had got Tarquin wrong when she'd said he had a spiteful streak. He seemed like a decent sort of fellow and was full of nothing but praise for Betty. "That's kind of you to say so. I…I had hoped to ask her if we could start courting tonight," he confided. "Seeing her so happy at Glan Mor has convinced me that I need to find a way to come and work in

Abertarron instead of at the colliery and bring my ma as well, so I can look after them both."

Tarquin nodded understandingly. "Betty said you were kindhearted, and I can see she's right." He thrust his hands into his pockets and sighed, suddenly looking doubtful. "The thing is, Betty is destined for greatness, Dylan. I know because Mama and I used to perform in the theatres in London. As soon as word of her singing reaches the London theatre agents, she'll be snapped up to be their principal performer…I expect they'll be fighting over her."

Dylan looked surprised. "I don't think Betty would want to go to London. It's too far from her family, you see. She cares for them, and they're very close."

"Of course, I understand," Tarquin said smoothly. "But she could earn so much more money in the London theatres…it would allow her to help her family even more than she already does." He named a sum that made Dylan's mouth gape open in shock. It was more than he could ever dream of earning.

"I'm sure that if you love Betty, you wouldn't want to stand in her way of success?" Tarquin added softly.

"No. Betty deserves to do well," Dylan said. He felt a hard lump of regret form in his chest as Tarquin strolled away, realising that his dreams of a happy life with Betty as his wife were nothing more than a childish fantasy. She was destined to be on the stage in London, not to settle for being married to a man who had never ventured further than Pencastle village and the colliery until today.

"We mustn't miss the train." Minnie bustled towards him, with Betty in her wake, pointing at the clock. "Mr Crundell would never forgive you if you're not back on duty at the pit again on Monday morning, and I promised Mary I would complete Lady Flora's gown tomorrow.

"I'm sorry Ralph interrupted us," Betty said, taking Dylan's arm. "What was it you wanted to say? Ralph is already talking about how we can get Ma and Jack down to Abertarron to see a show, and maybe I can come home for a visit soon as well. I miss the village…and you," she added quietly.

"Yes…yes, that sounds like a good idea," Dylan said briskly. He tried to recapture the feeling of certainty that he should declare his love for Betty, but the moment had evaporated like the hot sun burning off a morning mist. All he could think about was Tarquin's firm advice that the kindest thing he could do for Betty was to make sure he never stood in her way.

"Are you sure there's nothing more you wanted to say?" Betty searched his face for clues in his abrupt change of mood, but for once, she found his expression hard to read.

Dylan felt wretched as he saw Betty's eyes fill with hurt, but he knew that if he didn't leave now, he might end up ruining her singing career by declaring how much he adored her. "No, there's nothing more to say," he muttered. "I'll write to you soon and look forward to your visit. But now Minnie and I must leave. It's been a wonderful day, Betty. You sing so beautifully...I'm sure you're going to go far." He brushed a kiss on her cheek and hurried away, feeling as though his heart was being torn from his chest.

Betty stood in the doorway and resisted the urge to run after him. The thoughts racing through her mind felt so tumultuous she could barely catch her breath. She had been so certain Dylan loved her, but his brusque farewell seemed like nothing more than friendly politeness. She stumbled several steps along the cobbles. *Wait...come back...I never had a chance to tell you that I love you.* The agonising thought filled Betty's mind, but she knew it was too late. Dylan was returning to his own life, and she had to remain in Abertarron to keep her promise to look after her family. She touched her cheek where he had kissed her, wondering if she had imagined that they were still destined to be together.

CHAPTER 19

"*P*inch your cheeks to get some colour in them." Felicity looked at Betty in the mirror with a worried frown. She patted Betty's hand. "Don't give up on him. Men can be terrible fools sometimes, but I know what a man in love looks like, and Dylan loves you very much, I'm sure of it."

"He seemed so happy to see me, but then his demeanour changed just before they left." Betty gave her a wan smile. "Perhaps I was hoping for too much…it's just…I was sure he was about to say something important. I rather hoped that it might be for us to start courting officially," she confessed, looking glum.

"I saw Tarquin talking to him, but they looked

like they were getting on like a house on fire," Annie said, pausing from curling Betty's hair.

Betty's heart sank. She'd had her doubts about why Tarquin had seemed so friendly at the summer fête and now she wondered if he had said something to put Dylan off. "I'll write him a letter saying how much I enjoyed seeing him," she said, feeling brighter. If Tarquin thought he could spoil her chance of happiness, she was determined to prove him wrong.

"Ten minutes until the show starts, ladies." Abe stuck his head around the door. "Are you enjoying your promotion, Annie?" He smiled good-naturedly as Annie nodded.

"She's a godsend, helping us all get into our costumes and doing our hair," Felicity said, doing a twirl.

"I'll still help you sweep after the show, though," Annie said hastily. Abe had looked after her like the grandfather she had never known and she would always be grateful for the way he had helped her settle into theatre life.

"I've got a new book for us to read together," he said, pulling a penny dreadful novel from his pocket and waving it at her. "It's about a group of sailors who get shipwrecked on an island." His cheerful whistling faded as he hobbled away to make sure that David, Mrs Snape's youngest grandson, was doing his jobs correctly as Annie's replacement.

"Come on then, Betty, let's give them all a show they'll never forget." Felicity gave her a hug and checked her reflection one last time.

When they arrived backstage, Betty felt her spirits lift as she always did before a show. Her head had been spinning for the last few days as she tried to imagine how she and Dylan could be together if he was still working down the pit. It was evident that he had found Abertarron a charming town, and she knew from Ralph that there was plenty of work to be had. But even now, she still thought of Pencastle village as home, and it would be a lot to ask of Dylan for him to move away."

"Tarquin looks unusually cheerful. If I didn't know better, I'd say he's had a nip of brandy," Felicity said, breaking into Betty's reverie.

No sooner had the words left her mouth than Tarquin made a beeline for them. His cheeks were flushed, and he twirled his cane, doing a couple of light-footed dance steps as he got closer. "Good evening, ladies. I have a feeling tonight's show is going to be one of the best we've ever done." His eyes were slightly glassy, and Betty realised that he had indeed been drinking.

"We always put on a good show, Tarquin. I was wondering...you were speaking to Dylan just before he left to catch the train. What were you talking about?"

Tarquin tapped the side of his nose and chuckled. "Nothing you need to worry yourself about, Betty, dear. I was merely telling him that you're the star of the show...and never more than tonight, I fancy."

Felicity and Betty exchanged puzzled glances as Tarquin hurried over to Camilla. "I know we should be pleased he's not in one of his tempers, but I've got a horrible feeling he's up to no good," Felicity said darkly.

"You look delightful, Mama," Tarquin said, slurring slightly. He fussed around his mother, adjusting her shawl. "Our fortunes are about to change, just like I promised," he whispered loudly, beaming at her.

Betty tried to put his strange behaviour from her mind, removing herself to a corner behind some props where she could think about her songs. She hummed lightly, warming her voice up and allowed the music from the orchestra to soothe her. It was a full house tonight, and she didn't want to disappoint the audience. She knew that as soon as she stepped on stage, all her worries would melt away, and she would lose herself in the songs that meant so much to her.

As the second half of the show started, a sudden commotion near the doorway caught her attention, and she was surprised to see a scruffy urchin dart towards Tom. He looked familiar, and as Betty stared, she realised it was one of the boys from the gang of pickpockets she had encountered when she'd first met Annie. Tom bent down, and the boy whispered something in his ear, gesticulating as though it was urgent.

"Is everything alright, Tom?" Betty hurried over with a sense of foreboding, especially as she saw Tom frown.

"Thank you, and remember, not a word to anyone." Tom slipped a coin into the boy's grubby palm, watching as he melted into the shadows and darted down the hallway that led to the back door.

"I thought you didn't mix with them anymore?" Betty heard Ralph announcing the next act and raised her voice to make herself heard over the raucous applause from the audience.

Tom pulled her into the passageway behind the stage. "I've been paying Mr Westwood to find out information about Tarquin," he said urgently, ignoring Betty's shocked expression. "There's been nothing to report until now. Just that he was mixing with some rather unsavoury characters at the gambling tables."

"He seems cock-a-hoop about something tonight," Betty whispered. "Felicity thinks he's up to no good." She looked across to where Tarquin and Camilla had been standing, but they had gone.

Tom nodded. "I think I know what it is. The young lad you just saw was in the pub where Tarquin drinks earlier today. He overheard Tarquin boasting that he's just had all his gambling debts paid off by a man called Andrew Waverly."

"Andrew Waverly?" Betty felt her head swim. "That's Wynn Parry's cousin. Dylan told me he lives in Abertarron but that they're not very close. Why do you think Mr Waverly would do that?"

Tom placed his hand under Betty's elbow, noticing that she had turned white. He wondered whether she was about to faint and fanned her with his cloak. "The lad said all Mr Waverly wanted to know in return was where you live."

Betty gasped, and her legs started to tremble.

"That means he'll tell Wynn I'm here, and then who knows what might happen…he's a very vengeful man. I'd hoped that after all this time, he might have forgotten about me…but—"

"Betty, you're on next," Ralph hissed. "Hurry up, the orchestra is already starting your first song." He strode over and propelled Betty towards the stage. "The audience is calling for you already," he added happily.

"The Nightingale of The Valleys," Ralph announced, guiding her into the spotlight. He clapped and bowed, holding one arm wide to introduce her as the audience cheered and stamped their feet in anticipation of her act.

Betty blinked, stunned by Tom's revelation. But before she could give it any more thought, the orchestra started the rousing opening bars of her first song, and she took a deep breath, launching into the first verse. As she progressed through her songs, Betty felt her initial fear subside. Looking out at the hundreds of faces of the audience, she realised she was a very different person from the scared young woman who had only ever known valley life. She lifted her chin and filled the theatre with her sweet voice, determined not to live in fear of Tarquin or Wynn Parry for a moment longer.

"Encore…encore." As per usual, the audience shouted for one more song, and Ralph nodded from the wings for her to go ahead and give them what they wanted.

"I shall finish with a heartwarming lovesong," Betty said, smiling as a young girl in the front row of the audience looked up at her with a rapt expression. She glided to the centre of the stage and nodded for the orchestra to play the song she had agreed. The conductor raised his arms, and the pianist struck up a lively tune, but before Betty could start singing, a shout rang out.

"Betty Jones…stay right where you are."

A ripple of annoyance over the interruption ran through the audience and Betty shielded her eyes against the glare of the gaslights to see who had spoken. Suddenly a burly figure strode towards the stage and clambered up the steps. Her heart sank as she realised it was none other than Constable Booth.

"What on earth are you doing?" Ralph cried, running across the stage. "You can't barge in like this in the middle of our show."

The audience started jeering and whistling. "Get him off…"

Constable Booth's face darkened. "Be quiet," he

bellowed. An expectant hush fell over the crowd as they leaned forward to watch the unexpected events unfold. "You're harbouring a criminal, so I shall do as I please," he snapped at Ralph.

"I don't know what you mean, I'm doing no such thing." Ralph gave the audience a nervous smile. "This is all a misunderstanding, Constable. Can't we deal with it after the show? Why don't I put you in one of our best seats, and you can enjoy the rest of the performance...free of charge, of course."

"I hope you're not trying to bribe me, Mr Hughes." The constable scowled and turned to Betty. "Betty Jones, you are under arrest for acts of wilful destruction of the property of Lord Griffiths. You're to accompany me to the police station, where we will deal with you." His lip curled in contempt, and he looked her up and down. "I've had my suspicions about you ever since you told me that pack of lies about those pickpockets last year. I'm never wrong," he added triumphantly. Grasping her arm firmly, he bundled her offstage.

"Get the next act on," Ralph hissed, gesturing to the Burton Brothers. "Fill in for Betty...do whatever you need. We can't let news of this get out."

Alex Burton shot Betty a sympathetic look as

he sprang into action. "Sorry, Betty, I'm sure it's all a mistake. You'll be back before you know it." He rushed to the front of the stage, and a moment later, the audience roared with laughter as he and his brother began their act, quickly forgetting about Betty's fall from grace.

Once they were out of sight of the audience, Betty angrily threw Constable Brown's hand off her arm. "Was that really necessary?" she demanded. "I have never damaged any of Lord Griffiths' property. Who has been spreading these terrible lies about me?"

"I'm not at liberty to say, Miss." Constable Booth grasped her arm again and marched her towards the corridor.

"Ah, poor Betty." Tarquin was lounging against the wall, watching with amusement. "It looks like your past has finally caught up with you."

"Was this your doing?" Betty looked at him coldly, even though she wanted to rail about the injustice of what was happening.

"I believe it might have been," Tarquin chuckled. "It's nothing more than you deserve, Betty. You might have fooled your uncle into thinking you were a decent performer but did you really think I would just stand by and do nothing while your cheap little music hall tunes stole the show? You humiliated Mama, and you seem to delight in making the Covington name worthless." He pushed himself off the wall and nodded at Constable Booth. "You can take her away now."

"You're making a terrible mistake," Betty cried. "All I ever wanted was to help my family...my Pa died from the dreadful work we had to do at the colliery...and I almost lost my ma and Jack as well. You have no idea what you've done, Tarquin."

"That's where you're wrong, Betty." Tarquin strolled around her, his gaze full of contempt. "I want to make sure you never set foot on a stage again. The public will see you for the cheap, talent-less pit girl you are," he whispered into her ear, his voice full of venom.

Betty knew there was no point in trying to protest her innocence anymore. The constable had probably been paid handsomely to arrest her so publicly, so her reputation would be destroyed, and she realised with shocking clarity how much she had underestimated Tarquin's dislike of her.

"There's no need to manhandle me," Betty said, hurrying down the corridor, her cheeks burning with shame.

"Where are you taking her," Ralph demanded.

"Betty is my niece, and I can vouch for her character."

"It's nothing to do with you. I have to follow the laws of the land," the constable said gruffly.

The sound of running footsteps made Betty turn around, and she saw Tom, Felicity, and Annie rushing after them. "Let her go," Annie yelled.

"Tell us where you're taking her, please," Felicity begged. "What can we do to help you, Betty?"

"That's quite enough," Constable Booth snapped. "I won't have this arrest turned into a circus performance. Miss Jones has committed a grave offence, and Lord Griffiths demands justice. She might have thought she'd got away with it, running away from Pencastle and making a new life for herself here, but Tarquin Covington has done the decent thing and brought this to my attention, so I have to follow the law."

"That snake, I knew he was up to no good," Felicity cried.

Betty squared her shoulders and gave them a tremulous smile. "I know I've done nothing wrong. Perhaps it's time I was given the chance to clear my name, so I can go back to Pencastle with nothing to fear."

"Please let her go," Annie sobbed. She threw herself at Constable Booth and tried to wrestle Betty from his grasp, but he knocked her away as if she was nothing more than an annoyance.

"We'll do whatever we can to help," Tom said firmly. "You won't have to go through this alone."

A moment later, Constable Booth bundled Betty into the awaiting police cart and signalled for the driver to leave. Without needing any second bidding, his colleague clicked his tongue, and the horse trotted smartly away, leaving the others in stunned silence.

"What should I do? Fay will be distraught. I have to help Betty, but we don't even know where they're taking her." Ralph paced back and forth, running his hand through his hair.

"I know," Annie piped up. She waved a piece of paper and grinned. "Once a pickpocket, always a pickpocket. I took this out of Constable Booth's pocket just now." She skimmed the contents hastily. "It's a letter from Lord Griffiths, saying Constable Booth is to take Betty to the back room of The Red Dragon Pub in Pencastle Village tomorrow afternoon. He intends to ask her exactly what happened in the Blaeny shaft on the day of the flood last year, and if he thinks it was her fault, she will go before a judge and most likely be sent to prison."

Annie's voice broke as she read the letter out loud a second time, imagining Betty in a rat-infested cell until she was an old woman. "How will Betty survive? Tarquin and that horrible Wynn will probably tell a pack of lies, and we'll never see her again."

"We have to go to Pencastle as well," Tom said. He looked at Ralph, who nodded.

"You're right. I never really knew the full details of why she had to leave the village, but now that I've got to know Betty, I don't believe she would have done whatever it is she's being accused of. We shall cancel tomorrow's show and travel to Pencastle to support her. And as for Tarquin...I need to go and tell him to pack his bags. He's no longer welcome at Glan Mor Theatre." Ralph turned on his heel and strode back towards the stage with a face like thunder.

CHAPTER 20

"*S*hame on you, Betty Jones…"

"How dare you show your face back here again…"

Betty winced as a rotten egg splattered against the side of the cart, filling the air with a sulphurous stench. She stared resolutely forward, her cheeks burning with shame, even though part of her wanted to see which villagers were shouting insults at her.

"Just sit tight, Miss, we'll be there in a minute." The constable from the nearby town glared at a couple of young boys who were running alongside the cart, but they just laughed and shook their fists at her.

"Your scandalous behaviour left our village

without the money we should have had." A toothless old crone who Betty remembered from the colliery hobbled out of her cottage and started following the cart.

Word of Betty's return to Pencastle had spread like wildfire, and before long, a throng of people was walking hastily after her, reminding her of the rivulets of water pouring out from every nook and cranny the day of the flood.

"I thought I was just meeting Lord Griffiths?" Betty mumbled. She stared back at the angry mob and felt her courage wavering as the driver pulled the horse to a stop outside The Red Dragon.

"Nothing to do with us," the constable said cheerfully. "Constable Booth just told us to bring you here and then to take you to prison afterwards while you await your trial."

Betty's heart sank. It sounded as though her future was already decided, regardless of what she might say to try and prove her innocence. The constable helped her down and hurried her through the pub doorway.

"Betty, we're here to support you." Felicity and Tom rushed forward to greet her, but the constable brandished his baton, not letting them come too close.

"Why are you treating her like a dangerous criminal?" Ralph demanded, looking shocked. "I shall make an official complaint if you don't give her the respect she deserves."

Betty's eyes gradually adjusted to the dark interior of The Red Dragon after the sunshine outside, and her spirits lifted as she saw that all of her family were already there, as well as Tom, Felicity, and Annie. Fay looked grey with worry as Jack supported her by her elbow, and Minnie had her hands on her hips, with an outraged expression on her face.

"How did you know where to come?" she whispered.

"I found out," Annie replied stoutly. "We ain't going to let anything bad happen to you, Betty." Her eyes were suspiciously bright, and she blinked back tears.

"Bring her up here." The barked order came from a tall gentleman who was sitting at the front of the room. He was wearing a finely cut suit, with a gold signet ring on his left hand and his face was stern. He gestured to a chair opposite his, clearly used to being obeyed.

"As you wish, Lord Griffiths." The constable nodded obsequiously.

Betty sat down quietly, clasping her hands on her lap so nobody would see how much they were trembling. She lowered her gaze as the villagers shuffled into the pub, eager to witness the meeting for themselves. Risking a quick glance around the room, she saw that the place was packed, full of the people she had grown up with...who she had regarded as friends. She searched the faces for Dylan's, but he was nowhere to be seen.

Our love is over. The weight of the past is too much for us to be together. The realisation felt like a shard of ice in her heart, and she felt tears pricking at the back of her eyes.

"I realise this is rather an unusual matter," Lord Griffiths began, looking at Betty dispassionately. "I was led to believe that you left the shutter door open down the Blaeny shaft when we had the flood last year, which caused all the terrible damage." He didn't wait for Betty to agree or deny his statement. "Before I had a chance to speak to you, I then found out that you had run away from the village...I can only assume it was to evade justice. I feel it is only fair for the people of the village to hear the truth from your own lips, Miss Jones."

Betty swallowed, but her throat was dry. "It's not true…I promise I didn't leave that door open."

"She's lying. Tell everyone, Ezra."

Betty flushed as she saw Wynn elbowing his way to the front of the crowd, dragging Ezra Crundell with him.

Mr Crundell nodded vigorously. "Like we told you at the time, Lord Griffiths, Miss Jones was the only person who could have left the door open." He rocked forward on his toes and continued pompously. "It was such a terribly careless thing to do…her own brother almost died, which just goes to show that she's quite without morals."

"That's not true." Betty jumped up, determined to make herself heard. She looked at Lord Griffiths and then at all the villagers, wondering how much to reveal. "The only thing I was guilty of was working extra hours after the shift ended. After Pa died, we couldn't make ends meet. So I persuaded Mr Crundell to let me and Jack bring up extra loads of coal after hours. It was just so I could keep up with the rent for our cottage, Lord Griffiths. I promised Pa I would look after my family."

"I…I've never heard anything so preposterous in my life," Ezra spluttered, turning beetroot red.

"She's touched in the head, Lord Griffiths, don't listen to her."

A ripple of whispers spread through the villagers, and Betty noticed that a couple of them were nodding and even eyeing her more sympathetically.

"It is true, Mr Crundell," Betty said firmly. "Not only did you agree we could work after the shift, you said that we had to pay you some of the extra money we earned. It served you very well to condone what we were doing."

"She's a blatant liar," Mr Crundell shouted, looking around wildly for support. "We're here to talk about her negligence, Lord Griffiths. It's her fault that all that damage happened to your mine and you deserve justice."

Lord Griffiths stood up and glared at Ezra Crundell. "I intend to pursue what Miss Jones has just told me, Mr Crundell. You know very well it's now illegal for women to be down the mines. If what she says is true, *your* careless disregard for the law could have the whole place shut down by Mr Morgan, The Mines Inspector."

"You're missing the point," Wynn Parry said hastily. He raised his hand and pointed at Betty. "She is the cause of all the misfortune in this village. Her careless behaviour damaged the pit and made us a laughing stock in the valleys, with all Lord Leyfield's investment going to the Ferncoed Colliery instead. It was an utter scandal, and she must pay for what she did."

Suddenly there was a commotion at the back of the room, and the villagers parted to let someone through. Betty felt a surge of renewed hope as she saw Dylan and Dai carefully supporting Catherine, helping her to the front of the room.

"What are you doing, boy?" Wynn's face was dark with anger. "Take that wretched woman back home where she belongs immediately."

Dylan ignored his father and one of the villagers quickly pushed a chair in his direction so Catherine could sit down. Only once she was comfortable did Dylan stand up and look at Betty, giving her an apologetic smile that made her heart skip a beat. "My Ma and I have something we need to tell you, Lord Griffiths."

Wynn crossed the flagstone floor in three long strides. "My wife is a very sick woman," he blustered. "She barely knows what day of the week it is, and my son panders to her, Lord Griffiths. I'll make sure they leave right away—"

"No." Lord Griffiths's command cut across

Wynn, making him jump. "Let them speak. I want to hear what they have to say."

Wynn tried to rest his hand on Catherine's shoulder, but Dylan stepped forward, shielding her from his father. "Ma is very weak," he said, addressing Lord Griffiths directly. "But she is of sound mind."

Catherine smiled up at her son, and then at Betty. "I may not be much longer for this world, which is why I must speak up and tell you that my husband, Wynn was drunk when he went to work on the day of the flood. It was him who left the shutter door open," she added quietly. "He told me that if I ever revealed his secret, he would make Dylan and I regret it for the rest of our lives." She cast an anxious glance up at Dylan, and he gave her a nod of encouragement, taking her hand in his own. "I've had enough of Wynn's bullying ways. Betty Jones is a kindhearted, hardworking young lady, and she doesn't deserve to be punished for my husband's cowardly actions. I would also like to add that Mr Crundell has always known about this but chose to let Betty take the blame."

After a moment of stunned silence, the room erupted with angry shouts as the villagers turned on Ezra and Wynn.

"Quiet!" Lord Griffiths waited until the noise had abated. "I appreciate it must have taken a lot of courage to speak out against your husband today, Mrs Parry. And you too," he added, looking at Dylan. "Constable, please arrest Wynn Parry and Ezra Crundell. I will speak to the judge to decide what will become of them."

"Get off me...you'll be sorry for this, Catherine. I'll make sure you and your snivelling son get your comeuppance for getting me in trouble...after I've cared for you all these years..." Wynn's angry protestations fell on deaf ears as Catherine turned her back on him, and she didn't even glance in his direction while the constable carted him away.

"Please help me up, dear," she said to Dylan. She struggled to her feet and beckoned for Betty to come closer.

"I don't know how to thank you," Betty said, feeling humbled. "How will you manage without Wynn's wage?"

Catherine shook her head and hugged her. "I'm only sorry it took me so long to speak up. The truth is, Dylan and I have been getting by on his wage alone for a long time. Wynn spent all of his money and more at the pub." She paused to catch her breath, coughing and wheezing, before taking

Betty's hand and tucking it into Dylan's arm with twinkle in her eyes. "It makes me very happy to see you both back together again."

A moment later, Betty's friends and family surged around them, thanking Catherine and exclaiming that they could hardly believe the turn of events.

"I think it's high time we all went back to Mary's house and had a cup of tea, don't you?" Dai called. "Lead the way, Jack." He nudged Betty. "Look, he doesn't even limp anymore, what did we tell you?"

They trooped off happily down the hill, chattering loudly as they caught up on all the news.

"Emrys would have been so proud of you, Betty. Ralph has told me that the theatre audiences adore your act and ask for encores." Fay looked between her long-lost brother and her eldest daughter, scarcely able to believe they were both in the front parlour of Mary's cottage.

Betty felt a pang of regret as she remembered how her pa had always encouraged her to sing, even when it was just for the family. "I wish he could have seen me on stage, Ma. But don't forget everything that you and Minnie and Jack have overcome too. I think Pa would have been very proud of all of us."

"Betty certainly does have a beautiful singing voice," Ralph said again. He shook his head slightly. "I'm sorry I left it so long to visit you, Fay. When Papa disagreed with my career choice, all I wanted to do was get as far away as possible. I kept meaning to write to you, but the longer I left it, the more I thought you'd rather not hear from me."

Fay poured her brother a cup of tea and handed it to him. "Let's put it behind us now, Ralph. What matters is that my family is back together again... although I don't know how long for." She let her words hang in the air, wondering what Betty would say.

"Betty must carry on at the theatre," Ralph said hastily. "Her talent is too good to waste it by coming back to work at the pit, even if her name has been cleared."

"Of course, I would never want Betty to return to Nantglas, but she must make her own choices."

Dylan hadn't stopped smiling since he had settled Catherine in the armchair in front of the hearth and he hurried over to thank Fay and Mary for their hospitality. "Ma's looking happier than I've ever seen her, now that Pa's out of our lives," he said, sounding relieved. He gave Fay a shy smile. "May I steal Betty away from you for a few minutes, Mrs Jones? There's something I want to show her."

"Of course, Dylan, you don't need to ask, she's a grown woman now." Fay smiled fondly as she watched Dylan escort Betty out into the garden.

"Am I about to lose my best singer because she'll want to stay here with her beau?" Ralph asked with a chuckle. "I hope not because I heard this morning before we left that Camilla and Tarquin are heading to Paris to try and find a theatre manager there who will take them on."

Fay looked shocked. "Oh no, I'm sorry to hear that, Ralph. How will you manage without your principal singer?"

He shrugged. "Camilla might be a good performer, but her tantrums and demands made her hard to deal with…and as for Tarquin, from what I've learnt about him lately, I would never trust the fellow not to bring the theatre into disrepute with his gambling debts and mixing with dubious characters. I was rather hoping Betty might enjoy being top of the bill instead?"

.   .   .

DYLAN LINKED ARMS WITH BETTY, and they strolled through Mary's garden. The roses were in full bloom and tumbled over the pathway, releasing their rich damask scent as Betty's dress brushed against the petals.

He reached into his pocket and pulled a small pouch out. "I'm sorry I rushed away after your show the other night. I wanted to give this to you, but then you had to go and speak to Mr and Mrs Washbrook, and the moment was gone."

Betty opened her hand and he carefully placed the primrose brooch on her palm. "It's just something I made. When your pa used to pick a primrose for your ma, to tell her that he loved her...I used to hope that one day I would be able to do the same for you." He took the brooch and pinned it on the collar of her dress and his eyes crinkled with his smile in the way that Betty found so endearing.

"Are you saying that you love me, Dylan?" Betty held his gaze and felt her heart skip a beat.

"Yes, I love you very much. Betty and I always will." His face creased with regret, and he sighed. "Tarquin said you were destined to sing on stage in

London, and I don't want to stand in your way. I know that I have to let you go, Betty, even though it breaks my heart. You deserve to be successful and being with me would only hold you back. This brooch is just a little something to remember me by."

Betty took Dylan's hands in her own and looked up at him, thinking about all the years they had known each other. "I'd give it all up tomorrow to be with you, my love. Singing and being on stage is meaningless to me if we can't be together—"

Before she could finish her sentence, Dylan swept her into his arms and pressed a lingering kiss on her soft lips. The moment of passion pulsed between them, and Betty could feel their hearts beating together as she melted into his embrace.

"I don't know how, but we'll find a way to be together and for you to carry on singing," Dylan declared. "Will you do me the very great honour of marrying me?" He stroked her cheek with his thumb, watching the way the dappled sunlight fell on her rosy cheeks.

"I will, Dylan. Even though fate kept us apart, my heart has only ever belonged to you…since the first time you kissed me by the river all those years ago." Betty leaned her head against his broad chest, before giving him a mischievous smile. "We'd better go and tell our families, don't you think?"

Dylan took her hand and placed it over his heart. "I never want to be apart from you again, Betty. Wherever your singing takes us, we'll go together."

She sighed happily and touched her primrose brooch as though it was a talisman, finally bringing good fortune into their lives. "I've been thinking...what with your ma and mine both suffering with poor health...maybe the fresh, sea air would be the perfect tonic for them. And Mrs Snape desperately needs someone to help her make the costumes for the theatre."

"Maybe it's time for a fresh start for all of us," Dylan said, his eyes sparkling at the thought of being able to provide a better place to live for his ma, away from all the bad memories of how Wynn had treated them.

"Let's go and tell everyone our wonderful news. There's a lot to arrange." Betty stood on her tiptoes and kissed him again before blushing as she spied everyone coming into the garden.

"Didn't I tell you there would be a marriage

soon?" Tom said to Felicity, who was dabbing away her tears of happiness with his handkerchief. He winked at Annie, who cheered loudly, sending two plump wood pigeons clattering up into the air indignantly.

"We've known it would happen for years," Fay said, linking arms with Catherine. "Do you remember when they were young…and as thick as thieves…we could never keep them apart."

The swallows swooped and chattered over Mary's garden in the summer sunshine, and Betty felt her heart swell with happiness. She could hold her head up again without the villagers blaming her for what happened with the flood, and she was back with the people she loved most in the world. Dylan squeezed her hand, and they shared a private smile. It was a perfect day, and she would treasure it forever.

EPILOGUE

"*B*ravo, Betty, what a wonderful performance." Lord Griffiths lifted his hat and bowed over Betty's hand, full of admiration. "To think you have such a talent and yet you never had formal training. You are indeed The Nightingale of the Valleys."

Betty accepted his praise with a demure nod of her head. Even though she had been the principal singer at Glan Mor for almost five years since Camilla's hasty departure, she still found it strange to be fêted in such a way, especially by people like Lord Griffiths and their other wealthy patrons. "It's very kind of you to say so, but I still have to pinch myself that I can do something I love every day."

Lord Griffiths beckoned Ralph over and shook his hand enthusiastically. "Thank you for a splendid evening, dear fellow. I can see I've made a very safe investment by putting money into the Glan Mor. Abertarron is busier than it's ever been, and every time I go to London, the high society ladies and gentlemen tell me it's the place they all want to visit to get away for some wonderful seaside air."

"I'm glad you're pleased with what we're doing with the theatre." Ralph glanced around with a gleam of pride in his eyes as the performers milled around backstage after the performance. The costumes were good enough to rival anything he had seen in London, and they had smart new seating and gold-edged curtains, which only added to the air of sophistication. "We sell out practically every night, Lord Griffiths. It was a shrewd investment, and now that you've added the new gardens to the business, it will only get better."

"Did I hear someone mention the gardens?" Jack turned from where he had been chatting to Abe and walked over to join them. He only had the faintest hint of a limp these days, and his face was tanned from working outside.

"I was just telling Lord Griffiths how popular the Nantglas Gardens are with all the town's visitors."

Jack grinned, always happy to talk about his favourite subject. "I'm adding more tropical plants to the orangery, and we're hoping to put a band-stand in the rose garden. Also, the new apothecary garden I'm creating is already attracting a lot of attention. I might need to take on a couple of extra boys to help me."

Lord Griffiths nodded without hesitation. "You've proven yourself to be an excellent gardener, Jack. I wasn't sure when Dai first recommended you, but you did wonders with my country estate, so you were the obvious choice to create these new gardens here in Abertarron. Just let me know what help you need, and I'll let you find the right people. I'm sure you have a few in mind from the town."

He turned to Betty, looking suddenly serious. "I hope you will accept my apology again for that day in The Red Dragon. Ezra Crundell turned out to be a real scoundrel. It transpired he'd been pock-eting some of the profits from the mine for years, and he should never have broken the law by sending women below ground. The new manager is far more reliable, and I've invested in many of the improvements you and Dai suggested. It was the least I could do after those terrible events."

Betty nodded and patted his arm. "Dylan and I have a saying, Lord Griffiths…learn from the past, but don't dwell on it. I know you're a very benevolent employer now, and I admire your philanthropic work for the poor. It's very commendable, and I hope you're enjoying your appointment to Parliament."

He put his hat back on and pulled out his pocket watch. "Goodness me, is that the time? I'll thank you again for a wonderful show and bid you goodnight. My dear wife and I are dining with friends, so I must leave."

As Betty watched his retreating back, there was a sudden commotion in the wings, and her two daughters darted out. "Pa…Pa…lift us up." She smiled as she saw Dylan scoop them both up and balance them on his shoulders as though they were no heavier than a feather pillow.

"Spin us around," Katie squealed excitedly.

"Make us dizzy, Pa," Mary added, wriggling like a fish.

Dylan's eyes met Betty's across the stage, and his mouth lifted in a smile that made his eyes crinkle with amusement.

"Goodness me, girls, you mustn't run onto stage like that...what if it was the middle of a show." Fay hurried towards them, followed by Catherine, both of them looking apologetic.

"They just slipped away when we were talking to Abe," Catherine said, sounding flustered. "It's past your bedtime, Katie. And Mary, what did we say about climbing up your pa?"

"We'll let them stay up late just this once," Dylan chuckled. "We did promise them they could come to the first show of the new summer season. I hope you all enjoyed it?"

Fay and Catherine both nodded enthusiastically. "Abe gave us the best seats in the house, backstage, of course," she added hastily.

"Pa is the best strongman in the whole of Abertarron," Katie said solemnly.

"I think the audience thought so as well," Ralph replied. "That was an excellent idea of yours, Betty, to give Dylan his own act. Marvel the Mighty And His Amazing Feats of Strength has a very good ring to it."

Betty gave her uncle a wry smile. "It's good to know all those years Dylan was dragging tubs of coal up from the pit didn't go to waste. It certainly made him stronger than most men."

"Glan Mor has become very much a family affair," Ralph commented. "And to think it all started when you showed up announced with Annie, looking for work."

"Do you ever hear news of Camilla?" Speaking about the past had reminded Betty just how much things had changed. Occasionally she still felt a shiver of fear at how close she had come to losing everything if Tarquin and Wynn had succeeded in spreading their lies.

"As it happens, I did read in the newspaper recently that Camilla is doing well, singing at the Paris opera." He lowered his voice slightly. "I also heard that Tarquin is being pursued by an irate gentleman for having a scandalous affair with his wife, a wealthy Countess. He always did have aspirations of grandeur beyond his standing."

Dylan chuckled and put his arm around Betty. "May I escort you to dinner, my love? Shall we get changed and kiss the children goodnight."

Betty nodded. "I won't need long to change my gown, and then I'll be ready. Tom is fussing like a mother hen that Minnie will have their first baby while she's still sewing costumes if she doesn't start her confinement in good time. I shall have to tell Minnie she must rest and let Annie take over. That is why Annie has learnt dressmaking, after all."

As all the other performers and patrons strolled away, Betty and Dylan were left alone. Betty gazed out at the empty auditorium, casting her mind back over the hundreds of shows she had done. "Can you believe it's almost five years since our wedding, Dylan? And now we have two beautiful daughters and all our family living and working here with us in Abertarron. I've truly never been happier." She nestled against him, enjoying the feeling of security and deep contentment she always felt in his embrace.

"We've come such a long way from those long hours down the pit." Dylan looked down at her and brushed a kiss on her mouth. He knew he would never tire of looking into the hazel flecks of her eyes, just as he had when they were children, laughing as they walked up the dusty lane from the river back into the village. "It was those backbreaking days that made us who we are, though, so in a funny way, I'll always be grateful we grew up under the shadow of Nantlas Colliery."

"I love you, Dylan Parry," Betty said dreamily.

Dylan dipped his head, and their lips met in a kiss that melted their hearts and bound them together.

"And I love you too, Betty. Always and forever."

READ MORE

If you enjoyed The Daughter's Courage, you'll love Daisy Carter's other Victorian Romance Saga Stories:

The Daughter's Courage:

Ruby's family is poor but happy. But when powerful people want to cause their downfall, will she find the courage to save her family from ruin?

Ruby Wheeler knows that she's more fortunate than many. Even though they've fallen on hard times, she has a close-knit family around her, and their grandfather's silk dyeing business still makes them well-respected in town.

But life quickly unravels when her father, an artist, takes on a new commission to paint a well-to-do lady and a terrible accident befalls someone they all rely on.

Beset by scandal, things go from bad to worse when a mysterious stranger unexpectedly takes an interest in Hamilton Silks.

Ruby knows that she must step in to save the business and her childhood friend, Danny gives her all the encouragement she needs.

But although Ruby does her best, she is no match for the greedy, powerful people who want to see her fail and will stop at nothing to get their way.

Will Ruby manage to hold her family together in the face of adversity?

Can she trust those close to her or will they betray her for their own gain?

Torn between love and friendship, betrayal and hope, Ruby is determined to make the best of her life and save her family from ruin.

The Daughter's Courage is another gripping Victorian romance saga by Daisy Carter, the popular author of The Maid's Winter Wish, The Milkmaid's Secret, and many more.

* * *

Do you love FREE BOOKS? Download Daisy's FREE book now:

Get your free copy by clicking below

The May Blossom Orphan

Clementine Morris thought life had finally dealt her a kinder hand when her aunt rescued her from the orphanage. But happiness quickly turns to fear when she realises her uncle has shocking plans for her to earn more money.

As the net draws in, a terrifying accident at the docks sparks an unlikely new friendship with kindly warehouse lad, Joe Sawbridge.

Follow Clemmie and Joe through the dangers of the London docks, to find out whether help comes in the nick of time, in this heart-warming Victorian romance story.

Printed in Great Britain
by Amazon